TWO GUN
PUBLISHING

# THE FOUR WINDS

JACK BALLARD JR.

For information, please contact twogunpublishing@outlook.com



In association with Two Gun Publishing.



9798404964653

Author Notes and Acknowledgements:

I did my best to strive for authenticity and accuracy, and any historical mistakes are mine alone. While the characters are fictional, the settings are not and really happened as documented or were possible, if fictionalized. For example, the falls under which the gold cache is found is a real place in North Georgia (Raven Falls), as is Kennesaw Mountain and the infamous Dead Angle. The incident calling for a truce in the middle of the battle really happened as described.

I would like to thank Two Gun Publishing for the chance to bring to light this novel. It was borne out of many miles of walking and driving through battlefields all over the United States and I appreciate Jason and the team's work in presenting it. Speaking of walking, I'd like to also thank my daughters, Erienne and Heather, whose idea of varying "fun" included miles of wearing out shoes for the sake of Mom and Dad's hobby. I appreciate friends and family who took the time to read the MS in its various forms and were comfortable enough to critique it. Finally, I'd like to thank my wife, Lori, who joined me in periodic walks all over Kennesaw Mountain and its battlefield, the wilderness of North Georgia and the museums of Atlanta. I may put pen to paper, but this story is the culmination of all these individuals' contributions.

# THE FOUR WINDS

## Chapter 1

*February, 1864*

When old Ben used to light the incinerator in Helen, it smelled like this. The horse's ears lay flat against its skull and skittered constantly, no matter how tight a rein he kept on the gelding as he rode into the cove. But it wasn't until its eyes rolled back and Jeremy found himself on the ground did he really worry.

He looked up. The horse already pounded away through the poor imitation of a gate. At fourteen, he still had not quite the control of his dead grandfather over either the horse or himself, and the flight of the horse made him pound the ground. An expletive ground out of his lips at the same time that would have shocked his mother.

He brushed off the britches and stood up. The curve in the trail hid the open area in the holler, but the smell scared him more than anything. Another zephyr rolled by him and the charred wood smell carried others with it, reminding him of the smokehouse with its pounds of curing pork.

A walk down the road a couple of hundred yards brought him to the black hole in the ground, still smoking in its solitude. It was the foundation of the place in which he was born, one room though it had been at the time. The hole was partially filled with charcoaled timbers and ash and, if the horse's and his perceptions were any indication, worse.

He set his jaw, yet denying the possibilities such a sight might convey.

He looked around but nothing stirred except for the brown leaves above him as the wind picked up. He walked toward the wreck and looked into it with dread. Under a charred log a leg stuck out, naked but charcoal black, and obviously connected in some way to a hidden body.

Tears filled his eyes, but he was determined to not give in if there were important things to do. That was the start. As Jeremy began to pull away more of the charnel, more and more recognizable limbs and bodies showed. They were only recognizable in the charred clothing that was attached to them and he could not bear to look at the faces. He steeled his face and his soul and tied a ragged scarf around his head so the smell or worse wouldn't make him puke.

Four hours later, he still worked and he froze his heart as best he could. The count: his mother, two child sisters and a younger brother. He as the oldest had been allowed to leave for the business in Dahlonega.

More than a month ago, his father had finally made a decent strike southwest of Helen in a cove hidden from the main roads. The placer mining yielded about three pounds of gold before initially playing out, but it was worth the trip to register the cove in Dahlonega, Georgia, the closest governmental registry to the farmstead. Jeremy had to register it as a farming homestead in his name only; a subterfuge, since they didn't dare let it be voiced that they had discovered any kind of gold in it.

Aside from the Confederate government's desperate need to shore up the economy and buy materiel, there were plenty of raiders who considered life but little compared to the gain they might get for far less than gold. The proof was in front of him.

So, he traveled to Dahlonega while his father worked the cove for more gold, if there was any to be found. They could always bring the heavy gear after the war, which his father was convinced was ending. Jeremy registered his "homestead" and his father ordered him to return directly to the rest of the family. He wouldn't need to establish residency for some time yet if they could help it.

He bent to his work and as he pushed his feelings back into a dark corner of his life, his heart grew colder and colder until it became a frozen lump inside him, threatening to change into stone. The emotional bowed before the rational and the hate that was left over coldly decided to follow and kill those responsible. It was not revenge he wanted, but justice, a means of working justice on the men who had done this thing. And even though vengeance may be under God's ownership as he'd been taught, by God, he wanted to be the instrument!

He selected a large chestnut tree some yards from the creek with a soft ground underneath and began digging the four graves. Part of him nagged at the delay but cold consideration made him frighteningly methodical and unhurried. Instead of just allowing the bodies to settle in the four feet of dirt allowed by the water table, he turned again to the creek and fished out large stones. These he lay side by side on top of each fresh hill, as closely fit as the best mason. Such a monument would have to do and anything permanent must be done later, but for now at least no wild animals would desecrate the monument.

As he studied the place for a moment, his distrust of human nature hungry for gold kicked in. He had heard of Yankees and others tearing up ancient graves in the hopes of looting the gold mementos buried with the bodies and although his family was much too poor for such gewgaws, no one would know that until the corpses were exhumed. And if rumor of the strike was common knowledge in spite of their attempts at secrecy, there was no doubt that treasure hunters would eventually come, logic not dictating otherwise. Jeremy gave such a robber no excuse to do so. Minutes later, a large pile of freshly cut brush, rhododendron and deadfall blended into the tangle of briars and azaleas that bordered the creek area. The living plants would die and turn brown, but he hoped it would look like a neglected burn-pile and remain undisturbed.

While his mother would have been shocked at his language earlier in the day, she would not have recognized this human form standing at her grave. The eyes faded as the last bit of spirituality left and he became nothing more than an animal, living and moving, ready to kill, eat and sustain the flesh, but no more than that. His hate was the last: hate was still a vestige of humanity for while an animal might be aggressive, it cannot truly hate. Even that he tucked into some forgotten corner bereft of light. If it were brought out, it might even be the seed for a soul.

Now it remained to find the horse with his rifle.

*

The road opened before Henry as he topped the ridge. After riding for weeks, he figured he was somewhere in the vicinity of Asheville, North Carolina. As usual, he stuck to the woods, meeting only poor homesteaders or loggers in the granite hills. Towns meant armies and armies meant meddling.

He smiled as he remembered old Bart and the night he left.

The pile of tack had begun to fall, making an amazingly loud noise in the silence of the night. It was like a gunshot to his sensitive ears. He glanced in the direction of the stableboys' sleeping quarters and held his breath while his arms locked straight against the gear above him. Moments passed, but no door opened or voice sounded. He started to relax and then tensed again when the barn door creaked open. He opened his mouth and his throat to minimize the noise the necessary breathing would make. A lamp's glow sneaked through the crack and a pry-bar followed that, held by a very large black hand.

"Who's there?"

He relaxed a bit more.

"Who's there, I say?" The door opened a bit more and a very large shadow followed the very large black hand, wary eyes large in the darkness.

Henry stepped away from the tack and let it fall noisily to the floor. The African-American jumped and peered into the black.

"It's okay, Bart."

"That you, Henry?"

He sighed. "Yes, it's me."

Bart grinned. "Okay. Caught me. Scared the ghost out of me! What are you doing here this late at night?"

"I suppose you heard the row I had with my brother last night. It had a lot to do with, shall we say, my convictions. I criticized Father's and his dealings with the industries up north. I know of their swindling the government out of materiél. It's worse now that Sherman's pushing through Tennessee."

As he heated up once again, he forgot the presence of his best friend and the family's ranch manager. Bart and Henry had grown up together and this employee of his now listened to the tirade his best friend was on. Bart held up his hand.

"Henry, I know all this. I heard last night. But what does it mean?"

"It means I am leaving. Tom never liked me—why, I still don't know. I guess he thinks I mean to steal his inheritance from him or something. As if I want it! In any case, I believe he will try something in the next couple days and my comfort won't be worth too much in the future."

"You just got here!" Bart was astounded. He sat down on a sawhorse saddle stand. "It can't be that bad."

"It is. I know he's hired a bunch of toughs to threaten workers and other businessmen, but it won't be too long before they find something else to do and I'm probably the biggest target at this point. I know I'm in his way."

"I'd like to go. With you, I mean."

"No." Henry turned. "I need you here for two reasons. One, to put them off the trail, for as long as I'm alive they'll be afraid I'm coming back. Second, I need you to go to Pittsburgh for me if you can. You remember that maple on Henson's Ridge we used to play under, the one with the hole in the rock underneath?"

Bart nodded. Henry carried the tack to his horse and threw the saddle on.

"I've hidden a few compromising things in there that would definitely curtail the shady dealings my brother's doing. I need you to take those things to our solicitor; I've talked with him already and he knows what to do."

Bart was shocked yet more. "But what about the family? What about your mother? This'll ruin the reputation…"

Henry was suddenly aloof and cold.

"Reputation be damned."

He looked at Bart pointedly.

"And Mother will be just fine. This family will do just fine, and don't worry, their *reputation* won't be tarnished. Most of this evidence we'll directly use against his thugs for their strong-arming, but my brother will only receive a, uh, *threatening* letter. He's enough of a coward, he'll back off. At least I hope so. That's why I need you. You've enough pull, I think, with your dad to make sure things work out okay. But it's vital that Tom be stopped, or at least slowed down.

"I can't bear it, this hanging about, I mean, and I can't stand the idea of Mother dealing with the crash that would happen. But, make no mistake: I'm not running off. There are a lot of reasons why I can't be around. Tom's got to back off, because things like this will be found out by people with no affection for the family. And then they *will* lose everything. *Everything*. Do you understand me?"

"Yessir. I understand."

The mare shifted slightly as he opened the gate and threw the blanket on her back. Not huge, under seventeen hands, she was that odd combination of spirit and humor, rare in humans and practically never found in a horse. That's why she was his favorite and that's why he was so meticulous in saddling her every time, especially now.

"Besides, if I'm right, and Tom *does* back off, this will only encourage Washington to deal with this light in the darkness, what they'll see as one… 'honest' family. Financially, they may make out even better in the long run."

He worked quickly. To finish the job, he slid the bit into the horse's mouth and pulled the leather over her head. He worked the ears through the loops and patted her neck. He pushed open the gate and picked up the reins, leading the mare out of her stall.

"There's a third reason I'm leaving you here, at least for the meantime. I'm going in a direction that they would never pick. I'm heading South and I couldn't be responsible for your safety from Blue or Gray as a black man."

"What about *your* safety?" said Bart. "Your accent will give you away. You can't talk hick worth a darn and you obviously can't talk Negro. And pardon me for saying so, but you're not exactly the image of the Southern gentleman!"

"I'll be fine. It'll be easier by myself to slip through. I'll only have the packhorse and my mare so we can take back-routes and mountain paths. If nothing else, I can still pass myself off as a Union officer on furlough, or prisoner trade mission or something. If you want to meet up, though, I'll eventually be heading West. The South won't be any place worth going once Sherman's armies get through with it and there won't be any law and order down there for years."

He stopped and thought for a moment.

"I'm not a flatlander. I like the hills. I want to see the Appalachians down in the Carolinas with their granite cliffs and vast forests. But most of all, I want to see the

Rockies and the Sierras and the others out West. I've heard stories say they make the Pocanoes look like molehills and there are hundreds of peaks that send their tops ten thousand feet into the air."

He led the mare past Bart and into the yard, where the packhorse was waiting discreetly in the blackness under a tree.

"If you're really dedicated about this and want to follow me…"

"Oh, I am!"

"…then meet me in September at a place where they used to rendezvous for beaver-trading. Taos, they call it, just north of Santa Fe. Take some of the gold I've stashed at the tree. No, wait a minute. Let's meet *next* year. That'll give us plenty of time. *I'll* spend next winter there, so if you're late, I'll wait and we can still meet. Pull out $10,000. That'll be enough for anything we decide to do out West. I'm not worried about the rest. If someone takes it, God help his soul. Now I've gotta go."

Bart stuck out his hand. Henry pushed it away and grabbed Bart's shoulders.

"You're my best friend. You always have been. I'll miss you. God bless."

"Go with God, Henry."

They hugged and Henry, without pause, threw open the gate and led the horses out into the early, dark morning.

## Chapter 2

Jeremy leaned over the gray's neck and examined the ground. Not more than a day old, he figured. Makes sense, considering the ground at the farm was still smoking when he had arrived. At least five horses, all of them shod, likely a packhorse or two as well. At intervals there were marks of a wagon wheel that had dug into the ground as it bounced along.

They seemed to be hitting the ridges rather than the roads, and went fairly fast. He thought that was unusual if they were just casually drunk raiders bent on some money and a good time. The trail led in the direction of the gold strike and he figured someone in his family had talked before getting shot out of hand. Not that he blamed them: gold wasn't worth someone's life any way you looked at it. But apparently, these boys thought it was. It will cost them dear and taking the Old Testament adage far beyond its intention, Jeremy had decided they would pay: eye for eye, tooth for tooth, hair, skin, nails and so on.

He straightened up. This time of year could be gorgeous in colorful north Georgia, with the new buds greening the forest in that bright chartreuse of early spring, but it made no effect upon his numb soul. He had little regret for it, too, as he tapped the horse's sides and continued along the ridge at a brisk trot.

The spoor was solid and he wasn't too worried about missing the raiders in the woods. They definitely rode like white men without regard to anything but themselves. Obviously, they had no idea they were being tracked and had no reason to hide themselves. Which was fine.

He pulled on the reins suddenly as the ridge dipped into a saddle with a thick hedge of rhododendrons in the bottom. A bunch of broken branches and leaves showed the clear trail through the bushes, but he stopped before he entered. Snagged on the sharp immature bud of a rhodie was a tuft of… hair, was it? No, he decided, as he rode closer. He scraped off the fuzzy stuff from the branch. Wool. Blue wool. Yankees. No one else had this color or quality that he knew.

In his talks in Helen and around the community, he'd heard of renegade troops of both sides, either cut off from the main armies or bored with action or inaction and choosing to "get a little" for themselves. Deserters to be shot if found, inured by field gore to any sense of decency and deprivations of war having enhanced the natural tendency for greed all humans have: these would be desperate men by a number of definitions and no quarter would be asked or given on any venture.

Yankees, this time. Fine. It would make them that much easier to track than Southern homeboys, he thought. It was three miles to the strike and once they found it, they wouldn't leave for some time. He had all the time in the world.

*

The horses stood munching the last of the grain,

apparently oblivious to the slow drizzle. They looked okay to him so he turned his attention back to what passed for lunch and contemplated life.

He was pretty lost now. Sherman was marching south, west of here, he knew. He was definitely in or at least near north Georgia and he wanted to stay away from *that* war as far as possible. Although originally the tactical maneuver made sense as far as the family plan went, now heading South seemed pretty stupid. On the lines, he could be conscripted for either side, shot as a spy or as a deserter. It was certainly time to head West, if possible, where he would be just another trader, refugee, whatever. He could sign up again and fight Indians for all he cared.

He stirred the fire, trying to coax it into some sort of flame. Lunch wouldn't be so bad if its temperature was hot. The rain added to his personal gloom and the low, dark clouds made an atmosphere that seemed to never get out of a dusky, drizzly half-light. It had been misting for a couple of days and the fog and dripping of the trees got on his nerves. The fire never started without trouble and some of his food was starting to get moldy.

The big granite cliffs made navigation pretty easy, each mountain going up a thousand feet or more from the valley flats. Their bald faces looked intimidating to the casual observer: Henry couldn't imagine trying to climb any one of them. They broke up the monotony of traveling through the forest and he appreciated the stark faces framed by the dark green foliage.

He bit into the oatmeal. Not even hot, much less

tasty. Oh well. It filled the belly and would keep him going a few hours longer. But he wanted some meat, so would keep an eye out for game.

He was in an area now of waterfalls that were more heard than seen and the trees had thickened as he had gone higher, the flora transforming from oaks and pines into dense fir.

He finished eating the rest of the lukewarm sludge that he had cooked up and kicked out the fire. Another day, another few miles. Time to find a homestead and find out where on God's green earth he was.

*

Jeremy hunched under the azalea brush, his woodcraft skill tuned very high. Under the drizzle, four men in the butternut uniforms of the Confederate Army shivered over a smoldering fire.

"Shit, but didn't I tell you he was gonna powder?"

"Now, now…" began what looked like an officer of some sort. At least, he wore an insignia on the gray uniform cap, but his spectacles and his manner decried his leadership ability. One of the others piped up before he could form his sentence.

"Now, Sarge, you saw it. That gol-dang kiss-ass officer done took off to save 'is own hide. Left us high and dry and now we ain't got no idea where we are. Think we're on the wrong side of the line. Damn sure we ain't anywhere near the line no more."

To Jeremy's slight amusement—he didn't have much left—the sergeant bristled and seemed to work up some sort of fury.

"You… you," he stuttered, "you are all volunteers. You knew this was a reconnaissance."

"A what?" A naive lad of fourteen piped up.

"A look-see," muttered the first man. "Yeah, I know. But he's skipped and we might even be on the Yankee side and home's sounding pretty good right now, if there's anything left to go to."

At this point, Jeremy sneaked back to his horse. He'd heard enough to know these had nothing to do with his own home, nor were they bent on general savagery. Just some Southerners who caught the short end of the stick in the latest skirmish and wanted the least amount of fuss. He would give them a wide berth. How they managed to miss the Yankee troops, he would never know: darkness, maybe.

As he mounted his horse, he realized that any patrol of any size and any worth would have a sentry of some sort. He turned the horse around and backtracked a quarter mile before beginning the wide circuit around the Rebs, who never caught a hint that he had been there.

*

The mind gets dull as the body tires, and the body tires as it is pushed to the limits of endurance and pain. By the afternoon, Henry's discomfort in the wet and cold had turned into pain, and the rain accelerated this when it began freezing into pellets of ice that felt like grapeshot after an hour. His head drooped. This probably explained it.

He was trying to switchback down a steep draw, threading the horse between firs and rhododendron bushes. Apparently, the stream had cut away the bank in the bottom of the ravine and left nothing to support the tons of mud under horse and rider. He could see bushes near the bottom of the ravine move and even disappear, but his dulled mind did not comprehend the significance. The mud slid out from under the mare. Henry knew something was wrong, but not soon enough to do anything about it except let go of the packhorse.

"Ah, ssshh…" was cut off by a grunt and the mare went down. His head snapped back as the horse jerked to one side. She landed hard on his left leg, but the mud was too soft to do anything more than just bruise it. He was still above the horse on the hillside. What was painful was the way she thrashed as the mudslide picked up speed. The horse rolled on him, still lurching and tossing her legs, trying vainly to right herself. The thrashing hoofs flashed closer and closer to his head and he arched his back, trying to throw his head out of their range. He lifted his right foot as high as he could and tried to shove down on her torso, the idea being to pull the other leg out from under her. Then the mare started to pivot: soon he would be fully below her. He struggled to keep his head above the clinging mud and breathe.

This was not good. He had no idea if the mud would stop on its own or if there was something, a logjam, for instance, to stop it at the bottom. In the latter case, he had no wish to be between the horse with her thrashing legs and the log or whatever. He made one hard push and the watery mud allowed the left leg to pop out with a sucking noise, straining every tendon attached to it. He tried to crawl or swim out of the path of the still-thrashing animal. The streambed was less than thirty yards away and he gave one last heaving dive to exit the accelerating slide. The mare slid past him.

The horse suddenly screamed as she crashed into the river bed; as close as he was to the tossing legs, Henry could hear a clear "snap" as one of her legs definitely went, bent under by something they were crashing into. He slid on top of her as she stopped thrashing due to pain and exhaustion. The mud started to slop over them, but as they had been near the top of the slide, there was no danger from that. A terrified neigh reached his ears through the last noise of the slide. He turned his head in time to see his panicked packhorse inconceivably galloping down on him, desperately trying to keep its balance amid flying packs and a new torrent of sliding goop. He ducked as the flying hoofs missed his head by inches and looked up as the fresh sludge hit his face. He was blind and the heavy muck took control of his arms and legs. He gagged and panicked for a second, trying to get his breath. He struggled and lifted his head and shoulders out of the heavy red mud clinging to his clothes and his body, which penetrated even to his skin.

Suddenly, he noticed everything was silent: made more, not less, by the gurgle of the stream and the dripping of rain and mud. The mare panted, scared, pain daring her to move. Henry could barely breath, mouth and nose covered in claying mud. Like cement, the stuff held him in by his torso and legs and it was with much patience and much effort that he once again extricated himself from the trap.

He stood slowly. Aside from the fact he was cold, wet and miserable, with a few scrapes for show, nothing seemed to be all that wrong with his body.

"Oh, God."

The mare, on the other hand, was beyond hope. She was bloody along the neck: a one-inch branch stuck a few inches out of her neck. Even without the broken leg, she was gone. Even now he saw that she did not move because she was weakening.

The revolver was wet, muddy and worthless, and he did not want to draw any attention to himself in any case. He pulled his hunting knife from his belt.

"I'm sorry. I can't make it any quicker than this." He put his knee on the head of the mare. He stabbed at the jugular and continued drawing the knife over the entire throat, slicing as quickly, deeply and accurately as he could in hopes that loss of blood would bring faintness and death quicker than the realization of pain. The mare jerked in response, but weakly: between the bleeding wound in her neck, the pain of her broken leg and the knife, there was not much strength left in her. She trembled and the eyes glazed over as her head relaxed into the muck.

He got up and trudged over to where the packhorse

stood, trembling. There were a couple of scrapes but there seemed to be nothing wrong with the gelding. He walked it around a bit. Miracle of miracles, no sign of lameness. Henry sighed.

"I guess I go on foot now, or get rid of this stuff." But dumping the packs was not an option.

He plopped down on a rock at the edge of the stream. His feet were in a foot of icy water, but circumstances being what they were, he did not notice. The horse had about half of the total packs and these were in such disarray about the gelding, he was amazed that there was no injury to either the horse or the packs. The other packs were strewn up the hill, one partially buried in the mud. A lot of work to do, he thought, between salvaging the tack on the other horse and cleaning and repairing the packs.

"Thank God I'm okay, I guess," he said to the horse. "Could've been worse. Much worse. Coulda been *my* leg."

He got up and hopefully groped in one of the most intact packages for matches. The container he'd carefully oiled was still intact. A fire would definitely cheer things up and warm him.

He set to work.

*

Once again, Jeremy found himself under an azalea bush staring at a bunch of soldiers. It was night and the glow of the campfire the patrol had foolishly lit had attracted him from the ridge more than three miles away. Sure enough, it was the cove that his father had made the strike in. The blue Yankee uniforms showed black in the night. He'd found them, and he did indeed have all the time in the world. They weren't going anywhere until they'd found the valuable cache.

## Chapter 3

Henry wasn't about to leave that saddle. His butt over the last three years and hours of oiling and care had given him both a physical and emotional attachment to that hunk of leather and wood. He kept digging at the mud with a sharpened stick that sort of did for a shovel and for the first time, thanked everything above that it was cold and raining. Things were bad enough with a bloody, dead mare below him: he did not let himself dwell on the situation during a hot, muggy Southern day, with the body below him beginning to swell, and flies laying magg… stop it!

The cinch finally showed under the mud. Thank God it was near the topside of the horse! Hopefully, he could slide the saddle around the torso and slip the strap around the other side from under the horse. It took him about twenty minutes of digging in the mud to free the saddle and another ten of standing in the stream, cleaning the sticky clay from it. Because of the softness of the mud, the saddle was virtually unharmed, though dirty. It would have a red tint forever. The bridle came off easily now that he'd found it: the blanket he left as a lost cause.

The packhorse grazed in a small clearing that had escaped the forest and stream floodwaters, apparently forgetful of the excitement the hour before. For once, Henry envied its equine lack of intelligence. Steam rose off his back as the sun finally broke through the clouds. Henry waded through the stream with the tack he was able to salvage and climbed out on the bank. The fire sank lower and because he was chilled by his time in the water, he threw on more wood. He felt the clothes hanging on propped sticks: almost dry and even a bit clean. His coat would forever bear the stains of the infamous southern Appalachian red clay. It would serve to remind him how close he'd been to… not oblivion, but he supposed something better. Still, he didn't want to go there just yet.

*

"Hey Davie, you got a chew?"

"Naw, chew?" The man roared with laughter at his punny wit as his interrogator made a face and took another swig at the bottle. There were nine of them, total, a few more than he'd expected, but not that many. Three-quarters of the troops were three-quarters drunk and the party didn't seem to be winding down any time soon. It was the second day they had camped here, he figured, and they hadn't found the stash of gold Jeremy's father had hidden here among the cliffs.

He sat on a rock outcropping high above the valley floor, a perfect place to watch and observe. The drizzle had stopped and a light breeze swung around to the north. He was damp in his oilskin, but not really uncomfortable. The last night and day of watching the obsessive men dig around in the wrong end of the valley had given him facts he needed to put his plan into motion.

They camped at the opening of the cove where the rivulet ran into the main creek. The vale split farther up into two canyons, which disappeared into the ridge above. Huge chestnuts spread over the valley except for a tiny clump of firs in the bottom flats. Best of all, rocky knolls spread all along the canyon sides and along the bottom, making picturesque falls out of the splash of water in the cove floor. “Picturesque” was nice, but the important thing was the tiny hiding places in the rocks, hundreds of them. Perfectly situated in any of those places, he could do anything he wanted and remain hidden. And rocks leave no footprints. Add to the terrain his natural and learned woodcraft, he would be a virtual ghost to the targets below. The word gave him an idea.

*

Henry slept the night next to the fire. His clothes were somewhat dry, although smoky, but the fire at least provided the needed warmth. He was exhausted. The culmination of weeks of travel, the day’s adventure and the hours of cleanup from that adventure combined to throw him into a dreamless sleep. He woke once, during the small morning hours as some creature approached the fire out of curiosity and the packhorse snorted loudly. He rolled over, saw the green eyes in the dark and got up. He went over to the woodpile he had collected and selected a mixture of hardwoods and sappy pine that would make a hot, blazing fire and threw them on. The eyes disappeared and he lay back down.

*

The night progressed and the rowdiness died down as the alcohol disappeared. The men who didn't pass out around the fire managed to slide into their bedrolls. Good. Drunker, the better. Jeremy still waited. The three-quarter moon broke through as the clouds low on the horizon and, for Jeremy's purposes, was perfectly eerie. The blue light lit the trees and the breeze captured their branches, making the shadows crawl along the ground. The night was very quiet. Nothing moved in camp.

He hopped off the rock and moved into camp. Not a man stirred. There was a cart with its ample supplies parked next to the campsite. He would leave that. He didn't want to leave these men any excuse for leaving until he was done with them and depriving them of their staples would drive them off through hunger.

He moved to the horses, half asleep on their feet. He slid his hand under the halter and caressed the horsy face of the nearest mare. She opened her eyes but, as he'd hoped, didn't start. He moved to the next horse and did the same. It stirred as well but did not move or whinny. When all animals were awake, he gathered their leads and tied them nose-to-tail. Taking his time, he slowly led them down the draw. The *clop* of the horses was surprisingly quiet and did not sound any louder than if they were grazing quietly in their hobbles. Jeremy looked back at the camp. One of the men mumbled in his sleep and as Jeremy watched, he groaned and turned over, and was silent.

He concentrated on routes that led over damp leaves that made no noise. The valley grew steeper and the noise of the stream increased proportionately. They walked about a half a mile and then Jeremy turned up a small canyon. After an hour of walking up the gorge, they reached a saddle at the end, well out of sight or sound of the Yankee camp. He untied and slapped each horse on its rump. Even if they only moved another couple hundred yards, they would still be far enough from the camp to be lost and he expected them to take the easy route to water and head down the other side of the gap. After tonight, if he did things correctly, he didn't expect the soldiers to move anywhere.

He ran down the canyon and back up the valley, creating a circuitous route around the camp. His strong legs carried him quickly up the other steep side. He made it to his original sentinel rock, nodded as he examined the scene, now deprived of its horses, and moved farther up the valley. Staring across the canyon at each other were two rocky cliff faces, about thirty feet high each. These united with others below as the valley spread out, an escarpment face: a natural echo. It was now about three o'clock in the morning and he was ready to begin.

The unnatural scream pierced the night. The rocks magnified and echoed it, eliminating any way to pinpoint its source and making it eerier yet. The moon was brighter now, the clouds having dissipated and left a crystalline atmosphere. The wind moaned and the temperature was much colder than it had been earlier. The effect was not lost on the drunken men. One jerked awake, immediately.

"Damn!" he gasped. "What the hell was *that*?"

A second groaned, hung over.

"Go back ter sleep. You're dreamin'."

"*Help* me! I can't take it… ahhh!" The torturous drawn-out cry waned into a moaning, made somewhat indistinct by the rock echoes. This time, the second man's eyes grew wide. It was clear that it was no dream. Or, if it was, they were all dreaming it at the same time. The fuzziness excessive drink had left didn't help: it primed their imaginations.

"Wake up, boys!" the first man said. The others began to move. The moon cast its spectral light upon the campsite; the fire had gone out and the night had turned cold. It was not a happy awakening.

One hung-over private groaned, "What are you fretting about?" Two of the men were up by now and looking with wide eyes into the shadowy forest.

The echoes had died out and Jeremy waited until all the men were fully awake before letting loose again. A goodly amount of time. When he did let loose a shrill scream, the agony of the supposed tortured man splintered the fragile peace of the valley. The echoes again magnified and distorted the original yell and the remaining troops scrambled to their feet, the more alert grabbing the nearest gun. Several tried to back into the coals left in the firepit.

"I don't like this," one ginger-bearded corporal said, coldly.

"Nor do I. Count heads." This was obviously the leader. His auburn hair indicated his Irish ancestry, but the stocky, muscular build showed a stereotypical "right by might" mentality necessary in such examples of humanity. The others quickly checked themselves and even this far from command, some semblance of discipline showed.

A blond from the other side of the circle spoke up as he staggered to his feet. "All accounted for, sir. What the hell's going on?"

"I don't know." He pointed to the man whom Jeremy immediately labeled Blondie. "Take two men. Spread out and do a gradual search. Don't go too far and be careful. This used to be Cherokee country and those savages still haven't figured out how to be civilized if what I hear is true." He pointed to another two men. "You boys build up that fire. And what's the matter with *you*? You'll bend that gun if you grip it any tighter."

The man in question did indeed seem to be trying to break his gun in half. He tried to relax, but the tension in his shoulders and the look in his eyes still betrayed his personal demons.

"S-sorry, sir. My grandfather was raised down here and he heard stories." He licked his lips and paused as if what he'd said was enough. The leader nodded and he continued.

"Ghost stories, sir. Indians. Stories of vengeance and blood-justice." He rattled on, faster. Now, his mistake: "I *told* you we shouldn'ta done it, I *told* you." In spite of the cool February night, he sweated now.

Several of the others shifted on their feet; one or

two looked out into the moonlit forest. The leader couldn't let them lose it, not now. He decided it wasn't time for mercy. Even if it had been in his nature. He pulled a military dagger, stepped forward and before the man could react, had grabbed his hair, moving the chin up and the head back. The man's eyes watered as the hair roots threatened to pop the man's scalp off his skull. The leader swiftly inserted the point into the man's nostril before he could twitch. The man whimpered and tried to shy away from the razor's tip, his head writhing. The other gripped tighter on the hair. He wanted to whisper for intensity's sake, but it was important that the rest of the men hear the entire drama.

"I wouldn't wiggle if I were you, unless you want to lose more than your nose." His grip tightened on the knife and yet more on the hair.

"You talking about Indians?" he asked.

He paused for effect although the question, of course, was rhetorical.

"You know what the Indians do to an unfaithful squaw? They slit their nostrils. Like…"

The knife moved up suddenly, slicing through the man's cartilage and skin.

"…that."

He pushed the howling man back. The man dropped the gun he still clenched and howling, grabbed at his face, blood already staining his hand, his clothes, the ground.

The leader turned to the others. "You act like a woman; I treat you like a woman. You understand?"

The others nodded. No comments. No one dared. The object lesson, however, was minimized, if not completely lost by what happened next. The scouts were shouting. Blondie rushed into the blazing firelight.

"*The horses are gone!*"

Jeremy was back on his sentinel rock, observing the goings-on. He took careful note of the man with the slit nose and those of the others who at least showed some concern for their actions. Even if just scared. His very meticulous Old Testament justice had not diminished in Jeremy's mind.

He thought, *you, at least, have some conscience. You will die easily.*

*

The sun felt good. The steam still rose off the hills and things were finally drying out. Henry walked the packhorse slowly into the collection of small buildings and muddy byways. You couldn't call it a town. It wasn't quite deserted: a couple of old men sat whittling near a stump in the yard of a clapboard excuse of a house. They looked at him closely. Henry nodded. One continued staring. The other dipped his head minutely.

He continued on. He hoped he could find a wagon. He was tired of walking and wanted to consolidate his supplies. There were several problems.

He would get pegged as a Yankee the first time he opened his mouth; better play mute, hurt in the war or something. He was beat up enough from the mudslide to give the impression of poverty, so *that* wouldn't be a problem; the last thing he wanted to do was to give a desperate or amoral person an excuse for depriving a "rich" man of his supplies. Otherwise, barter was the only medium of exchange here in any case unless he was badly wrong. As poor as this place was, it still seemed to be remote enough from the war to have saved food, which was the only real thing he wanted to barter for. He would just have to wait and see.

As he walked along what passed for other cities' "main street", people began to trickle out of the houses. He smiled inwardly, thinking that the isolation of this place would make the inhabitants very welcome of any visitors, Blue or Gray.

One man walked up to him aggressively, the chip on his shoulder more than making up for the loss of an arm. Henry stopped. The man's beard crept into his neck and above his cheeks: trimming was obviously not a priority here. He wore homespun britches and shirt and he walked barefoot. He chewed tobacco enthusiastically and quickly, and as the face paused within six inches of Henry's, he seemed to convulse, his face writhing about in some sort of way. The explanation came when he, without taking his eyes off Henry's, sort of turned his head just enough to spit and miss Henry's boot by no more than a couple of inches.

"Hey."

Henry just nodded and smiled. The tobacco-filled mouth scowled.

"I said, *'Hey!'*"

Henry smiled and nodded. One-Arm was beginning to rile.

"I can still whip you with *one* arm, so don't give me nonathat *shit*."

Henry's face immediately changed from a sunny smile to an expression of clouds. Then he nodded his understanding, suddenly. He dropped the reins and pointed to his throat. The gestures began to fly, meaningless, apparently, to the man. An old man walked up.

"Cal, can't you be civil to a man?"

"Hell, I *was*! He warn't being civil *back*!"

"Yeah, he was being civil. Can't you understand him? He's *mute*."

The man stepped back minutely. The old man had his hand on his hips, looking intently at him. Cal scratched the stump of his left arm. Embarrassed now, he mumbled a "sorry" and stepped farther back.

The old man crossed his arms and spoke directly to Henry. He was chubbier than Henry would have expected in a poor town as this. He seemed better off than many people in the area, the store-bought shirt tucked carefully into canvas coveralls that, though clean, nonetheless had seen better days. His salt-and-pepper hair was swept back into a ponytail, revealing a like-colored beard, surprisingly closely trimmed. Above that, his eyes shone blue and penetrating, and Henry knew he would have to step very carefully around this patriarch. He looked straight into the wise old eyes.

"War?"

Henry nodded.

"Yankee or Confederate?"

Henry shook his head. He'd known this question would come and wanted to be both ready and honest. He pointed south.

"Seminole?" The old man was nothing if not shrewd as well as knowledgeable. Henry again shook his head and jabbed south. *Farther*, he mouthed. The man's face lit up.

"*Mexican!*" he blurted.

Henry nodded.

"Winnie's crew?"

Henry nodded again. It wasn't exactly lying. He had been an officer in the Mexican war under Winfield Scott and had both seen things he didn't want to talk about and learned the benefits of keeping your mouth shut. These folks didn't need to know that the cause of his muteness wasn't *physical*.

## Chapter 4

Henry leaned back on the porch. Not quite coffee, but there actually seemed to be a pinch of it mixed in with the roasted chicory and other odds and ends people made do in rough times. *Much* appreciated. He nodded to his host and gestured with the cup.

"Oh, don't mention it." The grizzled old man took his place next to Henry in his very personal chair (as he had earlier said, "It's a *sin* to sit in it unless your *me*"). He sighed.

"It ain't real coffee, but it sure does warm the innards, especially after a nasty morning as this one was. Sometimes anything hot'll do, even..." He winked meaningfully. "...*tea*!"

Henry nodded and smiled his appreciation of the joke at the Southerner's own expense. He looked out of the porch and across the wagon trail that what in this part, passed for a highway. The village had fifteen families in it. Each family made its living serving others who tried to work food in the fertile valley bottoms. Their storage was still comparably plentiful in spite of the war and the old man had brokered some agreements to help Henry out with food and, more important right now, a small wagon. He was glad he'd included some "peripheral" gear in his packs. Originally, he'd thought it was to barter with wild Indians out West who of course, might not have use for metal currency, much less paper money or scrip. It made sense, though, that it would also come in handy in an economically bankrupt South, especially in the backwoods towns such as this. He had a couple of mirrors, a sack of nails and a couple of other pieces of hardware the North abounded with. The people here were glad to have them.

"So, now business is over, we can talk. And that means y'all can talk, too." The man sipped, looking straight ahead as if he'd expected Henry's splutter of coffee all along. He continued after he swallowed, his former hick drawl sliding easily into a more genteel, educated accent.

"You do it pretty well, I must say. But it isn't perfect. I can spot a liah"—Henry assumed he meant "liar"— "a mile away. Comes from twenty years on a trial bench, prosecutor, defender *and* judge. Now, why don't you enjoy the rest of that brew, rest your butt awhile and tell me a story? A true one would be nice, now, y'hear?"

"Uh," Henry began. He was embarrassed, not so much of getting caught, but of getting caught by this particular man, one whom he instinctively liked and really did want to leave with a favorable impression.

"Relax, son. I know it ain't easy to spit out the truth once you've been caught, but believe you me, it's easier than some of the alternative. These folk hereabouts don't like being taken for fools. Nor do I." His bushy eyebrows stuck out as he looked out meaningfully from under them.

"Well, sir. I never actually *lied*. I suppose I just allowed you to draw conclusions," he shrugged, "ones that I didn't exactly discourage."

The old man ignored the obvious Northern accent intruding into the distinctly Southern town atmosphere. "Ah. Letter of the law versus spirit, eh? You don't believe in the spirit of the law?"

"Yessir, I do, I really do. But it didn't seem so smart to advertise my family heritage in a place that would not appreciate it, considering Sherman's army is somewhere west of here."

"Well, son, it's *my* place to judge, not yours. I would say you rather painted this town with an awfully broad brush, wouldn't you? For all you know, this is a town full of loyalists, not Rebs. They *do* exist south of the Ohiah, believe it or not."

Henry shrugged again. "I suppose. But your friend out there didn't exactly receive me cordially. And my accent rather sticks out."

The man snorted.

"Yeah, old Cal is carrying something a bit too big for him to tote. Lost his arm in the war. At Shiloh. At the time the doctors were chopping more than healing. Came back afraid others thought he was less a man with an arm gone. Literally. Willing to prove it on anyone, *anyone*, I say, who looks at him cross-eyed or bow-legged. He can do it, too. Used to be a bare-knuckler 'fore the War. He don't mean no harm. Got a good heart, it just needs some healing."

He looked over at Henry. "You coulda helped there."

"I don't understand."

"You don't listen, son. You *could have helped* there. You apparently didn't hear me. You don't *know* that Cal fought for the South. He *may* have been on the North side. Not likely, granted, but still a possibility. Haven't you learned yet that it's not our place to decide where the Good Lord wants us to help? If you were really in the Mexican War as you claim, y'all would have learned something along that line, I think."

Henry sat. He didn't know what to say. The last thing in the world he expected—especially here, miles from nowhere in the Appalachians—was a lesson in ethics. He wasn't sure he particularly wanted one, especially not now.

*

"Cherokee, for sure," said Ginger Beard. "Only they could've stolen the horses so clean."

"Keep your voice down," said the leader. "We don't need to be scaring the men any more than necessary, thanks to that 'woman' we got over there."

Ginger Beard giggled. He was a man whose encounters in blood only whetted his appetite. A hawk the leader loosed at prey when necessary but always tethered when possible.

"Yes," the leader said. "He needed a lesson. Won't last long amongst this bunch." He raised his voice at what he considered the least hung-over of the men.

"Jesse! And… Kevin!" The men in question

turned their faces. "You're the pickets for tonight. Stay awake and stay away from the bottle, 'less you want to wake up dead."

He pointed.

"Jesse, you take that ledge upstream. Kevin, hide yourself in the thickets somewhere across the stream where you have a good view. Protect the camp, looking in, not out. Shoot anything."

Jeremy smiled, watching the pickets move to their posts. The other men went back to their bedrolls. He was close enough to hear almost everything and they still didn't know he was there. He was beginning to enjoy himself, relishing the growing challenge as these seasoned troops adjusted to a threat. Should he finish one tonight, or let a few nights of fear and uncertainty build "dissension in the ranks?" He thought about that for a while. He mustn't get greedy.

The leader was good. Too good, in a way: it was a pity he spent his skills on evil. Without wondering about the incongruity between that thought and the morality of his plans, he backed away until he was back at his sentinel rock.

*

"Most of it's the truth, what I told you," said Henry. "The only difference was that I speak as well as you or anyone. I *was* in the Mexican War, with Winfield Scott, as an officer, a career army man who had just received his commission and all. And you're right. I did learn a lot in that war." Henry paused. He didn't really want to talk about it.

"So. What are you doing down this part of the continent, hmm? You'd think the way things are going it'd be the last place anyone would want to be." The old man cocked his head slightly, his eyes half-closed, but nonetheless piercing in their inquiry. Henry could see the intellect evaluating, considering. Judging, he supposed. He looked out from the porch at the road. No one was on it, the locals spending the time working and not traveling. There was nothing to see on the road and no time for townspeople and farmers to spend looking for things that weren't there. The judge's shrewd questions bothered him. He had not sorted the answers out entirely himself and was not particularly in the right frame of mind to tell them to someone else.

However, there were things he could say, and he knew intuitively that the judge was both curious and had the best for him in mind.

So, in spite of himself, Henry told him about his travels and the routes he had taken through the world. He'd learned a lot, he said, how different places had the same morals though different cultures, how people could be both kind and cruel and, contrary to his rather paranoid performance of the mid-day, how not to pre-judge people. He finally got around to the trouble with his family and the hurried departure from Pennsylvania.

"Between what I learned on the road and the things my grandfather taught me, not to mention a healthy regard for my body's welfare, I decided I could not stay or condone what my brother was doing in his business dealings. It also taught me to listen more and speak less."

"Hmm." The old man stretched in his chair, chomped his mouth as if awakening from an afternoon nap and leaned forward. "Why South?"

"It was a direction he and his men would never think to search for me."

"And…"

"It seemed like a good idea at the time." He shrugged.

"And now?"

Henry grinned. "Considering how lost I am, how the War seems to have followed me and how far I am from my ultimate goals? I don't know. At least they haven't found me and I haven't been bored, that's for sure!"

"It's your business, I suppose," said the judge. He stood up. "Well, son, you've learned a lot more than I think you know." He stood up and turned to enter the house. He paused.

"Too late to travel now. Stay for supper? Don't have too much, but we're better off in this valley than some places. Your story's well worth the vittles." He cocked his head slightly, entreating.

Henry nodded. The old man opened the door and

went inside. Henry stayed on the porch, thinking. Then, not wanting to seem ungracious by delaying, got up and went inside.

*

Kevin nodded. The cool air wafted gently about his head, moving his hair with a mesmerizing touch. For the first time since this venture, the weather was warm: he was warm. There was a slight rustling through the rhododendron bush in which he was hidden. He knew it was the wind. Maybe if he closed his eyes, just for a second… He jerked awake. It wouldn't do to fall asleep with the kind of leadership they had. He could be dead or maimed for such a dereliction of duty. He stirred and looked out at the campsite. Nothing moving in the area, he thought. Even the campfire had gone out again, its tendril of pale smoke drifting slowly up in the night, lost among the branches and new green leaves of the spring foliage. He nodded again.

Jeremy smiled. This one would be easy to take. But not significant, neither in honor nor in the effect he wanted to make. His skills had brought him within five feet of the dozing sentry, both a brash challenge to his woodcraft and a close reconnaissance in the early dark morning.

With all the skill he had, he backed out of the bushes and made a long circle around the camp to where the other sentry was positioned. Jesse was just sitting down and at this time of the morning—about four o'clock, Jeremy figured—reactions were at their lowest. He didn't figure there was too much trouble coming from him, but he would take his time, nonetheless.

Jeremy stepped from exposed rock to exposed rock until he reached the creek. This was probably the most dangerous time of all. He was wrapped in "rhodie" branches and the evergreen leaves covered most of him from sight. The night light took care of the rest. But what would happen if Kevin or Jesse noticed a bush moving in the middle of the stream below them? Jeremy smiled grimly and moved as quickly as possible across to the other side. He was about fifty yards away now and he moved even slower. The sides of the eyes were the most sensitive and he would give Jesse no excuse to wake from his semi-drowse.

Because of their greed for gold, these men had logically, but foolishly as far as he was concerned, based their camp amidst cliffs and boulders enclosing the stream. There was access to water, protection from the wind and nearby were the crevices and holes that allowed a feasible approach to veins of gold underneath, not to mention the cache of "placer's" gold his father had found. But these men did not allow for an enemy within their midst and these same rocks and noisy, rushing water allowed a stealthy man to approach the camp concealed.

He stopped, probably for the fiftieth time in the last fifteen minutes. Slowly, slowly, and they would never notice the changing landscape. Finally, about twenty yards from the camp, he slipped into a crack in the rocks and shed his bushy camouflage; it would only rustle now and noise was more important than sight, now that the moon was below the horizon and he crouched close to the camp.

When he left it, neither Jesse nor Kevin seemed to have moved from their erratic catnaps. Certainly, they had never stirred, much less given an alarm. If they woke now, they would not notice anything had changed, for sleeping men and dead men look very much the same from any distance.

*

"I'm sorry we don't have many fresh vegetables, being early in the year and all. The new crop's only just getting under way." The old man passed over a bowl of cellar apples and Henry selected one. "We also don't have meat all the time. I guess I'm luckily y'all came along or we wouldn't be having it now!"

From what he'd seen so far of the South, Henry now knew this old man was pretty well-to-do. The judge had apparently a good trust from somewhere built up, probably in England or the North, where investments were still fairly capable of growth and not too volatile in a wartime economy. *Nothing like a dern war to make money on,* Henry frowned, remembering his brother's philosophies.

The table had been set when Henry first came into the room for dinner, so it was with some surprise that he saw the fifty-ish thin black woman come through the door with a jug of the coffee-substitute. The judge noted it.

"Ah, yes, you *are* a Yankee, aren't you?" the judge asked. He gestured toward the black woman.

"This is Mary," he said and added quickly, "She's not a slave, she's indentured."

"Indentured? I thought that went out a century ago."

Mary poured the "coffee", left the pot and went back into the kitchen area.

"Yes. Well, I tried to give her freedom a couple years ago, but there were a couple of things that went against it. First, crazy woman likes me, says there's nowhere else to go and she likes working for me. Second, she had a fit, straightened up and told me in no uncertain terms that if she was going free, it was to be on her own terms, that she'll *earn* it. So, we put together a contract of five years—I wouldn't do the standard seven, too long, and she fought me for *that*—after that she'll go free. She's got about eight months to go. After that, I'm not sure *what* she'll do. I suppose I'll have to hire her. Or something."

Mary said nothing, but grunted.

Henry looked at him curiously. "You're a strange man," he said.

"Why?" replied the judge. "Because I live in Rebel country doesn't mean I'm a slaveowner. Okay, well, technically I am, but you know what I mean. I don't let it be known for obvious reasons, but I'm an abolitionist at heart." He paused. Mary put her hand on her hip and smiled at the man.

"Y'all read the Bible, sir?"

"I have read." Henry blushed slightly as he always did at the mention of some church things. In all his travels, he hadn't learned it was okay not to.

"You study it, you'll find much. It's a how-to manual for the world."

"How so?" Henry asked.

"It's a step-by-step manual how to put together and run things, not just yourself, but society as well. It's like your horse. You don't take care of your horse: it'll die on you. Everything, from feeding it properly to cleaning out the frog if it gets messy. Same here. You don't pay attention to some of the statute in the Book, y'all are going to pay for it."

"I think I see," said Henry.

"Anyway, to your statement. Do you remember the part in the Book of Acts where Phillip preaches to the Ethiopian?"

"I'm not sure I do," said Henry, feeling ignorant.

"In the States, we call the Negro 'Ethiopian' sometimes and in some cases, that's literally true. Well, if the Good Book says that the Ethiopian eunuch received God and went on his way rejoicing, what the hell gives us the right to enslave these people that are worthy of His favor?" The judge had worked himself up.

"I agree, sir. My best friend is part Negro."

The judge looked at him. Paused. Then smiled. He relaxed, a bit embarrassed, but had been too long a judge to let an outburst bother him too much.

"I suppose that explains a bit why I rode you this afternoon about being judgmental," he said.

"No explanation necessary," Henry rejoined. "You were right, although to be honest, I never would have expected such a lecture in such a place."

"That's what this war's done to our country—and it is a country. This rabble that's claimed a 'Confederacy' don't know what they're talking about: it was doomed from the beginning. Although I can respect 'states' rights' as an issue, the fight has been worse than the issue."

"Well," Henry raised his cup. "Let's drink to the end of the War and the healing of the nation."

The judge looked at him, smiled again and raised his cup. "I can at least drink to the ending of the War and healing. Unification? I don't know if it'll happen whether I want it to or not."

*

The shriek flew through the air and cut through the morning mist from the creek. Ginger Beard leaped out of his bedroll and without changing direction, grabbed at the rifle leaning against the tree. When he saw that most of the men were still coming awake and that the forest showed nothing beyond the mist, he relaxed, slightly. Then he noticed the single man, standing, staring at a form on the ground. The form in question looked normal, asleep, except for the wet blanket covering most of the body. The blanket was soddened with something dark: too little light this early to really see what it was. Ginger Beard stepped forward.

Even in this light, he could see the man's throat had been cut from ear to ear. Someone left nothing to chance. He looked around. The leader was at his shoulder now.

"What the…?" he asked, rhetorically. Other men stood around the corpse now. He recovered quickly.

"You, Johnson," he said. "Get Kevin and Jesse here right now." Johnson began to leave and then turned back, quickly.

"They're already here, sir."

The leader turned and looked at the circle of men until he found the two sentries, who were breathing heavily from their sprint into camp. They both looked as shocked as the other men. More so, perhaps, since they had apparently been awake all night and had seen nothing.

Jeremy watched as the rest of the men stepped back and the leader stepped forward. And watched him beat the ever-loving daylights out of Kevin. Doing his job for him. From the looks of things, Jeremy didn't expect Kevin to live through this one. Jesse stood, too scared to run—although almost too scared not to and afraid he'd get shot either way. The wheels worked in his head, wondering why he was being allowed to live.

## Chapter 5

The track dipped down into the vale. The sun was fading into the torn wool of clouds left by an afternoon shower. In front of him the huge granite cliffs shone black, silhouetted against the evening sky and crowned with a variety of trees: mostly firs and pines at the top, a blend of oaks and poplars in the valley. He knew he was fairly high up, higher than he'd ever been before, and yet his desire reminded him that the legendary Rockies were yet much higher than this.

He sighed. He was seeing beautiful country but his heart was already West.

Judge Anderson amazed him. In this wilderness of the South, the last thing he'd expected was the generosity, forgiveness and—he chuckled to himself—the lecturing in morality. If the judge only knew. The packhorse twitched its ears back at the sudden break in the backcountry silence, identified the sound and proceeded to ignore him. It plodded along as it had in the years since it had been a saddle horse.

Henry had left the little town in the early morning. The Judge was more than generous and was heartily offended at Henry's attempt to pay him.

"No, boy, you got something I ain't got. Youth. I know you're in your thirties, but that's still youth if you treat it right. I were even ten years younger, I'd be stowing away among your gear. I'd love to go West."

He pointed down the road, the opposite opening in

the buildings from the one he'd entered.

"Head down there three miles, or so. You'll come to a 'Y'. Don't head left, that'll take you East to Asheville and then into deep South, along the coast, where they *definitely* got opinions on Northerners." He winked. "Y'all 'll wanna go right. That'll take you up near Helen, and points West. You'll see some more gorgeous country 'tween here and there, and the people, tho' strange to our way of thinking, are good people as long as you stay in the backcountry. Lotsa community. You'll be tolerated at least, if not actually welcomed in most places. Just don't talk Yankee if you can help it! And stay away from Sherman's army! No one knows where they are at this point, but you can bet if they're anywhere south of Chattanooga, there'll be one hell of a long line of communications or logistics!"

"With that wagon, you'll have to stay to the road. Try to get another horse soon, you'll be able to avoid some of the patrols pressing people into service by staying off the main trail. That kind of thing'll happen more as you get out of the hills on the western side of the mountains."

He stopped and took a breath.

"I'll miss ya. We had some good talks. All in a day, I know, but good talks nonetheless. Sure you can't stay awhile?"

Henry had shaken his head. His heart was set West.

The horse shifted slightly as it guessed at the

footing of a steep section. The wagon bumped after. There was a mist in the valley floor. *Could be thick tonight*, he thought. All the better, he supposed. Better to go hidden the more west he got.

The cliffs on his right and left began to glow with that "orangey" pink a post-storm sunset will give. Although cooler, it was not cold, and Henry unbuttoned his top shirt buttons and rolled up his sleeves, better to dry off the sticky moisture the humid rainstorm had forced past his slicker. There was no wind, except that zephyr flowing past his ears caused by the patient stride of the packhorse. All was silent.

He jumped, startled, in his seat.

"Ride w' ye?" The voice came from behind and Henry cursed, unusual in itself. The stranger picked it up and laughed.

"Must be a preacher 'r something the way you stumbled over that last word!" he cackled. "I can cuss something *awful*." He raised his voice and seemed to scream into the gloaming, such was the contrast with that previous stillness.

"My name's Billy Hawg and I'm the best drinker, best fighter and ESPECIALLY the best cusser in the South."

He laughed, loud and boisterous. His horse was obviously used to it: it didn't budge from its slow walk. Henry grabbed his reins as his packhorse jumped and skittered, threatening to bolt if given the excuse. He wondered what kind of boor he'd run into. Or been run into by.

Hawg kicked his horse to a trot until he rode even with Henry. Henry stopped. Hawg did, too. Henry steeled himself against the stench of chewing tobacco, smoking tobacco, body odor and what else he couldn't identify. His eyes began to water when the wind drifted his way.

Hawg looked him over. Henry did the same to the other. Billy Hawg was a short wiry man, looking anywhere from a hard-living thirty to a well-preserved sixty. Henry stopped that thought. This man hadn't seen enough to be contemplative, much less humble as a forty-something man would be. His beard looked like an untrimmed hedge: thick and with just enough definition to make it look as if it had been cared for once upon a time, and wider than it was long. Brown with just a trace of gray around the sideburns, it matched the thatch of hair that grew around the head that was not covered by an old leather hat. The eyes twinkled, with humor or conspiracy or both, Henry couldn't figure. He had jeans above the boots—boots! Henry noted with slight alarm. Boots in the South were hard to come by these days. Unless you were into scavenging battlefields. And the man was definitely no Northerner.

"Don't look like no preacher." He tapped the horse into a slow walk and walked in front of Henry and his horse. He threw out his chest, then leaned over his saddle horn.

"Don't look like much o' *anything*."

It sounded like a purposeful challenge and Henry

sat up a bit straighter. He wasn't so naive as to travel without some firepower and his left hand was unobtrusively resting on it now. He was hoping the stranger didn't notice. He didn't want to precipitate anything. Glad he was not to have thrown away his service revolver when he left the army.

*

Ginger-beard squinted into the gloaming, trying to adjust his eyes to the diminishing light. The horses had never been found, as if they'd never existed at all. He suspected part of the reason was a certain disinclination of the scout to go too far into "Indian country." A small detail buried the dead men—the man with the slit nose that Jeremy had killed, and Kevin, whom their leader had beaten to death—together in a community grave on the hillside. If they'd been on the move, they would have left them to rot, but they were certain the mine lay in this cove and would not leave until they had found the gold. Tangible corpses were not good things for morale. Out of sight out of mind, he thought.

With sunset, the men had begun to drift back from the various rocks in the cove, unsuccessful in their hunt for the yellow metal. They were tiring of this game and Jeremy's nocturnal contributions made it even less enjoyable. Raiding farms was a lot easier, profitable and more fun in the long run. A mythical gold mine would not hold them here for long. Hell, they might as well *work* for a living! Ginger-beard grinned. The promised carrot was beginning to disappear from these soldiers' minds as the search progressed and the leader's stick was becoming ineffective against this Indian specter of death that haunted them.

The smoke from the fire disappeared into the dark sky overhead and that same dark brought out the red glow of the flames. As men crashed, falling onto their bedrolls, they dug into packs for the evening's ration of hardtack. A man who had been designated "cooky" grabbed some bacon and a cast iron skillet out of the wagon and began to fry. There was some low talk and Ginger-beard relaxed slightly. The leader's iron hand had quenched the nervous talk the slit-nosed man had begun and it seemed that things were at least wearing a facade of normalcy.

A man returned out of the gloom and approached. Ginger-beard nodded to him. "Yes?" he asked.

"Been out all day and ain't seen nothing. No horses, still. I didn't want to go too far, of course. I saw a couple of footprints, moccasins, looked like, downstream from here about a quarter mile. All mixed among the hoofprints. After that it gets real rocky and the trail—even the horse trail—disappears. They know what they're doin'. I'm just not a good enough tracker to do anything more."

The leader joined them. Ginger-Beard deferred.

"'Kay," said the leader. "You're the best tracker we got. You and Jesse are watch tonight. All night. I don't want to take the chance of a fuzzy-headed private just waking up missing something in the middle of the night."

He raised his voice. "*Jesse!*"

Jesse jumped up from the fire where he'd been soaking his hardtack in the bacon grease to make it softer. "*Sir!*"

The leader waited until the suddenly panicked man arrived. He looked at him intently until Jesse dropped his eyes.

"You saw what happened to Kevin this morning?"

"Yessir."

"Will that *motivate* you tonight?"

"Yes*sir.*"

"'Kay. I'm going to put you in Kevin's position: on the outside looking in. Any doubt as to what'll happen you make the same mistake tonight?"

"Nossir."

"'Kay. Get some sleep for the next couple of hours. I want you two fresh at nine o'clock and ready to *stay* fresh until dawn. Gottit?"

"Yessir," the two men replied.

Jeremy was impressed. Soldiers who came back to Helen from some battle or other talked of swapping watches through the night, and no chance for catching up on sleep if there was anything going on and then being asked to dig a privy or some other menial task. This man was bucking tradition by giving assignments to specific men on watch. That was their job: nothing else would be required of them, the more to concentrate on that assignment and the more to keep them fresh and awake.

Fine. Plenty of time to work, and he knew exactly what he was going to do.

*

Hawg leaned back in his saddle and appeared to relax, swinging one leg up onto the horse's neck. His eyes narrowed as he continued to examine the ex-officer.

"Hmmm. Army man, eh?"

He spat.

"I can tell by the way y'all's sittin'. Ready for *fun*," he said as he leaned forward. Henry still didn't say anything. He hadn't thought about it, but he was sitting on the front of his hams, leaning forward with his hand on his hip. The man grunted.

"Yep. Hell, I don't mean you no harm."

Henry spoke up now.

"Something I can do for ya?" He tried to slur his words and at the same time copy the inflections that he'd been listening to for the last week. But the rider picked it up right away. The obnoxious laugh broke through the deepening evening.

"Haw! Haw! Haw! I seen it! A *Yankee*! What the hell you doing down in Dixieland, boah?"

"Traveling." He wanted to add "boah" but things weren't settled yet. Not by a long shot. He smiled wryly at the pun. At this point, he'd just as soon make it a *long* shot: scare the man off rather than injure him. The stranger walked his horse forward a bit until he was by Henry's right side. He couldn't see Henry's sidearm from there and therefore, didn't know the left-handed man had his hand on it.

"Well, unless you're into sleeping and riding at the same time, I'm thinking it might be a good time to quit the riding and start the sleeping, if you know what I mean. There's a good clearing about a mile and a half from here. Got some venison, but I'd split that for a share o' tack or what-have-you from one of them packs."

"Fine, but I was planning on making my bivouac in the bottom of the valley here."

The man shrugged. "Fine, but it's your ass gonna be wet by morning. All bog. No good for anything but skeeters."

Henry slapped the reins on the gelding's back. The horse reluctantly resumed the long walk.

"It's amazing what a good oilskin'll do against the wet."

Hawg pulled farther up alongside the right side of the cart and rode, keeping pace. He purposefully had his back to him, Henry figured. Bravado or a show of faith? He wondered. Henry kept his left hand on his revolver. The voice from the hat continued.

"Wal, I imagine we can find a dry spot somewhere's on that crick. Some places just rise up above the water and drain pretty good. Yep, you can see that kinda place really easy and this time of year you got some grass that'll set you down to sleep light'n easy. Might even find some wood for a bit of a fire. Although most of *that*'ll be punk. Damp. No good except for getting smoke in your eyes. Although, I s'pose smoked deer meat is pretty good, you get it done right. Takes forever, though. Die of hunger before you get the meat to your face. Now, *this* place I got in mind. Get there in, say, half hour'r so. Bit farther, but much better. *All* grass. Good wood. Light the fire right away and stuff your face with grub afore the moon comes up."

Hawg continued. Non-stop. Henry bore it as long as he could, then abruptly stopped the cart.

"Look here. You intruded on my peace and if you got to ride along, you need *keep* the peace, you get my drift?"

Billy did nothing but just kept grinning, occasionally spitting a brown-colored glop to one side. He must have been the most irritating man Henry had ever met, and he had met his share.

"Wahl, now, if'n you don't like my comp'ny, thass alright. Now, I knew a man back in Texas, this was when I was down there, y' know Santa Anna and the Alamo? Tough time that was. I wasn't there, no, but I had a friend of a son of my cousin who died there." And he didn't stop there.

Henry's sense of danger from this man waned as the annoying side of him grew. He sighed with the infinite patience experience had taught him. He removed his hand from the revolver and pointedly interrupted.

"I don't trust anyone on the road I don't know better than my mother, no offense, and I for sure am not going to take the suggestion of a stranger to bunk up in a place I don't know better than my home town. We set in the creek bottom. Once we're set, I'll swap some grub with you, but until then: *shut up!*"

The annoying grin dissolved into the furry face and the green eyes drooped for a split-second. Henry hesitated for a moment. He didn't like to offend anyone and obviously that boundary had been breached with this man. Before he could make up his mind what to say, Hawg had dug his heels into the side of his horse and resumed the walk several paces ahead of the packhorse. Henry whirled the reins and the cart lurched forward.

*

This time, the fire was not allowed to burn low. It cast a bright light into the chestnut trunks and wavering shadows moved behind every rock and tree up the valley. That would not be a problem, first because his destination was not the camp itself and second, it had been Jeremy's experience that the brighter the light, the darker the shadow.

He didn't bother with camouflage this time. There was no need. He would stay among the rocks until he approached his target. The Tracker (as the leader had called him) would be the most vigilant, Jesse's terror of the leader and the "Indians" notwithstanding. He would be looking out and making sure that Jesse would be safe, as Jesse would be looking in at the camp, each covering the other.

As the shadows moved, he moved. Even the woodman's patience was sorely taxed as he waited for the variations in light a fire will naturally give. They had built the fire for maximum brightness and every minute or so there was a pop and a flare as gas pockets exploded from the interior of a superheated log. Though it would only last a second or two, Jeremy used the noise and distraction and the suddenly shifting shadows to move to the next cover.

It took him an hour to cover the two hundred yards to the target. By this time, he was in the rhododendron bushes that had hidden Kevin the previous night and now contained Jesse.

The man was visibly shaking and not from the cool night. He stayed in a constant state of terror. On one hand, he had the invading "Indians" to contend with, and he'd seen how effectively silent they could be. On the other, he'd seen what a lapse in discipline or skill had cost Kevin. Feeling a little bit sorry for the man, but much less sorry than determined, Jeremy moved forward, drew his knife and clamped his hand over the frightened man's mouth.

## Chapter 6

Henry closed his eyes. Billy sawed logs in the loudest way on the other side of the fire, but with a full belly and a long travel day, he would not have a problem sleeping. He reached into the holster he was still wearing and removed the revolver. He placed it on his chest and wrapped his hand securely around the handle and outside the trigger guard: he didn't want to shoot himself in the middle of a bad dream. Hawg changed the style of snores and the breathing stopped. Henry opened his eyes. He wondered if Hawg had just died in his sleep and half rose to go see. Billy twitched violently and went to a third type of snore that sounded like the cross between the squeak of a wagon wheel and his family's munitions factory, including the test firings. He chuckled under his breath, pulled the blanket up to his chin, over the revolver and his hand, and drifted off.

Music wafted by him. He closed his eyes and let it soothe him. He sat on the patio outside the country house of the commanding officer. Up in Virginia it was, a beautiful Victorian house with rolling hills around it. Blossoms floated along as the warm light wind moved over the fields. One of the wives was on the piano, an officer played the cello and another performed the clarinet. New from Europe, the popular "chamber" music of Brahms swirled around the garden. Henry sighed and opened his eyes.

A gust of wind grabbed the newly published music off the cellist's music stand. The audience breathed a gasp of horror at the social impropriety and the music faltered. The cellist stopped playing suddenly and made a grab at the paper, letting go of the cello at the same time. The instrument went over and Henry cringed as the delicate cello hit the ground with a loud…

…click.

Immediately, his eyes opened and the world came rushing back in on him as a full view of Billy half-lit by the fire towered over him. He shifted his hand immediately and the revolver barrel poked the blanket up at the specter that loomed out of the dark night above him.

"Don't move," he said, quietly.

"Hush!" For the first time, Henry noticed that Billy wasn't even looking at him, wasn't bending over him. His head cocked to one side and his attention was on something in the woods. He then saw that there was no gun in Billy's hand: it was still tethered at his leg. The click must have come from his stepping on a couple of rocks around the fire.

Now, he heard it, too. There was a murmur in the distance, voices, he thought, coming from the hillside above him.

"Time to move. Quietly." The ever-present obnoxiousness was gone in the voice. Henry didn't question, but rolled over and went to the wagon where he had left the rifle. Stupid! Getting it was a moment lost and he *knew* better. He retrieved the Winchester and floated back into the trees, unknowingly using the same technique in the firelight that Jeremy was using at the same time, some miles to the west.

The voices increased. The camp was completely empty and even the horses had been tethered a ways off on some new grass by the stream. The bedrolls and the dying coals were the only evidence of human activity. The voices stopped. They'd evidently seen the fire. A branch snapped in the distance and a short curse at the noise defined both the direction and intention of the intruders.

There was no hail, no "hello, the fire", or anything innocent travelers used to defuse the naturally tense situation of a camp in the remote woods. Henry didn't know whether they were random thieves taking an unexpected opportunity or if he and Billy had been tracked. At this point, he didn't even know the strangers weren't aligned with Hawg for some reason or another. He was still wondering this when a shape grew out of the dark of a tree.

Patience, he said to himself. We still don't know what they want. But then: Thank goodness the horses are down by the creek. They haven't seen them yet.

The shape continued to grow until the form of a man detached itself from the tree trunk. A flareup momentarily lit the figure, which then subsided into shadow. An arm was in front of it and what was obviously a revolver made it seem far longer than it was. A shadow behind it merged with it as a similar arm with a similar revolver seemed to attach itself to the man's head.

"Move, your dead." It was Billy's voice. Henry stayed where he was. He'd discovered many things in these few seconds. First, and most relieving, Billy was not likely part of the intruders. Second, he didn't seem by nature a killer, prone to shoot first and ask questions later, even in these extremely selfish, violent times. Third, this was only one down. At least one more sneaked through the woods behind, unless this one was simple in his head and talked to himself. And he didn't believe that in his remotest dreams.

Billy pushed the man onto the ground, face down. He stepped on the gun-wrist and applied pressure until the hand released the weapon. He kicked it away. He spoke very quietly to the man lying prone.

"I'll be watching you. You so much as stir, I'll blow your ever-loving brains out. You got any to believe me with?"

The man nodded. Billy melted into the forest shadows. Henry was impressed. Billy got around well in the woods and apparently had found out that this man was only reconnaissance, sent to find the strength of resistance in the camp. He was so confident that he didn't even bother to question the man. Empty bedrolls had lured the man in too far and he was paying for it now. The others would show when he didn't.

It took half an hour, but Henry was too charged with adrenaline to doze. The fire was almost gone, but the waning moon had risen, casting its blue light upon the bluer smoke curling up from the dying coals. Even the night creatures mellowed, tired or fed, and the night was silent except for the gurgle of the brook.

A change in the creek's splashing brought his attention to the front. It was not loud, but the variation was a cannon blast in the silence of the early morning. His head perked up and his sharpened hearing detected two sources flanking the camp. He strained his eyes and spotted a ghost descending the hillside. So, three additional intruders walked in the black woods. A rustle in the new spring grass showed the first two had crossed the stream. They approached the little knot of firs in which the camp was imbedded.

After a bit, he could see the ghostly shape against the moonlit grass by the brook. Although he still could not see the other two, his ears confirmed a continued approach to the camp. They sneaked up to the trees impressively quiet, in spite of the unnecessary noise earlier in the night.

The man on the ground was either asleep or so convinced of Billy's threat that he had decided not to press his luck. Too bad for him. A shotgun blasted the air, twice, and the man on the ground gave an involuntary grunt and went slack, oozing blood in dozens of tiny holes where the shot had pierced him. At the same time, small caliber gun shots snapped from another bearing and Billy's bedroll jumped as if there were snakes living in it. A shadow jumped out of the woods. A white man, fully bearded, wearing filthy overalls and no shirt, kicked at Billy's bedroll and gave a grunt. He turned to look at his compatriot by the fire. He immediately knew he had injured or killed the wrong man, even without examination. He cursed and immediately regretted it.

The curse was too loud for sense. He crouched, suddenly paranoid of the concealing forest. Before he could move, two more men moved out from the woods.

"We git anything?" One of the men ventured as he walked foolishly upright into the clearing.

"Yeah," he said, still looking into the forest. "We got Paul. Let's git. And *now*."

"Dern moonlight!" the second man said, with feeling. It was likely he was less feeling an emotional loss for Paul, than he understood the mistake they'd made. The men all began to run for cover, too late. This became obvious in the next blink of an eye as Billy Hawg fired without warning.

The man in the overall flung the shotgun into the air as blood splashed from his chest, black in the sullen light. The others spun around to the sound of the revolver, but before they could raise their guns, four more shots snapped from the same side of the clearing and they went down, each with a pair of leaky holes in the torsos.

The night was still again. Henry hadn't moved much beyond the slow attempt to raise his revolver.

"Bit slow, ain'tcha?" Billy's sneer popped out of the shadow that emerged from the other side of the clearing. He moved to the collapsed figures around the fire and began to loot the bodies. Not that there was much on these thieves besides the firearms and ammunition. Henry scanned the woods.

"Any more, you think?"

"Nah. If'n I know anything about the woods—and I do—ain't a deer within half a mile, much less human bein's."

Henry lowered the revolver hammer and moved out of the woods toward the fire pit. "Know 'em?" he ventured.

"Nah. Probably just some locals wanting to pack their money belts. You?"

"No."

Henry looked at the bodies.

"Look, with you blasting away with no warning, how was I supposed to get my gun up quick enough to give you a hand? Even if I was inclined to kill first and ask questions later."

His veiled accusation did not go unnoticed. Billy stopped his examination of the bodies and straightened up, looking at Henry. He did not do anything. Didn't make a move with his gun, didn't walk toward him, just looked at him. What followed was—albeit in less educated language than the judge had provided—the second most educational speech on morality he'd heard in his life. In its own way, this dealt no less with pre-judging people than the judge's speech did.

"Ya wanna know why I shot 'em so quick? Three against two and you *wonder*? We'd both be dead if they ain't been slow and stupid. Sometimes you get only one shot—*only one*—you hear the click and if you're lucky, you ain't dead 'cause the bastard missed and your picking up your gun and drilling him afore he gets the next one *off*. You, a military man, and *you* don't know that?"

He took a breath. Henry was a bit shocked at this sudden eloquence, especially from this cussing, chewing, rawboned man.

"Second, did you see the way *they* shot 'first'? Didn't you see them shoot their own and not even hesitate? Call *that* a fair shot? No, man was just lying there and they thought it was you or me. I gave them the same chance they'd 've given us. If they'd hollered the camp, hell, if they'd even 've drawn a bead on me lying there and done *anything* but shoot, at least one of 'em would be alive, if not kickin'."

"Now, dammit, 'fore you open your stupid trap again, help me drag these yokels outta here so we can get some sleep!"

*

The young soldier awoke in the early dawn, as Jeremy watched. He sat up in his bedroll and scratched himself, snapping joints as the muscles stretched in cause. His hair was frazzled from heavy sleeping in warm weather: no comb would untangle that dirty mess with the porcine habits these men had developed. His campmates yet slept heavily. Although harsh orders had stopped the extremely heavy drinking it had not minimized the stress of random and impending death weighing upon them. But the hard work of each day's search for the gold cache ensured the night would be restful and they did not stir until forced to.

The haze was extensive throughout the area and sagged into the little valley. It was not heavy enough to be fog and prophesied a warm day despite the early season. The boy stood up and looked around. He pulled his suspenders over his shoulders and, bladder being more important than boots, wandered barefoot off to the well-known collection of brush, trees, boulders and tangle that the troopers used as a privy. A fairly well-worn path ran up the slope to the ridge a couple of hundred yards away—even this ragtag collection of thieves knew not to foul their own nest—and the boy gingerly tiptoed as fast as he could. A muffled grunt or curse squeaked out as his toes hit roots and tiny but sharp pebbles pierced his soles. Jeremy did not move as the boy moved up the trail directly toward his position.

The escarpment that ran along much of the valley was fully thirty feet in height and varied from sheer rock faces to vine-covered mud. At the upper end, the highest cliffs formed a barrier over which the stream fell fifty feet through a cleft. As the valley deepened and the ridges fell away from the mountainside, clusters of ancient granite thrust up through the forest-covered soil. Abreast of the camp, rocks jutted up and their crowns overlooked the flat bottom of the valley where the campsite lay. A small rivulet melted through moss and algae in the back of a tiny alcove near their pit. Poplars overhung the niche and even this early in the year were sending green shoots from the smallest twigs.

The private unbuttoned his britches and began to

make water. He sighed with relief; his eyes closed. Fully awake now, he opened his eyes and began to look around as he finished and buttoned his fly. The morning progressed slowly and the light grew. He glanced down at the tiny pool at his feet. It was slightly discolored, a little reddish against the stone bowl in which it collected: the scum tended to grow quickly during early warm spells this far in the South, he thought. He snapped his suspenders back to the shoulders and looked up the little waterfall as he began to turn toward the camp.

Almost as unnerving as Jeremy's screams of torture the first night was this boy's screams as he ran heedless of stone, root or bramble down the path to the camp. Though tired and asleep, the camp was strung tight as piano wire, and instantly awoke. The leader leapt out of his roll as the private ran into camp. The blubbering soldier was out of control and without wasting the time to yell, the leader smacked him twice across the face to stop the mess of unintelligible drivel. Though faint, he could hear the report of each blow even from his post above the camp privy and for all his freshly acquired hardness, Jeremy winced at the ferocity as the boy fell back before his attacker.

The leader waited for the boy to settle down, his icy patience far more unnerving than a screaming order or physical blow would have been. The private stopped slowly, the hysteria settling to a sobbing, the sobbing to a scared but sullen silence. The leader spoke.

"Now, son, we need information to do anything beneficial, right?"

The boy nodded.

"'Kay. Whatja see? And…" he looked pointedly at the boy, his index finger in his face, "under control, hmmm?"

The boy nodded again, still mute. The leader gestured for him to continue.

"W-w-w-ell, s-s-sir. I was first awake here, dern birds woke me up and I went off to take a piss, sir. So, I went up the trail, up to the privy, like, as you ordered us to do to keep the camp clean, and I seen him."

The leader's eyes narrowed and he cocked his head slightly in askance.

"Yessir, I seen him, or at least one of them."

The leader held up his hand. "In order. Leave no details out."

"Well, sir, I was peeing and doing up my britches and all and was looking around and I looked up. At the top of the rock above there was this green man all painted up and crouched on the rock there. Couldn't see much of him, but just the eyes peeking out and then you could kinda seen the rest if you looked closely, I think. I didn't wait to find out. But above me, swinging from the poplar branches above the little fall was Jesse and Travis"—by whom Jeremy assumed he meant the "Tracker" as he'd thought him— "dead! Their throats were cut and they were d-d-dripping on me." He swallowed hard. The private was about to go crazy; he was dancing around, but the leader's steel control and stern countenance forestalled that temptation.

The leader stared at the boy. A moment lapsed and then he moved into action. He counted the remainder left: five of nine, besides himself and Ginger Beard. He regretted killing Kevin now. Albeit a harsh lesson to the others, it was foolish and merely an indulgence to his inclinations rather than an exercise for his infamous icy logic.

Now it was time to work. He pointed to two men.

"Four hours on, four off. You watch, the rest work and we'll rotate. All day and all night. You have an idea now of what sleeping'll cost you. So, don't. Your first duty is to dig us a new privy downstream up on that little ridge. We'll leave the bodies up at the old one. Keep the privy close, in sight. If you gotta use it, grab an armed partner to keep an keep an eye out. Now, grab your guns and let's move. Kyle and Richard, you do breakfast, for yourselves and for the sentries."

The men turned to obey and the leader stopped with a final order.

"This time, let's all stay in camp during the night. I have no idea how they got Travis: most likely lured him out. Remember, they can't kill or steal anything in the camp without coming into the camp. So don't get lured out. Indians are famous for luring a party out and then ambushing them."

As the men began their assigned duties, Jeremy slipped off the rock above the old privy and began planning his amusement for that night.

## Chapter 7

They didn't talk much as they set to breakfast. Tired and stressed from the adventure in the early morning, neither wanted to sleep in. Henry felt a mixture of embarrassment and curiosity. Billy either wasn't much of a talker in the morning, or he was still upset. In any case, it took a bit for things to warm up, both the breakfast and the camaraderie. Henry shared some of the oatmeal that was dry and unspoiled: mush was mush, North or South. Billy wandered off in the brush for a while and returned with a handful of newly sprouted raspberry leaves. He threw them into the smallest pot he'd already set on the fire to boil. Henry cocked an eyebrow. Billy grinned.

"Yep, you do okay in the woods, you guess, but you still got a lot to learn! Raspberry leaves make a fine tea when there ain't coffee to be had. Good for colds, too. You just don't want to get the old or dead ones. Cost you a stomach ache." He pointed into the woods. "Lotsa stuff in there."

Billy had killed the deer only a couple days before and the haunches he had cut were aging slowly in the cool weather of early spring and still very good. They sliced off strips and roasted them over the fire as the tea and the oatmeal cooked. Billy looked up, hopefully.

"Molasses, mebbe?" he asked.

Henry grinned. The tension cracked.

"Better," he replied. He got up and walked over to

the cart. After rummaging through a pack for a bit, he pulled out a small crockery jar sealed with a wax top.

"The last place I stayed in had a farmer with some bees. The town was so far away from anybody that some of the things they had were really abundant. I guess what I'm trying to say is he was really sick and tired of living on honey and desperate for a couple of things I brought south."

As he stepped over the log, he reached up to a fir that was mixed in among the poplars and broke off a small branch. The healthy tree ensured the needles on the end would stay fixed when they used it to dip into the honey and the needles would retain most of the honey without excessive dripping. Henry opened the crock with his knife and dribbled some honey onto the oatmeal pot. Then, he sucked the fir twig clean.

Now that they had broken the silence, they began to talk. They talked of the war and took educated guesses as to where Sherman's army might be. Billy had fought in the initial days of the war, but when given leave had deserted without a qualm. Two major battles and eternal skirmishes, he said, were enough to convince him that one could push his luck with Providence only so long and then even God would lose patience and call him home for an accounting. He also thought it was a rather useless fight: while the South could win battles, they could never win the war.

Since then, he'd been plugging along, living off the land and learning a lot.

"Ain't got a family," he said. "A good thing, I

s'pose, considerin'."

Henry decided to broach the sore subject of last night. Billy squinted at him in the early morning sun.

"I'll bet you think I ain't got no morals. Shoot first and don't bother with questions, 'cause it's fun er something? Hell, I seen enough in the war and outside the war to rub the 'morality' a little smooth, if'n you get my drift. But I still got 'em. Only difference is I'll match my 'morals' with that of my opponent if they make me. 'Cause they don't care what my morals are and'll take advantage of 'em. You ever hear of the saying 'Those who live by the sword shall die by the sword'? Well, that's what those dogs last night was doin'. They shot first, intending to forget the questions, and so I decided they should go by the same standards, eh?"

"So 'morals' change depending on the circumstance is what you're saying. Suppose some local constable decides to arrest you for acting as judge and jury? What 'morals' are you hoping that he'll use when it comes down to hanging you for killing another man? His own? Yours? The mayor's? Or the law of the land?"

Billy thought.

"I see your point. Still, we'd both be dead if I hadn't."

"I know that, that's not the point. Look, I fought in Mexico and saw the difference between cold-blooded murder and killing in battle, not to mention self-defense.

I know what it means."

Henry leaned over and picked up the messy pots. After washing them in the brook, he filled them with water and came back to the fire.

"Billy, I like you. So far, anyway. I think you have some great qualities that would make traveling with you enjoyable, and safer. But let's have a simple agreement. Let's hold off killing until the last possible moment. Knock them unconscious, shoot their thigh, tie them up and leave them, but let's not kill them out of hand. I think there are also some practical reasons for doing so, too."

He killed the fire and stirred up the ashes. He pulled the extra dirt over the pit until there was a smooth, level plain where the fire had been. Then he picked up the grass turfs that he had cut to make room for the pit and placed them like puzzle pieces over the dirt until there was a consistent field of green. Billy was impressed in spite of his earlier comments on Henry's woodcraft. After a day or two, the quickly growing spring grass would cover the seams between each turf and even cover the horses' prints. No one had been here.

Billy agreed to Henry's stipulations. Privately, he thought he could agree now to keep the peace for present and change as necessary to keep their lives. Besides, he wasn't going any place or doing anything.

The night's entertainment notwithstanding, he was a man of peace, as he called himself, although others usually used the word, "lazy." He instinctively liked Henry. There was something about him that seemed to settle things down: a comfortable "home" base, as Billy thought it. It was practical to travel in pairs. The night's adventure proved that.

It took them only a few minutes to pack and leave.

*

Ginger Beard searched with the exploring men. As the leader had ordered, two armed sentries protected the others. The other five split up into groups of two and three to comb the upper end of the valley. Their insatiable lust for the gold collided with their natural instincts for survival. Their explorations naturally inclined toward easily defensible positions.

The leader and Blondie explored the south side of the valley; Ginger Beard was on the north. *God, this was getting frustrating!* The old man had said it was in the rocks along the stream, but he died before they could get anything more out of him. After four days, they were no nearer than when they had started and now, they were sweeping the upper end of the canyon.

The stream itself had yielded nothing to this point. The only rocks at the top of the valley were in the stream itself and there was a large cliff. The cliff looked like a dam in the valley, cleft by a narrow chimney that stretched up seventy-five feet or so. Deep in this crevice, the stream poured into a basin that leaked out the bottom of the chimney.

Something clicked in Ginger Beard. It was here. He knew it, somehow.

He ran down the side of the hill toward the cliff base. The going was rough: between bushes and loose, sliding rocks he risked a broken leg. The cliff loomed over him as he slowed to a walk near the stream. The chasm was cold, much colder than the sun-warmed slopes outside and he could see that the vertical walls disappeared into the water. He didn't know how deep the pool was and he could not swim.

"Thomas!" He yelled at the private behind him, who desperately tried to keep up without twisting an ankle.

"*Sir!*" Thomas panted.

"Can you swim?"

"Yessir… I learned as a toddler." His breath heaved. "Like a fish."

"I hope your wind's better under water than it is running," Ginger Beard said, wryly. "See that pool? I think what we're looking for is in there. That old bastard told the truth. Sort of. It's in the rocks but nowhere you'd normally look for it."

Thomas' eyes grew big and excited, and the imminent presence of gold smudged away the haunting of dead men and vengeful Indians.

Jeremy looked down from the ridge. He had followed all the men as they hunted along the stream. He watched Ginger Beard and this man called Thomas from the north side of the canyon. He moved quickly until he was at the corner where the cliff face met the slope of the valley. He was still high up, about two hundred yards from the crevice where the two men let loose their avaricious thoughts.

He sat down upon the flat rock he had chosen when he first realized the soldiers would eventually explore the cliff area. He took out a homemade tripod made of several stout branches lashed together and spread in a teepee shape. One branch with a strong "Y" at the top intersected the middle of the teepee, solidly founded upon the rock beneath. His Kentucky long rifle's amazing characteristics were evidence of more than a decade's care and fine-tuning. With a good marksman behind it, it would drop a small animal from a long distance and Jeremy considered himself a good marksman. The heavy rifle gave the steadiness he needed, but he enjoyed using the tripod. It was a guarantee.

Jeremy reached into his makeshift pack and pulled out a length of soft wool cloth he'd taken from the uniforms of the men he'd slain. He loaded the gun, using a little extra charge than he was used to: he didn't want too loud a noise, but neither did he want a spent ball to hit wrong at the distance he was shooting. He inserted a peeled stick into the barrel. He wrapped the wool around the tip of the barrel and continued very, very gently up the length of the stick, a few inches or so, until there was a bulging blue tip at the end of the rifle. The stick was withdrawn and the wool slightly drooped, but not enough to matter. Between the weight of the bullet and the charge he was placing behind it, there would not be enough interference to throw his aim off.

His next job fixed a couple of three-inch tall gunsights onto the barrel. The ball of wool at the end obscured his target. These particular sights gave him more accuracy, their lengths a clear line-of-sight over the barrel and wool.

Thomas looked at the cold, cold water and the heat of greed died away as he imagined dunking himself in the winter spring.

"Well? Get on with it."

Thomas sighed—not too loudly—and stripped off his clothes until he was shivering, naked in the morning sun. He examined the water. It was clear enough and he could see to the bottom for the most part. The pool extended from inside the cliff where it was fed by the waterfall, bent in a dog's-leg to his left and disappeared in a series of boulders and mild rapids. Below, the stream plunged in a series of small falls to the valley floor. Knowing better than to dive or jump into a place he'd never been before, he took a deep breath and stepped into the shallow end of the pool. It was cold, but not as cold as he thought: certainly nothing like the spring pools up north. He waded into the deeper end of the pool. He turned the cliff corner and the waterfall suddenly thundered around him, magnified and echoed by the crevice walls. The cold water reached his groin and he gasped, stiffened and suddenly plunged in to get it over with. Ginger Beard followed his progress, walking up the creek until he was standing opposite the waterfall he could barely see. The cliff walls prevented his going any farther.

Thomas stood up and waded deeper. Soon, he had to swim. The total depth was no more than eight feet: he would have to tread water in spots, but there was little area to search. He looked around at the cliff walls. Smooth and sheer, the rock showed nothing at all to hold a money belt, much less any substantial cache.

"Under the falls, under the falls!" His commander suddenly ordered.

There was nothing for it and he ducked head under. The sudden thundering of the water and swirling of the white bubbles disoriented and blinded him for a minute and he dove below the chaos. The cimmerian walls of the underwater crevasse loomed indistinctly over his head as he went deeper.

Suddenly, he saw it. Directly below and behind the waterfall, there was a dark brown object. He reached out and grabbed it. It was very heavy. He pushed up from the bottom and grabbed a quick breath before the weight of the heavy package drew him to the bottom again. *So that's how it was going to be, he thought.* He changed his initial strategy and walked along the bottom, away from the falls, allowing the contour of the bottom to raise him toward the surface. It didn't take long. He broke the surface and sucked in air desperately. He shook his head and waded through the crevice and to the shore where his commander waited.

Jeremy placed the barrel on to the Y-stick in the tripod. He could make an adjustment of several inches in his target by merely breathing a little deeper or letting the air out: it was that precise. He lined up the sights onto

Thomas' chest, ignoring Ginger Beard's frantic tearing at the leather bag. The private hopped about, trying to get warmth back into his limbs. Jeremy did not move. Rather than trying to follow him with the sights, he waited until Thomas moved into them and stopped, even momentarily.

*Sure enough.* As the man warmed up, his tired body slowed down. He walked into the sights, curiosity and greed getting the better of him and he stopped, trying to see into the bag that Ginger Beard opened. Jeremy breathed in, shifting the barrel minutely lower. The sights focused on a spot slightly below Thomas' left armpit. Thomas was still, now. Jeremy pulled the trigger.

Ginger Beard was unaware of anything except the bag. Suddenly, without apparent cause, Thomas grunted, his chest appeared to explode from him and he hurtled to his right, dead before he hit the ground. A funny whipping sound echoed, lost itself among the cliffs and then nothing stirred. Thomas lay, his eyes open in shock, entry and exit wounds leaking blood profusely.

Jeremy didn't waste time. He picked up the rifle and tripod and ran in a slow lope up the cliff ridge and into the woods surrounding the box end of the canyon. He crossed the stream above the falls and set up on a similar rock on the south side of the valley.

He got one more soldier as the leader and his partner paused in their search, oblivious to the drama in the cliff area. Again, the partner dropped dead and the weird whipping sound echoed over the area. The two remaining—Blondie and the leader—were smart enough to get into the valley and under cover, searching for the remainder of their dwindling crew of now five.

*

Henry and Billy continued traveling throughout the day. They set a very relaxing pace as neither had any place to go. Billy was intrigued by Henry's desire to go West and "Lord willin', I'll go with ye!" If Henry exercised his rather limited well of patience to the ceaseless talking, he found that Billy's experiences were well worth listening to if not downright entertaining. Among other things, he discovered that yarrow takes the pain out of a scrape or other blood wound, that Billy was born in the year the British invaded New Orleans, knew the Cherokee well— "Like 'em, but I don't trust anyone with more and one kind of blood in 'em"—and had seen action at Missionary Ridge and Chickamauga.

"Yep, that's when I powdered. I knew we were lost right then. One thing to fight a cause you believe in, 'nother to be on the winning side. I warn't no coward—I think you'll agree with that—but I ain't stupid, neither."

Billy rode for a while in silence. He turned to Henry. "What's your story? Why ain't *you* been fightin'? I knew you was a army guy. Desert?"

Henry bristled a little. He was not yet so humble that he wouldn't take offense at such a suggestion.

"Well."

"Ah, don't wanna talk about it, eh? I don't blame ye."

Henry interrupted what he figured would be another hour of constant ramble:

"I fought in Mexico. Saw things I didn't want to see. Saw things I didn't understand and couldn't reconcile with, with, uh, with certain things," he ended, lamely. "I was an officer, fresh out of West Point. But there's a difference between military theory drawn out on a slate and a man dying on your right because he wasn't lucky enough to duck. Fact is, you get so you don't care what your commanding officer orders when you're just trying not to get killed. And when the battle's over, you know you've just survived. That's the first thing. Then, maybe you can think about winning. Even then, you only think about it to see how soon you have to fight again and whether there's enough time to sit down and eat and sleep the sleep of the dead, same as those lying around you but you know you'll get up again in the morning and have to do it again…" He knew he rambled, but couldn't seem to stop. He took a breath. The horses plodded along complacently.

"Short version is, I guess I thought too much, instead of just obeying orders. I got tired of the stupidity, the name dropping and arrogance, and worst of all, the fighting for self-promoting accolades and not even for the team, much less principle. Anyway, I quit. Soon as I had a chance there, I walked to my commanding officer and resigned my commission."

He smiled at the memory.

"He was not happy. Apparently, I had both a medal and a field promotion coming to me for some tactical initiative I took during one of the battles. I didn't even know about it. I think I just moved a certain direction because I thought I was more likely to save my butt if my troops moved that way. We argued for about an hour and I was about ready to walk out the door on him, respect or no respect. He gave up then… I wonder what ol' Dan's doing?"

"Anyway, I made it home and then started traveling. I had some means my grandfather left me and I spent most of it going around the world. I had some questions and I wanted answers and I knew I couldn't find them in Pittsburgh, in Pennsylvania, the Union or, hell, I couldn't find them anywhere this side of the Atlantic. So, I traveled."

There was silence. It was the first time that day that Billy hadn't filled up the space with inane facts of the flora they were walking through or the history of his life. Surprisingly, the silence lasted longer than five minutes. Billy stirred.

"So. Didja find 'em?"

"Huh? What?"

"The answers. Didja find 'em?"

"Yes. I did, as a matter of fact."

That evening, they found a homestead in the next valley over. The family was paranoid and it was understandable, if disconcerting, to find their greeting was long, had two barrels and was of a very large gauge.

Fortunately, the family was desperate for something beyond staple food and welcomed the opportunity to enhance their larder when Henry made an overture to that effect. Henry and Billy slept under the lean-to that sheltered the hay. There was no sign of stock. Billy said if they had any, the family had hidden them in some godforsaken cove farther back in the boonies where no soldiers or thieves could find it. They quickly fell asleep under the comfortable hay. Henry still slept with one hand on the revolver.

## Chapter 8

Bound to happen, it occurred in the deepest, darkest part of the night. Clouds obscured the moon and there had been a light, showery rain on and off during the evening. In the early morning dark, the fire showed little but the dying coals.

The leader stood watch, on the move in a circle around the camp. One of the three men stirred and stood up. He turned away from the fire and walked a few yards to answer the call of nature. Finished, he walked back and stumbled over a root or stone. Like a flash, one of the bedrolls exploded and the man went down.

The leader whipped his gun around and almost pulled the trigger before he recognized one of his men, leaning on one elbow and shaking, the barrel of his revolver just poking through the smoking hole he had made in his blanket. He just sort of stared at him.

"I think I got one." He was rattled but spoke in the calmness that some men manifest when they are truly on the verge of insanity.

Only the realization that they were down yet another man kept the leader from kicking this one's head in, but the hair-trigger imagination of the man finally made him realize the serious trouble he was in. Fact was, if he were the only one running off with the cache of gold under normal circumstances—Ginger Beard was not so foolish as to keep it for himself—he wouldn't mind so much, but now he had no idea if he could make it by himself through a forest full of wild Cherokees.

"You just shot Zach. Dammit." He said it with a calmness and habitual matter-of-factness that he wasn't sure he felt anymore. Whatever Indians were out there were playing weird. Real weird. No Indians he'd ever fought—and he'd seen his share in his stint in the West—had the patience he was seeing now. Usually, an Indian raid was a matter of slaughter and loot and all done with the attitude of a five-year-old on Christmas morning. The only patience he'd ever heard of regarding natives came in the area of torture, and Western Indians *were* good at that.

But these waited around the camp. It'd been near a week and they were weeding out the men, one at a time. He realized with a start that he, Blondie and Ginger Beard had not been touched and didn't think it was chance. He didn't like that. Not one bit. He'd heard somewhere that the lust for gold carried death. He began to believe it. For the first time, he felt a bit scared. No, not scared. Nervous. That's it. Yes, that's it. Nervous was healthy, too. Got you to think. Still, this man who'd seen just about everything, felt suddenly "nervous."

*

Billy and Henry approached a neglected homestead. The day warmed in the morning sun, and the trees leaned over the bottom of the cove where they stopped after a morning's ride. The grassy valley bottom showed signs of recent plowing, but new weeds already showed through the turned soil. For a moment, they thought it was merely deserted: men off to war, women and children in a local town with relatives. They turned with the road and saw the house itself, or lack thereof. The gate stood open. Many hoofmarks indelibly scored the hard Georgia clay. Billy raised his eyebrows as some recollection rudely interrupted his thoughts.

The charred remains of the log house still smelled sour after a week of settling. Billy was unusually silent and a bitter twist in his mouth marred his rugged face. He dismounted in the yard and Henry stopped the wagon. He got down when he saw that Billy approached the mess.

Billy stepped over the burnt log that outlined the dimensions of the house. He looked around and kicked at items, the rare metal ones making a resonant clanking in the silence of the cove.

"What happened?" Henry asked, although this close to the war, he thought he knew. He walked around the periphery, looking at the walls. When Billy spoke, the normal flippancy was gone from his voice.

"Deserters and raiders, I'm thinkin'."

"Thought so. We're still too far from any battle for it to be a direct cause."

"Close enough for some SOB's to clear out on the war figuring to do their own work. For fun and profit."

He bent down in the hard packed dirt, looking closely at something. Henry stepped over the sill into the "room" that Billy was exploring.

"What's the matter?" he asked.

"Someone's been here. Prints are only days old and happened after the fire. There ain't no bodies, but I saw some blood outside and I don't think they's chicken blood. There should be bodies."

He straightened up and looked toward the creek. Examining the ground as he went along, he followed the marks he found until he paused under a chestnut tree leaning over the stream. Henry followed.

At the creek, they found a tangle of branches, leaves slowly wilting and not yet brown. Vines and weeds were already trying to obliterate it but the overall effect interrupted the consistent spring growth of the forest. To a woodsman like Billy, it was obviously a man-made item. He pulled aside some of the bracken; Henry leaned forward to help. It didn't take long to expose the graves in the ground.

They stared at it as conclusions pieced themselves together. Billy pulled the mess of branches over the graves, reverently, and he tried to make it look as natural as possible. He strode to the creek and, stepping to a flat rock in the bottom end of the pool, crouched down. He splashed water over his long salt-and-pepper hair and worked it through his beard. He took a long drink. Henry watched this without comment, the burials too near at hand to entirely erase the incident from his thoughts. Billy stood and walked off to his horse, stepping up the sandy bank and wading through the low shrubs.

Henry called, "Now what?"

He had been repulsed, but the scene had clearly made more of an impact on Billy.

"We git the sumbitches 't did it."

"'Scuse me? They're long gone and unless I'm entirely incompetent, I can read signs well enough to know that someone had to bury the dead. Sure, and no raider would do it. Whoever buried them is going after them and likely they don't want our help." Billy ignored this clear piece of logic.

"Ye got something better to do?"

"Well, no, but…"

"I go. You don't have to."

He spoke in that tone of voice that invited no discussion. Henry was wise enough not to, but followed him and seated himself in the wagon. Billy grabbed his horse's reins and, eyes glued to the dirt, followed the days-old hoof prints up the hill and into the forest.

*

Jeremy followed at a distance of two miles. The four men hoofed it through the forest depths, following the river downstream as it grew, eventually joining, as it must, the Chattahoochee. Northwest was the Union army, even now beginning a final drive toward points north of Atlanta and, dressed as they still were in issue uniforms, these renegades were not good enough liars to convince anyone that they were not deserters. One maybe, but three wouldn't have a chance. And because of their greed, the gold wouldn't allow them to separate, not yet. Honor among thieves, Jeremy supposed. That, and none would leave if there was a chance to get more of it from the others. As soon as they came upon a homestead or a small town, they would steal civilian clothes and try to fake their way to the coast where they could sail to England or Mexico and spend the gold, Union blockade notwithstanding.

Their prints showed them heavily laden, even if Jeremy had not seen the desperate divvying of food and gear that morning. They possessed the gold and now they could leave, sooner the better. Maybe the Indians would leave them alone if they left their grounds. The "Indian" smiled. The warm afternoon was turning into a warm evening and then the fun would start again.

*

The trail that allowed the Yankees' wagon through also allowed Henry's wagon and he and Billy followed that clear blaze, Billy still leading the way. Easy to follow, it kept to the ridge and allowed them to move at a very fast pace. It wasn't until evening fell that the road dipped into the gloaming. Like a cloud over the bird above them, the unlight enfolded them. It was utterly silent and both of them could feel an attitude of some kind, whether man, beast or nature, coming from ahead of them.

Somehow, the wagon stayed level as they went down the steep hillside to the creek. Ahead of them, rocks grew out of the loam and interrupted the constant background of trees. As the trail crept along the hill, they heard the trickle of water yet hidden by the curve of the hill and the edge of the rocks. Faces forward and obsessive in thought, they did not notice the cleft on their left down which a thin trickle flowed. But the horses did. Ears flattened, Billy's horse skipped, his tight hand on the reins being the only thing to keep it from galloping. Henry took note and pulled back on his reins before the packhorse could panic. Now they did look around, jarred out of the still trek. Billy saw it first, and the stench hit both of them at the same time.

Far gone in decomposition, the bodies hung from the trees above the spring. Hardened though the two men were, both suddenly breathed through the mouth in shallow breaths. Henry suddenly groped for a handkerchief; just in case. He forced himself to look up. A large crow—big enough to give buzzards competition—perched on the increasingly fleshless skull and disdained the two approaching men. As they neared the cleavage in the escarpment, the crow glanced at them once and proceeded to rend the red mush for its next bite. Henry swiftly threw up.

Billy kicked his horse into a trot and made his way to the valley floor. Henry wiped his mouth and took a drink of water, still holding tightly to the reins. It would not do to let the trembling packhorse loose at this point. He took a deep breath and guided the wagon to where Billy had dismounted, walking around the campsite. He parked the wagon and got down.

"Didja see the clothes?" Billy asked, not looking at him.

"No." Henry felt as if he needed to excuse himself for not noticing, but couldn't think of what to say. The moment passed.

"Yankees. I was right." He continued walking, widening the circle of his transit in gradual sweeps.

The campsite had been wiped clean of vegetation by the sloppy living of eight men over the course of a week. They had scattered utensils and cans of sorts, mostly around the campfire. There was a wagon parked several yards away from the site itself and as Billy and Henry continued looking, they noticed the area where the horses had been kept: a small defile covered with last fall's leaves and encircled by small and large trees. Billy stooped to look closer.

"Old. At least a day." He pulled on the corner of one leaf that had been ground into the others by the shod hoof of a heavy animal. It came up easily.

"How can you tell that?"

"Leaves're springy. If this was a fresh print, it would be creased still, well pressed into the print. This ain't. The print is duller in appearance 'cause the other leaves've sprung back to their old shape."

Henry straightened and examined the rocky bed downstream of the site. He shook his head and moved away from the stream. The valley flattened out slightly into a "U" shape, escarpments still prominent on either side. The stream itself spread out into a shallow flow over sand. This early in the year it was fairly low and stretches of flat sandy deposits ranged widely along the valley floor. In one of these, Henry found what he was looking for.

Peeking through the light layer of autumn leaves was a patch of sand about three feet around. In that were more prints. The crumbling sand around the edges of the prints helped Billy establish what time the horses were gone. More importantly, he saw at once that they were unladen. He also saw the moccasin print.

"Ten horses," he said. "Considering the weather and all, I'd say the horses were taken five days ago. Injuns, too, I 'spose chasing 'em. They'll be pissed. Musta been friends to those in the cabin'r something."

As they continued looking at the prints in front of them, Billy also noticed something that he disgustingly considered obvious. "Shit." He said this without somehow making it a vulgarity: merely a description of his personal disgust.

"What?" Henry asked. He was learning an amazing amount about tracking from this man, but many things still needed interpretation. Billy pointed to the moccasin print.

"The horses' prints are old, but that's fresh," he said. "I shoulda seen that right off. This new one's no more'n a day old, and if I'm any tracker at all, I'd say last night or this morning."

"How do you tell that?"

For an answer, Billy pointed upward. New leaves spread out from the branches, but had certainly not formed the canopy it would be later in the summer.

"No leaves above us worth speaking of. Although the sun's still pretty low in the sky and this is a deep valley, it'll still peek through for about two hours in the mid-day. Now, wet sand packs. Dry sand crumbles. Two hours of sun'll dry a damp piece of earth, but this close to the stream, not too much."

Henry saw. The print was firm all around the edges, except for a minute landslide here and there where the sand was no longer wet enough to hold. If it had been more than a day, the print would have disintegrated into a vague shadow of what it had been.

As they looked farther, they found the boot prints, Yankee, they both assumed, several of them, heading down the valley. Henry was tired, and hunger bit at him in spite of the macabre vision they had seen. It was now nearly dark, but Billy seemed obsessive and fey, his personal destination at the end of the trail with which he was intimately involved. He returned to the campsite and mounted his calmer horse. He moved down the trail. Henry hesitated, then got on the wagon and slapped the horse into a walk, following, of course, Billy.

*

The men had been afraid to light the fire. They had been afraid not to. In the end, the morale boost caused by having one far outweighed the negatives. As the flames flickered in the darkening night, shadows played on the canyon walls and rocky halls as before. Now, every moving shadow was a stealthy Cherokee. The leader did his best to portray nonchalance, taking his modified pack and slapping it on the ground for a pillow. He leaned back casually and closed his eyes. The day tired him, but the tightened muscles in his back subtly portrayed his disinclination to sleep.

"One of you keep watch. I'm knocking back."

Ginger Beard and the other men looked at each other, nerves frayed by the day's hike of ten miles under the expectation that they could be murdered at any second. Sleep would come hard, if at all.

The leader thought that another morning's hike would bring them to the Chattahoochee, and civilization. It wouldn't take much to steal some clothes from a farm: they would still have to be careful. Up until now, their Yankee uniforms were not a problem. If they were going to murder someone, it didn't really matter if they'd been seen, and in Southern country the uniforms would only help instigate fear. But they definitely needed some sort of disguise if they were going to pass through hard-core Rebel countries. Gold was useless if they were dead or captured. Which pretty much meant the same thing around here.

Wan light from the moon flickered as wisps of cloud passed over it like the shutter on a tintype. It might rain tonight, he thought. Things couldn't go worse. Although, they *might* be able to slip out in the storm without being noticed. He doubted that. They were dogged too hard. They needed speed, now. If they got to a town, the Cherokee might leave them alone, but they would have to move fast. They'll have to leave early in the morning, after a couple of hours of sleep at the most.

They can rest up later. They can't rest if they're dead.

The clouds built up with great intensity and the air became even more still than before. They obscured the moon and shut off the little natural light it gave, leaving the flickering shadows more eerie in their loneliness.

Jeremy continued watching. His body had gone without sleep for the last two days and without food for much longer than that. Nonetheless, he did not feel particularly tired. Rather, his mind and his body were detached, the one able to think objectively and critically, while the other merely obeyed the commands given it. It tuned him to an extremely tight pitch and it would not take much for his fourteen-year-old body to collapse, given the excuse. He could not let that happen. Not yet. He had to do much, but there were only four men he needed to do it to, and he can last this remaining night.

## Chapter 9

The clouds seemed to scrape the stars from the sky and the moon disappeared completely. The bushes in the hollow the men lay in seemed to move of their own volition; the wind was that subtle. The rustling startled Blondie and he looked wide-eyed at the moving shadows. He threw another log on the fire for comfort's sake and was alarmed to find the action of the shadows increased in response. The silence overwhelmed them.

Ginger Beard leaned against the only tree, dozing on and off as the night dictated. Closed eyes weren't distracted by the moving shadows and although hypersensitive to the sounds of the night, the light sleep allowed his body to begin recovering from the exhaustion he had forced on it during the day. The leader snored and the fourth man was very awake and aware.

The earth suddenly seemed to shake: at least that's how it felt as the low tremble of thunder made itself known rather than heard. Distant lightning added to the fire's dancing shadows, enhancing the imagined Indian behind every tree and rock. The remaining man had yet to close his eyes.

The wind increased to violent proportions in a matter of minutes. The leader merely turned over in his sleep, muttered some half decipherable obscenities and was lost to the world once again. Ginger Beard woke briefly, recognized the wind for what it was, noticed had not yet begun to rain and drifted off again. The third man looked, panicked, at the fire and although it was burning brightly, threw several more fagots on. The fire was hot from the burning hardwoods they had used and the pitch from the occasional conifer crackled and flared.

The noise of the wind had increased and the lightning was approaching quickly. These intense storms were usually short and violent in nature at this time of year, sweeping wind and rain before them as they marched across the land in echelon form. Jeremy moved. Two of the men slept in the land of whatever twisted dreams such men have and the third was well awake. Blondie had drifted off, too tired to keep awake.

Again, he moved stealthily and above all, slowly, allowing the shadows from the fire and the lightning to hide his movements. The noise of the wind allowed him to move faster without betraying his presence. He moved through the rhododendron bushes and down the hills. The brush was thicker than he'd expected but this only turned to an advantage for him as he moved, the wind whipping the branches around, creating more noise, generating more movement. He made it to the stream where more noise and damp leaves masked his progress. None of the men had moved, three still asleep and one trapped in his waking nightmare.

The lightning flashed frequently now and a pattering in the leaves showed where the precursors of the storm hit hard. He must go quickly, lest the sleepers wake to protect themselves from the hostile environment.

The man awake actually felt nothing as a hand suddenly covered his mouth and a razor-sharp blade pierced his throat. A wet warm flow spread down his side and he drifted off into the permanent sleep.

Instead of leaving this one, Jeremy pulled him back into the bushes toward the stream and once on the other side, shoved a pile of leaves over the body. He examined his trail by the blue lightning and covered any traces. Then he crawled far up the hill to a rock outcropping from where he could see the sleeping men and built a fire.

*

Henry reached back into the wagon and pulled the oilskin off the packs. He slipped his arms into the protective garment and hopped off the step. He chocked the wheels of the wagon and walked over to Billy, who had dismounted and was pulling out his slicker. Henry was slightly surprised to see an oilskin of excellent quality emerge from the saddlebags. Billy noted his look and grinned.

"Wet, your dead. Don't skrimp on quality and your fine," he said, re-buckling the pack in question and putting on his own 'skin. "Buy cheap stuff and you'll suffer for it. The end of the day comes and if your dry, you can do anything. It cost me a lot, but, by God, it's been worth it."

The incongruous conversation amid the howling wind, incessant lightning and rain, not to mention the morbid quest they seemed to be on, struck Henry humorously and he chuckled.

"Well," he said. "Well. He turned to the

packhorse and began to unbuckle the harness. Billy came over to help. Henry looked at him in surprise.

"We're close, real close," he said. "They're on foot and we're on horses. They've gotta stop. And we can't go any further with the wagon, not on the trails they're taking. Can this horse take a rider?"

"No, unfortunately. I'm afraid the time we would spend getting it to settle into the tack would be better spent on foot. It can pull well, but it doesn't like a rider at all."

"Well, we'll haveta hoof it. My horse can't take two. But I don't think it's necessary if they're as close as I think. We'll hobble the horses here to graze. Lightning don't seem to be bothering them and this part of the canyon is pretty well protected."

They secured the stock and made sure they had a rifle and revolver apiece. Neither was quite sure what they were getting into, and if either had opinions about the morality of the situation, he kept them to himself.

Henry worried. What would they do if they came up to… whatever? If the signs were interpreted correctly, there were several soldiers up front, probably Yankee, on foot, fairly heavily laden, moving quickly. In all likelihood, they were the ones who had decimated the household they'd found. Second, at least one Indian tracked them for vengeance. The bodies they'd found at the campsite showed evidence of that. The question: if and when they found them, should they allow the Indians to take vengeance? It was justice served, apparently. But should anyone, no matter how bad, have to go through the kind of torture Indians were capable of? Should Henry and Billy mete out justice on *all* of them, the marauders for the crime and the Indians for the killing of the criminals. Or was killing the murderers, murder? If so, then when does it stop? If Henry and Billy shot the Indians for killing the murderers, then they in turn should be killed for murdering the murderers who murdered the murderers. When does it stop?

Henry smiled, grimly. Such a debate in morality would be good at Pennsylvania College, but downright impractical in a place where the practice of that morality *really* determined who lived and who died. Mexico taught him that if nothing else. He determined that whatever happened, he would try to stay alive himself and stop whatever violation was going on, just to iron things out. Pretty hopeless, maybe, but it was the best that he could do. After all, the last seventeen years had taught him that he had a conscience of sorts. He didn't always listen to it, but it had become a… personal companion, he supposed.

The rain became heavy and the lightning lit up every other step they took down the drainage. Billy hurried lest the wet sand become saturated by the heavy drops and obscure any signs. The canyon deepened as the walls rose to both sides, and the wind dropped, frustrated by the narrow cleft in the earth.

*

He walked through London town, the omnibuses passing him on his right and the businessmen in top and bowler hats brushing him on his left. A manicured park appeared, the type where the gentry walked their horses and the ladies rode in buggies for the afternoon parade.

It had been a nice life since the captain who had smuggled him aboard in Florida dropped him off in Liverpool. He was no dummy and would not spend the gold on whores and parties. With his newfound wealth, he quickly bought into a couple of profitable businesses and put the rest in trust: he was now a man of the world and made sure people knew it. Women hung on his arms: none of the tarts that he'd had in the States, but real classy women, and now men nodded as they passed him on the street.

One man passed him and looked at him pointedly but did not tip his hat. For some reason, this bothered him and he turned to look as he passed. Something caught his eye down the street and as he looked, he noticed several American plainsmen approaching him. That was the oddest thing. Here. In London of all places.

Not plainsmen, he saw with a start. Indians. Warpaint covered their faces and oddly, nobody in this London business district gave them a second look. He backed away and turned, walked, and then ran, running for his life. Suddenly, a hand snaked out of the alleyway to his left and covered his mouth.

Blondie awoke. The hand covering his mouth was the merciless reality and another on his throat squeezed and pulled him quickly into the bushes. Jeremy continued dragging him to the stream ready at any time to break his neck should he prove to be a problem. Blondie was a smallish man, less than 130 pounds, which boded well for Jeremy's plans, for he was not large himself at 120. He believed his native strength, surprise attack, and woodcraft could take care of things.

The leader's snore suddenly cut off as he awoke to a particularly close boom of lightning with a vague sense of impropriety. He looked around and saw that he reclined alone with Ginger Beard, who snored. The fear that years of experience and evil deeds had suppressed welled up in his throat, but training—self-imposed and of military origin, both—kept him from running completely insane into the dark woods. The storm did not help, but on the edge as he was, he at least knew the benefits of staying put. Alert and awake, but staying put. He pulled out his watch and looked at the face. Still ticking, it comforted him with a façade of normalcy. It settled him a bit. Four-thirty A.M. Still a couple of hours yet until dawn, when he would feel comfortable about leaving this comparably safe spot. The trees still moved around him, the wind not yet settled at all, and he saw that the rain had drenched him. It had not yet stopped. He was surprised he had not awakened sooner. He must have been more exhausted than he thought. He pulled out a piece of hardtack and his canteen and began to munch at it, as much to kill time as to fill his stomach. Then, he drifted off, nervously.

Ginger Beard woke. He, too, had been dreaming of the good life, his variation being in San Francisco, California, where the gold rush of almost fifteen years ago had made the city urbane and, if not world class in the eyes of the snobs back East, at least presentable. He'd buy land and with the booming economy would make out like a bandit. He woke, smiling at the ironic phrase.

The ground had scuffmarks where two men had been, as if something had dragged them into the brush. It didn't take him long to figure things. The leader was dozing again, his head on the pillow made from his pack: the one with the gold-laden leather satchel. There was no way he could get that gold, Ginger Beard thought, without waking him. His hands twitched as his dream beckoned him: promising to turn into reality if he had just the guts to take the pack. He could try to kill him, he thought, but he knew he was no match for the man. Even the movement of a gun, not to mention the "click" of the hammer, would alert him. Dead with gold did not appeal to him as much as "alive".

He hesitated, then looked around in the woods. He, too, noticed that he and the leader were left and he did not like that, either. The gold may carry a curse, and he did not want to be a part of whatever curse the Indians thought they were fulfilling. He concluded he would powder, hoping the "Indians" would leave him alone, since he would then have nothing to do with the gold. He could always try to get it later.

He gathered his gear: his makeshift pack held little more than food—water was plentiful—and a bedroll. He wore his service revolver at his side and carried a rifle. He hoped, beyond hope, that the Indians would ignore him. With a last look at the leader, he figured who was doomed in any case, he melted into the woods.

An hour later, the leader was still waiting. The rain had settled to a drizzle and the warm humid evening air had given way before the cooler air behind the front. The clouds above cracked now and then to bring forth glimpses of pale blue moonlight. Fog began to build, a mist crawling along the valley floor swirling empathetically with the flow of the river. It was eerie. As he watched, fascinated, each swirl would mount up, like a ghost in some macabre dance. To his worried soul, some began to look even human, his mind conjuring a face where there was really none to see and voices began to murmur through the gurgle of the stream.

He shook his head to stave off the dream world that threatened his consciousness. He pulled his cloak tighter and tried not to think of things unthinkable. That could only lead to madness, he knew, and that way led to death. Exactly what his adversaries wished. In spite of his chill, he still felt much better than he had when he had first awakened. He had taken stock of his situation and believed—true or not—that with a short haul to the Chattahoochee, he would be fairly free of these Cherokee that seemed to be hunting him. He was still a bit afraid, but, he rationalized, a good fear was healthy. It kept one alive if one kept it under control.

That was at first. Then, the screams began. He may have underestimated his ability to control himself.

*

Billy stopped short, listening. Henry could hear the shriek in the distance, maybe half a mile. Billy began to run. Henry grabbed his arm.

"What are we to do?" he asked, his questions on morality not yet having been answered.

"Save that poor bastard first."

"We don't know how many Indians there are."

"Not too many, no more'n three, from what I read."

"'Kay. How do we do it?"

"Well. He's on the slope on that south side from what I hear. You go up top and come down from above. I'll slide along the creek and see what I see before moving up. Human nature being what it is, they're more likely to take the lazy way and come down the hill. 'Sides, ain't got no reason to go up."

"You think. 'Kay." Inwardly, Henry didn't care for the physically tougher part. Not the time to fight about it. There were more important things to do.

They split up, Henry heading straight up the south slope, intending to traverse along the ridge and coming straight down. That way he would have his breath back and a bit of his energy, and it was always an advantage to look down upon a hostile situation than up at it. He thanked God at this point that he'd been riding in the wagon earlier. No sleep on top of a healthy walk like that would do no good to anybody.

The woods dripped heavily, but the damp leaves softened any noise he made. He moved as swiftly as he could, but days of sitting in a wagon severely hampered his wind and the muscles in his thighs and calves began to ache. He slowed to a walk and angled up the hill in the direction of the chilling and still distant screams, easing the steepness and giving his legs a little break. Ghostly forms of gray trunks moved by him and the occasional wet leathery leaves of the rhododendrons brushed his coat as he passed. The human noise in front of him was diminishing now, but he was still too far away to discern anything else.

As he closed to within a hundred yards of the place, he moved straight up the hill again so as to approach it from above. There was a glow in the trees, a fire in a little nook in the rocks that flickered light through the trees above. He saw no one, much less Indians, and wondered.

He was close enough to hear the occasional pop of a fire gone cool and as he stepped over the rock ledge to peer into the nook, he saw the image that would stay with him for the rest of his life.

## Chapter 10

Billy stood at the mouth of the nook, his gun hand raised, and as Henry looked, shot into the rocks.

The rocks formed a U-shaped escarpment not unlike the cleft in which he and Billy had found the hanging bodies. A couple of trees grew in the upper end of this nook, only the size of a small house. The dell had a flat floor; sand, leaves and new grass were mingled together. Under the largest tree, an area the size of a kitchen table was scorched by the large bed of coals. Coals of chestnut and hickory, they gave off an intense, sustaining heat and served as the ultimate source of the screams.

Even had he known him before, Henry would not have recognized Blondie now, for the form hanging above the fierce coals was virtually unrecognizable to anyone as a human, much less any particular one. He had been tied by his feet to the lowest branch of the big tree suspended over the dell and his head hung a scant foot above the ground. A fresh bullet hole in his forehead dripped, but he was beyond pain and beyond this life. Billy turned, his face cold and unreadable.

"See anyone?" he asked.

Henry pulled his eyes of the body of the tortured man with an effort, and looked at Billy. "No." His voice was raspy. He swallowed. "I didn't see any sign at all."

"Better skedaddle," Billy said. "I only saw one set of prints," he added.

There wasn't much Henry could say to that. In one sense, it relieved him; in another, it was a bit nervy if one person could take out a whole troop of soldiers in less than a week, give the impression it was a group of hostile Indians and most importantly, never get caught. There was something odd about the whole thing and he wondered what to do about it. In any case, Billy moved quickly away from the horrible place and Henry was glad to follow.

They continued on down the hill and moved through the newly leafed bushes, the moonlight becoming stronger as the wrack of clouds above tore into wisps. The wind merely flurried now, and the rain had diminished into sparse showers that didn't seem to wet them. Dispersed among the bushes of leaves were bushes of mist that swirled about them as they passed through.

The creek's gurgle increased as they approached, Billy still following the sense of trail that Jeremy had left. The boy was good, but Billy was up to the task and it held them in good shape as they progressed down the streambed.

They hiked to a flattened area where the rocks were less precipitous in the valley floor, and there grew firs in the wet bottom, poking through the sandy soil. Billy halted and motioned for Henry's compliance. Henry stopped suddenly, and opened his mouth to make his breathing less noisy. Even he knew they were up against a formidable… enemy? He still had trouble thinking of his quarry in such terms. As yet, the tracked didn't know he was being tracked himself, so intent he must have been on the trail of the soldiers. The puzzle began to assemble itself in Henry's head: who had done what and why.

It was evident that the soldiers were pillaging homesteads across the South, as he and Billy had surmised. It was also obvious that a single person was tracking them down and exacting his own vengeance upon them, devouring them piecemeal. But who was this stealthy avenger? He was awesome in woodcraft, certainly better than the soldiers themselves, determined in vengeance and good at killing. But who was he in relation to only one of probably dozens of raided farms in the north Georgia hills? Why should a single Indian care about white homesteaders?

The avenger in question approached the now terrified leader who was unaware—or perhaps his guesses were all too aware—that he was among the last of a contingent of nine men. Jeremy saw Ginger Beard flown, and he cursed under his breath. He was not worried about a stab in the dark: Ginger Beard had clearly left to save his own skin. Jeremy would have to track that sadistic—again not perceiving the irony in his choice of invective—bastard down. What a nuisance.

As far as the leader was concerned, he was a lone man struggling against a hostile wilderness. Any branch could turn into an arm with a strangling hand if he looked at it too long. He wouldn't have been surprised to see something materialize out of the sand beneath his butt and drag him into hell. For he was beginning to believe in such a place and he had no doubt that that was where he was headed. Perhaps he was already there. Perhaps it was only this thought that kept him from pulling out his service revolver and ending things. But the screams permeating the dark taught him that, his concept of hell notwithstanding, there might be reasons staying alive could be worse.

The night encroached upon him and the mists grew, extending vines from the stream and circling the clearing. They showed as condensed, starkly white things, still metamorphosing from shape to shape, hands, torsos, heads, faces, ethereal forms that defied gravity as they approached him like accusers. A skittering sound swept from left to right, behind him, and he started, the clammy sweat trickling down his face in spite of the chill night. He breathed heavily. He was losing control, he knew, and his growing terror of the clearing matched his complete terror of the forest around him. He could not move to save his life: even life was a very secondary thing to one who had long ago given up the last shreds of humanity and was now a mere biological function.

Jeremy watched with no small satisfaction the all-consuming fear. His goal was not to physically torture this man, but to allow the mind to do things to him that Jeremy could not. The moon blew free of clouds and although the sky was yet dark, dawn was not far away.

Suddenly, his head jerked up. The shot sounded from the same direction as the fire over which he'd left Blondie. His treatment of the man was incidental to the effect it had on the man he was now watching. But something had changed and he realized that he was no longer alone. There was not enough time for Ginger Beard to move obliquely in that direction and he had not passed him in the forest if he had taken a direct route.

He grimaced in indecision. If he made his way back to the fire, he would not be able to examine the place and see how things stood, and dawn would come before his planned prosecution of the man in this clearing. That would be too bad. The man would recover and to bring him to such a state again would be far too time consuming to be practical. He did not want to rush the job here, but he no longer had any choice.

The leader was catatonic in his fear. As he looked into the moonlight-bathed clearing, the mist lowered to the ground and began to crawl toward him. Jeremy picked his time. He lowered himself to the ground and began to crawl with the mist, slowly, toward the man frozen on the ground.

The troop leader saw a glob of mist. Exhaustion, fear and the unusual stress of the last week shaped themselves into a hallucination in the form of a face. The face resembled to some degree the old man they had killed in the quest of freshly discovered gold. But it also resembled people in the homestead where they'd found out that gold existed in the first place. It looked like all of them and, new in his experience, guilt manifested within his being. An unholy guilt, it was formed of an instinctual need for self-preservation, the mere act of a body containing cellular function and barely an ability to react to external stimuli, much less able to do what men would call "thinking". And light-years beyond reflections of the soul.

Nonetheless, his benumbed mind, detached and

dispassionately examining the actions of the animal as from far away, was faintly aware of the concept of guilt as something others had spoken of in a long distant—in time and space—past. The conclusions it drew were not good, for "guilt" was also for the first time associated with the sense of doing something wrong and thus, an equally uncomfortable sense of impending punishment and retribution. The hell it dreaded became instead the only avenue of escape and the mind watched the body pick up its service revolver, place it to its head and…

"No!" Henry came rushing out of the bushes in time to see the body performing its last function.

…pulled the trigger.

Billy came running behind. If there had been, as they had originally thought, a score of Indians, they would have been very foolish men or very brave ones. But there was only Jeremy, one quarter Cherokee and three-quarters Scotch-Irish, who stood up in the mist which flowed about his waist as Charon flows about the Isle of the Dead. He looked at the two men who stared in amazement at the fourteen-year-old man. Jeremy saw nothing but the dying soldier and none of them moved as the leader's body slumped, leaking from his temple the watery blood of a dead man over the rain-wet sand.

## Chapter 11

The sunlight slipped over the ridge, filtering through a green canopy of new, small leaves. It was cool, not cold, comfortable and not humid, the storm leaving a very spring-like presence in the valley. The atmosphere caused Henry to reminisce about growing up in western Pennsylvania.

Billy walked somewhere out and around, looking for horses: theirs, the dead soldiers' and this young man's from what they gathered through his ravings. Unless some local family took opportunity of a few lost "strays," he didn't think they would go too awfully far. They would be hidden: he knew that. From the signs and the murmurings of the prostrate lad, he thought he pieced together the events of the last week.

He shook his head in admiration and concern. The kid was no more than mid-teens, he was sure, and yet to fulfill such an agenda of meticulous hatred as it seems he had done took the determination and skills of a full-grown experienced—and motivated—man.

The boy lay on as comfortable a bed as they could make in this part of the forest and boiled up with a fever. *Probably a combination of no food, lack of sleep, excitement and an element of guilt all thrown together*, Henry thought. Add on top of that the wet and rainy night and it was no wonder the kid was sick. Billy had set up some snares for birds— "poultry's broth's the best thing for getting food down a sick kid"—but now they tried to feed him broth from some potted meat Henry hadn't traded away. He looked at the boy. He looked pale and drawn, motionless, wrapped in the bedclothes they had fashioned out of their own gear.

Through the spectral mist, they had seen the boy collapse, his brown eyes turning up in his head the moment the man on the ground had expired. A crumpled heap, wasting away in mind and body, was all that was left of this talented half-breed woodsman. Although Henry and Billy did not know it, Jeremy had not eaten for the better part of the week and his sleepless reconnaissance had taken their toll on the fourteen-year-old. He had gone from lithe to downright skinny and his painted face betrayed shadows of exhaustion under his eyes.

They left him where he was, albeit straightened out, and covered him with a blanket. The leader of the soldiers, they examined and carried off to a modest burial. It was in removing the very heavy pack that they had discovered the gold.

"Well," Billy drawled slowly, "looky here."

The dark leather pouch was still damp from the water and its excessive weight indicated an item or items probably important to a carrier whose trekking interest should lay in a pack full of only essentials. Billy unrolled the sticky wet material and deposited three small items on the ground. Henry reached for one of them, a leather bag, and undid the leather string around the top.

The metal seemed to glisten even in the low light of the false dawn. Henry blew a low whistle. "The plot thickens," he said.

"Yup, sure does."

*

Ginger Beard saw the sparkle of the metal in the morning sun, even as far away as the abutment above the valley. He could see that they were white men and since he could not hear their voices, assumed they were part of the "Indians" that killed eight men over the previous week. His frustration was only matched by his amazement that *white* men could pull it off. He knew he was no match for such men in the woods: otherwise, he would just steal up and plug them. He was *that* good a shot, he thought. As it was, he wasn't sure if he could kill one such man, much less two without being detected first. And their vigilance was at its height right now. He would just watch and observe and see where they were headed, and try to come up with some sort of plan.

*

"Zee gold, she keels, no?" Henry murmured in a bad French accent.

"Huh?"

"Nothing: something I heard in my travels. But it's true. Well, whatever this is from, it's a pretty sure bet it wasn't honestly come by."

"Why d'ye say that?"

"Figuring on the nature of *this* beast," he said,

pointing to the leader, "I'd say he wasn't much for diligent work in the mining field."

"Whaddya wanna do with him?" Billy asked.

"Bury it."

"Why? Ain't worth the effort. And if morals have anything to do with it," Henry glanced swiftly at the man, catching Billy's obnoxious grin, "buzzard bait's too good forim."

They decided to take him up to where the tortured man was and push rocks and dirt over the both of them as they lay in the recesses of the cleft. It satisfied both of them: Billy who wouldn't have to dig anything (Henry didn't blame him but didn't say much about that), and Henry who wouldn't leave the bodies for carrion. Above all, the whole night's adventure had left a distinct mark on both of them and they didn't want the body anywhere near their camp.

They had returned to the soldier leader's last camp and decided to resurrect the fire and "hole up" for a few days until things got satisfactorily ironed out. In any case, the boy was out of his mind and unable to travel and, "morals" notwithstanding, Henry didn't wish to leave him in such a state, even if Billy was (which he wasn't).

While Billy cut fir boughs from the copse surrounding the place, Henry got the wagon and found a way down into the valley floor, which wasn't easy. The creek spilled in a series of small and large falls and even if the cliffs weren't prohibitive, the volume of spring runoff would have been. Fortunately, the ridgeline was fairly gentle and he followed it faithfully until he was peripheral to the camp, then switched down the side until he found a spot within a hundred yards of the place. He pulled out the blankets, tarp, oilskin and some of the cooking supplies and moved quickly to the site. Billy finished the job of piling the fir boughs into a fragrant, soft couch.

"We'll set a back screen behind him to reflect the fire. I don't think it'll rain for some time yet. The air's much drier and it'll hafta build up water afore it can rain agin. By that time, I figger we'll have something built."

Henry nodded. Clearly, Billy's woodcraft skills came in handy. Hawg was definitely an interesting man. For example, although obviously not a man of means—*apparently*, Henry corrected himself—he was not hurting so bad he would steal. As dawn had approached, he had laid the packet of gold to the side without a second glance, as if it had been filled with stones instead of metal. Either he was rich or, contrary to his claims, he had a far higher degree of morality than he let on.

They lay a blanket on the boughs and moved over to the sandy couch on which the boy lay. Billy lay his hand on the forehead.

"Burning up."

They picked him up and lay him on the couch, then covered him with several blankets and the oilskin. Covered as he was, the emaciated frame shook in spite of the fever that held him. Henry pulled out some matches and began building a fire from the warm remnants in the pit in the middle of the clearing while Billy collected logs for a back screen.

Not long after, some nightmare had coaxed the boy into mumbling portions of a terrifying account of the last few days. Henry had started some sort of breakfast by this time of the morning and he and Billy turned their heads to the tormented figure on his bed of fir. It was amazing, just the little bit they heard, and it served only to increase their curiosity.

Now, in the mid-afternoon, Henry smiled grimly. During one of these eloquent moments, they had learned of the horses and Billy determined to find them if they hadn't strayed too far. He'd been gone most of the day and left Henry to tend to the kid and catch whatever sleep he could. Which meant "zero".

The day got on and the sun seemed to move faster through the lacework of the leaves. He moved to the wagon with its supplies and grabbed an extra blanket. The sun waxed, and the ground was warm and inviting. He laid the blanket down as a ground cover and lay on it. Ginger Beard watched from a distance, even less sure of himself now that the ugly one had left: he had no idea where he had gone. He didn't know, but what if the one in the glade was faking it. The Indian affair of the previous week left him very unsettled and unsure of himself.

Henry woke with a start. Even as tired as he had been, Henry's senses were tuned very highly and the distant rustle was like a cannon to his sense of being. He merely opened his eyes and moved his hand to the grip of his revolver.

The next thing he knew, Billy stood in front of him. But this was very different from the night earlier in the week when they'd had to fight for their lives against a trio of raiders. Henry lowered the gun under his blanket. Billy grinned from ear to ear and as Henry's somewhat fuzzy brain began to clear, his peripheral vision took in the rope that trailed from Billy's hand that led to a horse face, which presently obscured the mountain man as it approached. He shrank away from the ugly specter and tried to sit up. He shook his head.

"W-w-where did you get him?"

"Wal, downstream from here there's a little crick that branches up from this'n. It's all rock, but I had a hunch they might be up there. Shore 'nough, I saw a tiny print about fifty yards up—hard to get to, too, them horses went some pretty rough places. Anyhoo, I just followed the crick and shore 'nough in a little meadow about a quarter mile up was them horses. They was hobbled and the grass is new so they didn't go nowhere last couple a days."

"How many?" Henry asked. "They got brands?"

"Nope. Only one of them got a brand, and that's U.S. government. I 'spose we gotta give that back and how, I don't know, we're liable to be hung for nothing—but the others we can keep."

He pointed to the far end of the herd. "It's that palomino gelding yonder, so, pretty animal as it is, you can't have it."

"Hmm. What about tack?"

"Wet, in a pile of leaves. They wasn't soaked too bad and then, only the top ones. The country's too bad to ride 'em, steep and rocky and all, so I packed the tack on their backs and led 'em nose to butt down the crick." He grinned wider than ever.

"*We got horses!*"

Henry grinned back. He wondered about taking them—they weren't his—but the owners were doubtless long dead and it would be impossible anyway to find them without brands. He got up and walked over to the line of animals. Not too bad, but most were definitely not the top-of-the-line animals. Obviously, the soldiers had been infantry sitting on horses' backs, and not horsemen *riding* by any stretch of the imagination. He grinned. What a bunch of saddle-sore infantrymen there must have been those first couple of days!

He didn't hesitate to pick out a saddle-horse. He looked at one mare, medium-sized and sturdy, a paint splotched with brown, white and black. He wasn't particular about the color, but this horse, judging by the teeth, was young and had enough spunk to hold her own with and without a rider. He reached out and moved his hand along her face, gently, and when she didn't flinch, walked down her side, caressing her neck, shoulder and flank.

*Sure beats riding in a wagon*, he thought.

They re-hobbled the horses and turned them out in

a small grassy area near the creek. Then they turned to the boy. He was quiet, now, the dreams and demons resting quiet in this fevered brain, but he was pale and cold to the touch, shivering violently even under the spring sun and wrapped in blankets.

"Looks like we'll be here awhile," Billy murmured.

"Yup."

Billy pulled out some tobacco and stuffed a pipe he brought out from his pocket. He lit it and puffed a while and they stood for a while in indecision, considering the circumstances and the solutions. Except for the occasional breath of wind, stirring of the horses in the distance and the murmur of the stream, it was quiet.

"Saw something up a 'ways y'all should know about," Billy said, quietly.

"What's that?"

"Saw marks heading up yonder ridge; fresh, last night at the earliest."

"So?"

"*Fresh*, I said. Ain't no Injun, neither. 'Less I'm a much worse woodsman than I think I am, there's a white man about. Seems to me the boy didn't get 'em all."

"'Kay," said Henry. "Let's set up a more or less permanent camp. I wouldn't mind staying here a couple of days, and we're still a ways from the nearest town, I think."

"Catch some sleep, I'll take the night watch."

"Why, you think he's still somewhere around? If I were one of these boys, I'd high-tail it outta here, quick as I could."

"Yeah, but you like your hide better'n your wallet. If'n y'all was one of these here boys, and knew there was a fortune in gold you just stole from someone, do you think y'all could walk away from it just like that?"

"No. I see your point."

"'Specially now that you think your 'Injuns' was just a few white men having fun, eh?"

"Yes. I suppose he won't try anything in the daytime, if—and I say 'if'—he's still around."

"I call you lucky he didn't decide to pop into camp and plug you," Billy chided.

Henry shook his head. "I was ready. I haven't made it the last fifteen years in the world by being stupid. I was ready for you."

"Not for a rifle, you weren't. I'll go find some grub, check the traps and see if I can find some birds, if y'all will stay awake for about half an hour," said Billy. "Springtime's a good time of the year for plant foods and such. Ever had a fiddlehead?"

"Um, no," Henry replied.

"Baby ferns. You fry 'em up on a greased pan: ain't nothing better."

"'Kay. I'm willing to try anything once."

"You'll like 'em." And with that, Billy disappeared into camouflage again. Henry turned his attention to the boy.

*

"Dad?" His grandfather's form appeared in the darkness. Jeremy squinted, trying to make out the ethereal image in front of him. The picture drew clearer and he could make out the green leaves of a forest and the grassy slopes of a hill behind his father. The forest was weird. The trees looked like the firs of his home, but were taller, thinner and… *tighter*, more compact. Farther back were higher hills and beyond that, mountains, true mountains. Jeremy had never seen such peaks, craggy and massive, covered with snow and ice. They rose high above the comparably mean hills and gave an impression of a goal, of secrets to be found and appreciated, not exploited, secrets that only led to more secrets: of discovery. He tore his eyes away. There were more important things at hand. Weren't there?

His grandfather did not look at him; he faced the mountains and walked toward them in a determined, yet not hurried pace. Jeremy set out after him.

"Dad? Dad!"

The form turned and looked at him. "Who are you?" it said.

"Don't you know me?" Jeremy said, an unfamiliar panic rising in the back of his mind.

"I see death," said his grandfather, and turned away. Jeremy tried to follow, but the form turned back.

"You cannot follow," he said. "Hell cannot enter into the Great Mystery."

The panic grew.

"I don't understand!" Jeremy cried, desperately. Some unreasoning fear dominated his thinking and although he knew—as in dreams one does—that what he wanted so desperately was over the mountains, he had no idea why it was so important. But it was.

"There is blood on your hands. And not only blood of others, but blood of your own, shed by your own deeds."

Jeremy did not know what he was talking about. A fog settled about them and the air grew cold. It was the same fog as after a storm, but there was no storm and it seemed as if there never had been one in this place. The cloud increased and his grandfather faded into the white. Which turned gray. Which turned black as night. The fear that tainted his being now grew to consume him and he shrunk within himself. The worst thing was that he still didn't know why. He just knew that his grandfather traveled to go over the mountains and he himself couldn't. The black was opaque and, in his blindness, he stopped stumbling the walk and fell, full length onto the ground.

But the ground seemed to melt from beneath his feet and he kept falling, falling into the new (or had it always been there?) abyss. It came into his mind: "I am in hell." And he wept.

*

The fever broke later that night. After a long afternoon nap, Henry felt fit enough to volunteer for nurse duties that night. Billy brought back a couple of small birds they roasted and threw into a pot for stock. The fiddleheads were okay, but Henry was not thrilled with them. He ate them with outward relish and evaded Billy's enthusiastic inquiries into his opinion. When the stock finished and the horses had been seen to—they were short on grain—Billy lay on his bedroll and Henry did his best to try to feed the boy some broth. He hoped that the body would accept it even if the boy were unconscious.

With a spoon, he placed the greasy liquid on the lips of the boy and then pulled the lips apart with the spoon. Some dribbled in and the boy swallowed reflexively. Henry was happy with this sign and painstakingly continued to feed the boy, wiping with the spoon the stray dribble when the lips wouldn't open. When the broth disappeared, Henry wiped the kid's mouth and went to the stream to clean up.

Jeremy opened his eyes. His mind was still fuzzy, but the dreams and demons haunting his catalepsy, fading as they were, hovered about his mind like a bad taste from bark medicine tea. His eyes began to focus. The firelight flickered in the night and illuminated the bottom of the leafy ceiling above him but his peripheral vision registered very little. He turned his head to the left.

Standing near the fire, gnawing a smoking pipe, stood a bearded man, someone he had never seen before in his life. His mind did not process beyond a faint curiosity and he wondered how he had gotten here.

Henry returned with the cooking gear, rinsed if not washed. The pot contained water. Oblivious to the awakening invalid, he positioned a couple of hot stones in the fire and set the pot on them. Then, he took a green forked stick and maneuvered it under a promising small stone baking in the midst of the hottest coals.

Jeremy watched this, inexplicably fascinated. He wondered who on God's green earth *this* man was, whom he'd also never seen. Henry lifted the stone and quickly put it in the water. It did not take long to boil and he threw in the "tea" that Billy had gathered from the flora that afternoon. Set on the fire and prompted by the hot stone, the water merrily boiled the leaves. Henry let it be and stood up. As his eyes noticed the boy, they widened slightly and he grinned.

"Up, huh?" he said. Jeremy said nothing but looked at him.

"Well," said Henry. "How do you feel?"

"Okay, I s'pose," Jeremy replied, haltingly. It was the first time he had spoken a word in a week. Henry heard the clear drawl of the country folk of the South.

"You're up quite a bit quicker than I expected, considering things."

"How'd I get here?"

Henry turned his head slightly and looked at him sidelong. "You don't know?"

"Not sure I remember rightly."

"Do you know this place at all?"

Jeremy looked around. "Don't know. Sometimes seems like I've seen it before, but really don't remember."

The evening passed fairly tranquilly and Jeremy told Henry his name, but nothing else. The last he remembered clearly was trotting home from Dahlonega after registering his father's claim. Beyond that was like a dream: fuzzy moments blinking in and out of his subconscious, giving him feelings, but not knowledge. He did remember the dream of his grandfather and the high, snowy mountains, but although it was clearer in his memory than the other shapes, he knew it to be a dream. Unless it was a vision. But this was his problem; he could no longer differentiate between the real, the dreams, the visions and their places in his memory. It troubled him because the memory was often of things unpleasant, things that needed resolution if not absolute restitution.

It is not for nothing midnight is thought of as the "witching hour" and it is true that—whether self-fulfilling prophecies or truly events of the spiritual—things happen at such times that are uncanny.

Jeremy felt comfortable and drifted off into that strange area between waking and sleeping. Suddenly, he saw before him the same landscape that had haunted his delirium. Oddly, the mountains were yet clearer than before: were they nearer? The figure with its back turned to him was definitely his grandfather, and definitely moving away from him.

"Dad?" Jeremy cried out.

The figure gave no sign that it had heard him, but stalked on, neither increasing nor slackening its pace.

"*Dad?*" Jeremy cried louder and began to run toward him. The figure turned, finally. Jeremy stopped, in surprise: he was no closer to the man nor the mountains for all his panicked sprint.

"Leave me," the figure said, "you who do evil."

Jeremy, as bewildered as before, was shocked nonetheless.

"I don't understand."

"No evil can enter that land to which I am called."

"What is evil? Why can I not enter? Please tell me."

"Do you really wish to know?"

"I do."

*

Ginger Beard crept toward the forest clearing with the stealth of, if not an Indian, at least a white man doing his best to imitate one. With the boy and the blond man asleep, he saw no reason he should not sneak by the hairy one. He approached the fire and understood for the first time how it was possible for a man to approach unnoticed in the flickering shadows.

Billy cocked an ear: something had disturbed that contemplative vigilance he was in the habit of exercising. The night changed imperceptibly, but something was out there. He rose from the rock he sat upon and looked over the fire into the wilderness. The fire's glow and the tiny light from his pipe ruined any night sight he'd had and he closed his eyes to restore it and to enhance his formidable listening skills. The boy moaned in his sleep, caught in the dreams such tormented young men have.

Ginger Beard froze, holding his breath. Billy turned his head slightly, one sensitive ear toward the human statue no farther than fifty feet away. The breeze picked up slightly and Billy cursed the slight rustle of the bushes. Ginger Beard let his breath out slowly. He thought better of this endeavor, but a panicked thought realized he was a penny away from being caught anyway. He would be caught leaving as well as approaching. Nothing ventured…

Billy seemed to change his mind and sat down again on the rock, but this time, facing away from the fire. Ginger Beard lifted his foot and, twisting it awkwardly to start a venture *away* from the camp, set it down. It crackled, slightly. Billy's head suddenly came up.

The blood curdling scream shattered the silent night and, experienced men that they were, Henry jumped from his bedroll and Billy turned, revolver in hand, both ready for anything. The boy sat bolt upright, staring into the dark, sobbing as if his heart was already broken. The two men relaxed, and deep understanding came to Henry as he listened to the boy cry.

Ginger Beard fled heedlessly, his legs banging rocks, ankles twisting as he ran through the black woods. The scream was the same that had come to him the night they burned the homestead, and it carried all of the deaths since. But the terror and despair in the voice reached even him and he ran. Billy jumped up and started after him, then cursed again, and headed back to the boy and Henry.

The next day, the boy was gone. In spite of Henry's vigilance in the early mornings, this young woodsman was better at his craft than any white man and most Indians. He had taken his horse, tack, rifle and gear that Billy had discovered with the rest of the horses. Nothing else was gone, not even food. Henry wanted to go after him right away, worried about the boy's state of mind, but Billy argued. He insisted that for his healing, the boy needed to work things out for himself, no matter how raving mad he might have seemed at the time. For some reason unappreciated by Billy, Henry felt a responsibility for this young man, lost in a moral, psychological forest, one that he had never been in before and every bit as alien to him as the southern Appalachians would be to a born-and-bred city dweller. Henry prevailed. He had been in that virtual wilderness.

They packed and headed west, tracking the boy as they went.

## Chapter 12

In the day or so after leaving Henry and Billy, Jeremy's mind went through a medley of thoughts, some sequential, some entirely disjointed and he wondered if he was losing his mind. Whether the dream resulted from the fever or merely replayed the events in his mind, it still told the buried story of the previous week. He knew it all. He sorrowed over his family, weeping the tears that he had buried deeply at the homestead, and they flooded his homespun shirt and mixed with the perspiration of the new journey. He wept over his father, whom he was sure met death at the hands of the greedy soldiers: their conversations had left no doubt. Mostly, however, he wept for himself, a man guilty of blood. The dream of his Cherokee grandfather brought back principles that had been taught him from the earliest days of his youth and he had taken God's wonderful gift of woodcraft that he had in untold measure and perverted it for the sake of blood vengeance.

He did not feel sorry for the men he had murdered—and yes, he admitted it in his heart: *murdered.* But there was no justification in the killing he had done, such as self-defense or even the protection of kin and property. Though there might have been justice going by the "eye for an eye" principles he had been taught, he also realized that he himself had lost more by pretending to exercise that principle than the dead soldiers ever lost themselves when their lives had been taken from them. He did not yet know what that loss was, unless the dream held more truth than most fevered apparitions. Another thought: was his “eye” now forfeit for what he had done lest he find himself in whatever hell there may be?

Part of him wanted to die. Life had no interest for him any longer and he felt unwanted by both humanity and nature. But he was afraid of death, too, for he believed enough of his grandfather’s teachings to realize there was something after that big journey, and a *reckoning* was one of them. The same sense of justice that he had used to justify murdering those soldiers condemned him now. And even that was less for committing murder than for betraying… himself? He had no idea, but he suspected that betrayal was the more bitter sin.

The horse jogged along the ridges and the valleys and Jeremy bounced along on its back. He headed west, why, he did not know except that there lay vast unknowns, and the setting sun confirmed an urge to go in that direction. The leaves slowly unfolded into the large canopy it would be in the summer and the azaleas bloomed, but Jeremy had no more appreciation for them than he had the week earlier. This time, it was for a different reason. Before, he had been consumed in the obsessive fire of revenge. Now, he was all too aware of the growing beauty in the woods around him and it saddened him to think he had betrayed even this one facet of his life for his own selfish purposes.

So, over the days, he wandered through the hills along the Tennessee border, using his skills to only hunt, fish and gather. He ate, but received no enjoyment; it was only a means of fueling the body and a way to stave off the death he so feared. He drank, but only because responsibility to his body demanded it. Like the soldier leader, his mind had detached itself from the body and walked in a contemplative world of its own while the body went through the motions of living and wandering through the woods.

*

It seemed that they were up against a snag. They stopped outside a small town in northern Georgia, seemingly at a crossroad. For personal and other reasons, Henry had been determined to avoid any patrols from either side of the War, not to mention the armies themselves. But the boy was moving generally West and that meant they would either run directly into the line of logistics, which even now ranged from the hub of Southern supplies, Atlanta, to Nashville and beyond.

"Aw, hell," Billy muttered as they poked along one day. "Ye never know, we could bluff our way through."

"Yes, and get conscripted into the Confederate army—that would be God's joke on me—or shot for spies in the North. No thank you."

"Well, for sure, the longer we poke around here, the more likely some skirmishing patrol's gonna find us."

"No other way around, unless you want to go to the sticks and wait out the War. No history of that happening soon, though. There's no way out by sea, the Union's got the blockade shut down more than ever. We're going the right way," he affirmed.

They rode a while in silence. Henry didn't like it, but Billy's flippant remark was likely to be the best way. They were as likely to get caught on their way north or south as trying to sneak through. The kid headed that way, as well.

"We can't make a decision until we find out where the armies are. You're more local than I am. I'll get supplies, what we can find and you get some information from the locals."

Not wishing to show off their wealth, they tied the extra horses to trees in a hidden cove about a mile from Jasper, Georgia. Nearby, in a hollow tree, Henry cached the bulk of the supplies left from his home in Pennsylvania with the satchel of gold buried under a layer of dirt at the bottom.

Henry selected his packhorse, loaded again with the rest of the supplies and Billy rode. They hoped their appearances would be non-threatening, but not vulnerable. They rode in separately, Henry first, and he hoped that there would be some sort of black market that had some of the things they needed, in spite of the tendency in places like this toward some sort of post-winter leanness.

The town of Jasper was a collection of clapboard shacks, although there was some sort of pretense at industry. The sun beat down upon the mud and transformed it into a fine powdery dust that puffed every time a hoof struck the earth. There was no wind and, early March though it was, the still air was warm. Residents came out to watch the two men, hoping for news in a place that was too far out of the beaten tracks to get it.

Billy watched Henry wander down the only street in the town and turn in to a place that seemed most likely to sell supplies of the sort they would need. He dismounted and led his horse down the same way. He looked pointedly at the first homespun-clad native to look him in the eye.

"Know where I can get a bit of rotgut in this place?"

The native jerked his thumb down the street. "Ain't no place I know'f here'n town," he said, "but ol' Sam Kinsen makes some mash out his place ain't bad."

"And where's 'at?" Billy inquired.

"Take track half mile past end of town, and turn at the ol' lightnin'-blasted chestnut. Track'll take ye' up a hill and ye'll see's old shack." The native jerked his head vaguely up the hill, apparently indicating the general direction to give emphasis on his words.

Billy was a backcountry woodsman himself—the close quarters of *this* place actually made him feel a bit claustrophobic, not to mention his times in Asheville or even Dahlonega—and knew he could find the place. Yes, he was thirsty, but more important, he knew from long experience that the place for news was the place men hung out and that was either church or a drinking hole. And it probably wasn't Sunday, he thought, given the slatternly demeanor in this place.

"'Bliged." He remounted and kicked the horse

into a modest trot. As he passed Henry, who seemed to be in earnest conversation with some sort of proprietor, he nodded to both of them and headed out of town.

"Toon a day, eh?" said the proprietor. Henry looked after Billy, wondering what in the hell he was doing and not paying attention.

"What's that?" he said.

"Said *two*!" said the man. "Ain't often we get a stranger, much less two in a day."

"War's probably coming down," prompted Henry, solicitously.

The shop owner looked at him. "You Yankee, ain'tcha?" he asked, suspiciously.

"May have come from there, but I don't consider myself much of anything at this point."

"Lessee your money."

Henry plopped a couple of gold dollars on the counter. The owner's eyes widened.

"Hell, ah cain't make change for that," the man whined. The gold was a comforting sight: he didn't take script or even paper money of the Confederate variety and it could be dangerous to be caught holding Yankee bills. But the coins were good metal, if authentic, and were tradable in any form, in any city in the world. The shop-owner practically drooled.

"I'll figure the change. First, forget I'm from the North. You don't know nothing about me and I don't believe you should be judging me just yet."

The shop-owner cringed slightly as his perspective "changed".

"Yessir, it seems your accent is disappearing as we speak, cousin, and as a matter of fact, didn't you just say you was from Asheville, or some sich place?"

"That'll do. Don't be stupid. Here's what I need."

Henry laid out a list and read it out loud. There really wasn't that much, mostly long-lasting items. He wasn't foolish enough to expect powder or lead in a rebellious country, but it was possible he could find some things "behind the counter". Grub he was short on, and the man knew it. His eyes confirmed this.

"Sor' sir, ain't got but a little bit of flour and beans. Might be able to find…"

Henry quietly leaned forward and one of the coins disappeared. The man squeaked and quickly shut his mouth up. In spite of himself, this intrigued him. Usually, if he held out, *more* money was likely to open his black-market storeroom. He was worried now. He didn't know if the man was bluffing: he looked willing to ride Houston before he would get supplies just to spite him.

He cleared his throat. "Um, well, sir, mebbe there's something in the back, just my own, you know, for the family and such, that I could rummage 'round and find somewhat. Be willing to work w'ye on that."

Henry didn't say anything, but when his hand left

the wooden counter, the coins were paired again. His point was made.

From that point, it was academic. Henry bought most of the supplies they needed and cleared out the place. The total left a small amount of change, but Henry allowed the man to keep it to ensure his confidentiality. One coin bought the supplies and the other was promised upon delivery. He made arrangements for the man to load the wagon and keep an eye on it while he went looking for Billy and whatever "noos" he'd found. He had the nagging suspicion that the soldier Billy had detected was still somewhere around and he made the man's silence an exchange for the money.

*

The soldier in question followed Henry and Billy as closely as possible, but they made fast time through the woods and he, on foot, couldn't hope to keep up with them. He didn't consider the boy: the boy was nothing and he had no loyalty to his former comrades-in-arms to prompt revenge. What he wanted was the gold, and the gold traveled with the men in front of him.

Months of raiding and the last week of scrounging through the woods sorely beat up his clothes, and in truth, he looked the deserter he was, and one who had had a pretty rough time of it. His makeshift pack gouged into his shoulders and he tired pretty quickly now, not having the skill in the woods of Jeremy, Billy, or even Henry, to feed himself. He slept nights on the bare ground using the pack as a pillow, and this stingy supply of food would last him no longer than a week if he hoarded and was lucky. A wiser man would have stopped and built traps, or hunted, but Ginger Beard was driven by his lust for wealth and his body suffered because of it.

The small remuda left significant prints and he had no problem following the trail of the stolen gold. It bothered him that they were heading west, but as malnutrition set in, he began to forget why he wanted to stay away from there.

*

One evening, after weeks of his meandering, Jeremy became aware of a commotion in the woods ahead of him. He heard shouting and the noises of horses being heavily worked. Creaking and working machinery came to his ears as he slowed his pace and the mere sounds of human activity served to suddenly bring him back to the present circumstances. He still did not know where he was, much less that Sherman and Johnston's army fought in the great running battle to the sea, in this phase encroaching upon the lifeblood of Southern commerce and materiel: Atlanta.

For the first time, he looked at the sun and saw he was heading north-northwest. He pulled off into a small cove and dropped off his horse. Then, using his stealthy woodcraft skills, *sans* gun, he moved through the blooming rhododendron bushes toward the sounds.

There stood Yankees, their blue uniforms starkly

obvious in the somber green of the forest. Curses and grunts accompanied shouted orders as men pushed the large wagon-wheels of their cannons through the newly churned muck. The horses strained and grunted as much as the men, but it was only through concerted effort and the assistance of assigned infantry that they were able to make headway along the newly hewn road of Sherman's march south.

Jeremy watched for a while. There were more men in this one short stretch of road than he had ever seen in his life—more, even, than in Atlanta, or so it seemed to his very rural eyes. As he looked upon Sherman's men, he was impressed with the discipline the officers held over soldiers that—in appearance, at least—were not that different from those he had murdered. Another, familiar now, wave of shame swept over him. These attacks had lost their emotional impact by sheer repetition, but merely served to reinforce the logical condemnation.

He sat back and thought for a moment. These were invaders and even in small Helen, he had heard stories of Union armies "living off the land" (only dead men in the South were not constantly informed of the war for freedom.) This meant that a large, vulnerable train of supplies and materiel was virtually nonexistent and therefore, not the weak part of an invading army. A by-product of such a policy also resulted in what was later referred to in military schools as "burnt earth". By depriving them of home and food, local civilians had to scrounge for sustenance, with no time for uprisings or guerrilla warfare, and, more importantly, supplying the defending army. Later in the 19th century, this policy was enforced in the Indian Wars, as natives frustrated the army as it fought against a highly mobile nomadic people with the best light cavalry in the world.

He had been too young to fight in the war and even at fourteen his father had laid down the law against taking a stand. The motives were the usual: escape from the family farm, desire to see the world, glory and honor for the young men and excitement. Plus, he might have even been paid, however little. Very low on the local man's list was a vague impression of a tyrannical North imposing restrictions on a virginal South. To the rural folk, this usually meant changing of the guard and nothing more, for the war was far off and only the government in Virginia might see something of that change.

But now, they were here. They encroached upon the lands that he was comfortable with and that he knew well, for he had grown in them and lived in them and knew them more intimately than he knew his family.

Opinions and philosophies collided in his mind and in his heart. From his experienced grandfather, who had seen something of battle during the 1812 invasion, he knew that killing men in time of war was a different thing from cold-blooded murder. Very different. Still more, he knew that killing in defense of land and home differed as well. Finally, killing to keep from being killed was the last justification, as was invariably the case when men are ordered by commanders to march into death's way—without political, strategic or tactical justification, men will kill, for the victor is less likely to leave his body for the wild janitors of the field.

What made his mind up, however, were none of these reasons. Men do amazing things, dare wonderful deeds, and show incredible courage for this universal reason. Quite simply: he had nothing better to do. And to do was far better than to think.

He dropped back into the trees and made his way to the horse. He led the animal away from the road, vaguely surprised that there were not outriders scouting for such as him, and did not mount until he was a full mile away from the progressing army. He was not sure where the defending army camped, but logically, the Union Army probably came from the north. He knew nothing about military strategy, but he did have that innate sense of logic especially manifested in the mountain people. Either they marched south to meet the Confederates, or they flanked them as the Grey was entrenched in an unassailable position. He flipped a stick and it landed small side to the north. He took a deep breath and rode that direction.

*

Henry loaded the horse and walked out of town in the direction he had seen Billy. He was nervous in a place that knew he had money: didn't matter how much. He unfastened the strap on his holster and loosened the gun. No quick draw, he nonetheless obtained some comfort from the gun and it would be a deterrent in a robbery.

"*Psst!*"

He immediately moved to a crouch as he whirled in the direction of the sound. Billy huddled behind a shrub of azaleas in full bloom. He motioned to Henry. Henry obliged.

"Y'all look *purdy* with all them flowers," Henry said, mimicking Hawg's drawl.

Billy whispered, "Let's cut cross-country. Don't want none of these yokels to have an easy ambush out on the road. They been looking at both of us a little funny, if y'all git my drift."

Henry answered, "Can we do it? Looks like some rough country."

"Steep, but that ain't gonna kill us or the horses."

"'Kay. Where are we going?"

"Man's farm up the valley. Makes whiskey and so, probably got noos."

"News we can get in town."

"Yeah, but we cain't get whiskey. And the noos is probably better."

Henry sighed. He never was one for alcohol: he'd seen his share of ruined careers in his stint in the army among enlisted and officers alike. Still, although he'd trusted Billy to some extent, he didn't know him well enough to dictate temperance. He wasn't his mother. Leave it alone and let performance be the judge.

"'Kay, let's go."

They headed up the hill and it was rather a push. The undergrowth was not too thick, although prevalent, and it was easy to find a deer path through the forest. A sweaty hour through the mess and they stood upon the top of a ridge, looking down into a partially cultivated cove in the middle of which stood a log cabin. Built single-room as most homesteads were, it was well established and the fields of corn indicated the commodity of choice. The still they could just see in the woods confirmed it.

They led the horses down the ridge, keeping the cove on their left and angled slowly into the valley—deer can be as lazy as any other creature who lives in the southern heat, and the trails they found were easy and level enough. They switch-backed down the hill from trail to trail as needed, and as they reached the bottom they looked warily across the fields at the house, smoke curling fitfully above the mud chimney.

"Hello, the farm!" Henry hollered across the valley bottom. No one responded. They moved down the side of the flat bottom, the heat wafting over them as a breeze moved down the cove. They carefully approached the structure, wary of nervous landowners with shotguns and hair triggers.

When they got close enough, they saw a bearded old man without a shirt standing on the porch, tacitly watching them. His paunch hung over dingy pants tied with a rope and his long gray hair blended with that on his face and chest. He said nothing and they followed suit as they approached and stopped in front of the shaded porch. Billy cleared his throat.

"Heard y'all had some firewater."

The man looked at them for a moment. "Heard raht." He spat on the hard-packed clay road.

"Spare some?"

"Lessee your money. Don't take no scrip'."

Billy nodded to Henry, who flipped a small coin in the air. The man's hand snatched it from the air and in a single movement deposited in the pocket of the grimy canvas pants he wore. He stepped off the porch. He looked at the revolver Henry carried and his eyes narrowed. He looked directly into Henry's eyes and to Henry's curiosity and amazement, visibly relaxed. The moonshiner had been around and he knew a trustworthy man when he saw him. The man chuckled.

"Y'all come in now, give a try on the hooch, on the house, if'n you buy enough."

"'Bliged," Billy drawled and didn't hesitate to follow the man into the house.

The atmosphere inside the house was close and warm, even though the board windows were propped wide open to let the minimal cross breeze do its work. It was considerably more congenial than out on the porch. Over the rotgut—and that was the word Henry irrevocably applied to it: he wasn't used to the stuff and he didn't dare refuse the offered mug—they learned quite a bit. He sipped enough to look like he was drinking it, not enough to make his eyes water.

They found that Sherman was solidly into southern

Tennessee and Joe Johnston's army was having a bad time of it.

"Don't blame him," said Sam," 'cause his army's a lot smaller, but them delaying tactics only brings the blues down into our territory."

Henry asked how he was so sure. The man didn't seem to be offended at the question and answered, "Had a attack of some sort on the line. Too sick to fight. They sent me home. I don't do much of nothing now but watch the corn grow and make a little hooch to keep me fed. Got some friends coming down 'casionally, and they keep me up to snuff." He winked. "Gotta make sure the quality's good, too."

"There's a line from Atlanta to Nashville, a long one where they send ammunition and food and such stuff when they don't get 'nuff from the country. If you want to join up, that's the way to go. Otherwise, stay 'way from there."

*

The homestead was remote and poor. The family had been close to starving and all but the father and oldest son had left for relatives in the city. The crib had corn, but the level was extremely low and even the two hogs found two humans sharing what was nominally their winter store. They weren't far from eating their brood hogs. All other animals had been turned out to roam wild and the two men prayed that they would remain wild and not garnish the table of some thief.

One of the thieves in question approached the house in the evening dark. Poor stealings, but anything was promising at this point. He just hoped he was strong enough to do the job, starvation having weakened him to some degree. How much, only time would tell.

There was a tiny, faint glow through the cracks in the wall and a distant-sounding occasional murmur. He crept to the house and lowered his empty pack silently, and the dry grass beneath him crunched minutely as the weight of the pack settled. The thief looked through the opportunistic crack, low on the ground to minimize detection, and saw a man of about thirty talking in a low voice to a boy of twelve around a tiny cooking fire. The boy rose and said he was thirsty and wasn't there anything in the jug. The father said no, you better get some more. The boy crossed over to the table, picked up the jug and walked out the door. The thief—and killer—was already in motion as the kid turned the corner.

## Chapter 13

A couple of hours passed before Jeremy heard new sounds of men and machinery. He rode a ridge to the west of Dalton, Georgia and climbed the hills at a walk, resting his horse.

Unseen by Jeremy, a group of young soldiers watched him from a pile of boulders lying on the side of the hill.

"Yeah, yeah, I got him." This came from a nineteen-year-old in confederate butternut; a corporal and one gifted in shooting.

"Don't shoot yet. Who is he?"

"Ain't no one I know, but I can't see the face from this far. Probably a spy. I just know if I give him a holler, he'll take off and we'll be none the wiser."

A lieutenant sneaked up to the rock on which the corporal was balancing his long rifle. His upper-class urban accent betrayed inexperience in the trenches and he was desperately trying to show some practical leadership to these young frontiersmen.

"I dunno," he said. "With the variety of uniforms we got in this army, he could be a courier, even in that homespun. One thing's for sure: any horseflesh is hard to come by right now and that's a good horse under him. Gotta be official somehow."

One of the "boys" sat back and—foolishly, the

corporal thought—lit a pipe he'd stuffed. They may have been short on food but one thing the South had plenty of was tobacco.

"Hell, just shoot 'im," he drawled with a lopsided grin.

"One thing's for sure," said the corporal without moving his head from the sight. "I don't shoot him now, he'll smell the t'baccy some idjit just lit." The grin on the smoker vanished, but he snuffed the glowing tobacco and leaned back with a pout.

"'Tenant?" The corporal asked. The one word was an exercise in eloquence. The lieutenant sighed. He was much more afraid of looking "yeller" than he was wise. He took the violent course.

"Much as I hate to say this, take the horse. We'll find out what he is. Andrews and Tate! Start off to the left, circle him and when Corporal Mackey here shoots his animal, take him, *post haste!*"

"'Post haste'?" Tate crinkled his brow.

"'Quickly!' Now *move it!*"

And they moved.

Jeremy's quick senses immediately detected the men who were clumsily—at least by his standards—running through the woods. Instead of wasting time to rein up and figure things out, he drove his heels into the horse's side, wrenching the head around with the reins as hard as he could. The animal reared, startled by his unusual treatment after several weeks of wandering, but instead of righting itself and taking off through the woods, it crashed on its side, not moving. In the excitement, Jeremy hadn't heard the shot and wondered why the animal flopped under him with its great weight. Even so, his senses did not totally leave him and he jumped off the beast before it could pin him to the ground. He flipped onto his belly, but before he could get his legs under him for the inevitable escape to the woods, a blow knocked his head sideways. It felt as if his head left his neck. His last thought was rather one of relief. He was so tired.

"Dammit, don't kill him," the lieutenant shouted as he jumped over the rocks. Tate nearly hit Jeremy again, ensuring the silence and passivity of the prisoner, but his arm froze on the upswing. The lieutenant mistakenly—and for a moment, with personal joy—thought he was being obeyed until the amazed Tate cried out.

"Wh-what?" the startled lieutenant stuttered.

"I know this man!" Tate exclaimed. The other men stood around him now and waited for the answer to the unasked questions.

"Don't know his name, but he's local. Somewhere east of here." One of the other boys snickered.

"Probably your sister and just don't know it," he said. The others snorted and chuckled. Obviously, Tate had been given grief for being a local inbred hick before.

"Damn your eyes," he said, tired of the play, for once. Although no one changed demeanor or stance, there was a general shift in mood as the surprised men realized Tate wasn't about to try to lick the joker. Corporal Mackey bent down to the boy.

"Coming around, sir," he said. Indeed, Jeremy stirred, Tate's "tap" to the head not sufficient enough to knock him out for any length of time.

His head was a dull ache and somehow his mind was detached from it. His neck really hurt; he must have wrenched it or something. Sound came to him gradually, like an approaching band in the parade he once saw in Atlanta. He heard something like "…ing drowned her…" and then the rustle of the new spring leaves in the bushes around him. His sight took marginally longer and a bright tunnel end approached until there was only a faint dullness about the edges of his sight.

"You're alright now." He heard a very faint brogue in the accent of the face above him and memories of an Irish great-aunt played in the distance. Mackey straightened up.

"He'll have a head like a pumpkin, sir, for a bit."

The lieutenant leaned down and examined the boyish face. Jeremy tried to focus as he looked back at the officer, without fear.

"Who are you?" The lieutenant stared into his eyes.

"Nobody," said Jeremy. "Nobody in particular, I mean. My name's Jeremy Kennedy."

"Where you from, boy?"

"Small town somewhere east of here, by the name

of Helen."

Tate giggled. The lieutenant turned on him in annoyance.

"Something on your mind, private?"

"Uh, no sir, except I know where I seen him, sir. He and his old man used to pop their heads in Dahlonega way. Small town. You get to know the strangers pretty quick, especially the backcountry folk."

"Is that so?" He turned back to Jeremy. "On your feet, boy, no matter who you are, you gonna walk wherevah. Tate, you and Johnson take him over to headquarters and have him talk to the cavalry liaison officer. He may have some intelligence in his riding about the area. Wheeler's probably up there after kicking ass on the Yanks yesterday and he'll be glad to hear any more news."

Tate gave a sloppy motion that was intended to pass for a salute and held out his hand to the prone man on the ground. Jeremy looked at him for a moment and, if not exactly reading friendliness, did not see any overt hostility in the man. He grabbed the hand and pulled himself up to his feet. He swayed as the concussed skull threatened to fly apart on his neck. At least that was how it felt. He felt his arms being grabbed by strong hands to either side—not for security's sake, but to help him stand—and gradually his legs were stronger.

"I can stand," he said. The hands loosened, but did not release, their grips. Tate spoke.

"Need you to follow me," he chuckled. "*Thought* I

knew you."

*

While Billy and Sam Kinsen got chummy, Henry rode back to town to pick up the wagon. As he passed under the spring growth, he loosened the gun in his holster, half convinced that someone still waited for him on the trail. It was quiet. Too quiet. Mostly his imagination, he knew, but he tensed anyway, ready for anything and he continued walking on down the trail.

On a hard turn overlooking a small series of falls he saw his ambushers-to-be. They faced away from him, intent on the trail below, waiting for the man who had bought up a certain storekeeper's black-market stock. *A little late for that*, he thought. Fortunately for him, the babbling of the stream and the configuration of the rocks in the canyon did not help in aural direction and their biases inclined toward the rich stranger coming up from the town. Not to mention the fact that they were the better part drunk, shown by the bottle at their feet.

Against his better judgment but very much in keeping with his sense of humor, he walked the horse up to them. They still didn't hear him and he thought he would do his best to help them locate the rich stranger he suspected they were after. He raised the gun in the air and it clicked as he drew back the hammer. One of the least drunk began to turn around as his sixth sense came into play.

It was not "jump?" but "how high, sir?" when the

revolver went off. Henry could barely keep from laughing, but an innate sense of professionalism ("thank you, Union Army") mixed with caution kept his face impassive.

"Looks like you boys are looking for something. Can I help?"

He still held the revolver, albeit at a relaxed attitude, but to the "boys" it must have looked like a cannon. They were now explicably sober.

"Asked you a question." Henry leaned forward, his acting ability giving a mean gleam to his eyes.

"Uh," a man with a beard stuttered, "we's just looking for my uh, my boy John, who's coming up the trail. Ain't that right, boys?" It was not a question; it was a hopeful request for affirmation. The other "boys" hesitated until they understood, then nodded with enthusiasm.

"Oh, so you live in that cabin up in the cove yonder, eh?" Henry queried.

"Uh, thassright, sir, thassright, ain't that right, boys?" More enthusiastic nods.

"Why don't I believe you?"

"Don't know what you mean." The man began to panic.

"Now, why don't you boys just go ahead and move on down the trail… no, you can leave those rifles, I don't plan on your needing them again." This, as the leader obediently leaned over to grab the bottle and his gun.

Henry continued. “You can keep the bottle: drunker you are the less likely you’ll come looking for your John and bothering me.”

“Y-y-yessir.”

“Now, *get.*”

The men scrambled as fast as they could and took off down the valley. Henry was tempted to let loose a shot after them, but it would have been arrogant and unprofitable, if gratifying. He dismounted and cleared all the firearms he saw and threw the ammunition into a deep pool in the creek. Then he got back in the saddle and kicked the horse into a walk, following the men he’d just chased off and leaving the rifles where they were.

The storeowner gushed gratefully at the sight of the extra coin, but Henry checked everything in the wagon just in case. He wanted to put the fear of God into him—he knew why the three men waited for him—but wearily felt it a waste of time. All the gear lay in the wagon and he headed up the valley. The road to the old man’s place narrowed and was rough in spots, but not impassable for the wagon and it took no more than an hour. He would wait until night to pick up the gold and the other horses, for obvious reasons. He got back about late afternoon.

Sam was affable, but Henry personally wondered if it was authentic or more influenced by the revolver on his belt. He felt badly: the last thing he wanted was to intimidate someone whose trust he wanted. They were able to buy a jug, but, although Billy was into “drinking and thinkin’”, as he put it, Henry was more inquisitive.

They found that although things weren't yet too bad as far as food went in the South, the encroaching armies were beginning to make a dent in the economy, since materiel had to be paid for with hard goods when it was to be had. The black market was clearly alive and kicking, as Henry had found out in Jasper.

By the time evening came, Billy and the old man had gotten pretty mellow. The old man probably was not averse to eliminating some of his own surplus occasionally and didn't need the cash for too much besides. Henry could see they were not leaving that night and, nodding to his host (who paid little if any attention to him), stepped outside.

The moon floated above the trees and a mist had risen from the moist valley flats. The air cooled, slightly, but noticeably. Henry sighed. It seemed "sighing" was a fact of life, his way of expressing hopelessness among other things. Not hopelessness in itself, nor hopelessness in himself, but hopelessness in others. Often, it was merely a reflection of the situation and the fact that he was helpless in the scene. In the meantime, he took stock of the situation.

They still needed to head west if they were going to catch up to Jeremy and that, he was determined to do. For some reason, he knew that he needed to straighten the young man out, so to speak. He'd only known him a few days, but still, if the last few years' experience had taught him anything, he had a sense of responsibility where none was expected. He just couldn't leave well enough alone, he supposed, as if the child was "well". Besides, they had the gold, which he suspected was the boy's or his family's.

The law was the least concern. No law in the South would condemn, much less convict, the retribution Jeremy had inflicted on a bunch of enemy combatants. It was all in the course of war. No, the damage done was to Jeremy himself, and Henry had been through enough experience in the last seventeen years to want to mentor others. And now, God had given him the chance to pay back.

He didn't dare take the horses west, especially one with a "U.S." brand: they'd get hung. He was sure of it. They needed to travel with a minimum of stock and supplies, enough for the month he hoped they would need to make the journey: he was confident that Billy could find the boy in that time. They could cache the rest.

He led the horses to the shack that passed for a barn and unsaddled Billy's. He pulled off all the packs on his horse until only the saddle remained with the rifle holster.

He hopped on the mare and headed down the cove to the main trail. He saw nothing on his way and Jasper itself lay in the moonlight like the sleepy small town it had appeared during the day. He continued through town and to the small cove where they had left their horses. The animals still chomped on the bits of grass and leaves they were able to snitch while on their hobbles. The gold and other supplies were still hidden in the tree where they had left them. He breathed a sigh of relief. He was *pretty* confident, but there was always that nagging "maybe" in the back of his mind. "Maybe" some local saw them. "Maybe" the man who might—or might not—be behind them had caught up. "Maybe" a dog dug it up and carried it off. He chuckled and repacked the things, distributing them among the horses.

He chained the horses, nose-to-butt, and bypassing the town, led them up to the house where Billy, he figured, was sleeping off a powerful drunk. Nothing happened and he saw nothing, except the ambushers' empty guns still on the trail where he had left them. He smiled.

*

Ginger Beard left only a rumor of terror as he passed like a ghost through the north Georgia mountains. He engaged in the practice of killing as a matter of convenience—it was prudent since no one could tell about or follow him—but he enjoyed it beyond reason. He had exchanged clothes with the father at the first cabin he'd raided. Now he was only some bum trying to escape from the War as best he can.

*

Jeremy learned that Tate grew up in Dahlonega and joined the Confederates as part of a Georgia militia. After the Battle of Chickamauga, when he had gotten separated from his troops, he'd somehow attached himself to these boys from the 15th Arkansas.

"Like 'em for the most part. Boys like ourselves. Even the lieutenant is okay, although he's a sissy booklearnin' type. He knows enough to keep his mouth shut most of the time."

As they walked, Tate proved a fountain of knowledge. Andrews said nothing the entire time. Jeremy learned that he had somehow missed the town of Dalton, Georgia on his trek west and they were holed up in a cleft in the hills called Dug Gap. It was May 10, 1864.

"Yep, we got this entire gap shut down and every time the bluebellies come up here, we just toss more boulders down on them. No one can pass through these gaps but what we know about 'em." He winked. "Got *you*, didn't we?"

Jeremy smiled. Jeremy had had no real interest in the War: it had hitherto been so far away that it had not affected their little part of north Georgia, barring the occasional drive for conscripts. He still figured to fight somewhere, again for lack of anything better to do, but there was no passion in him for it, nothing to drive him beyond exercising those skills God gave him and trying to forget his prostitution of them. His head still ached, but he didn't blame Tate for smacking him. He would have done it in his place and in fact, he was grateful for the lieutenant not ordering him shot out of hand. He was sorry for the loss of his horse, however. Walking was not fun and although he had never had any emotional attachment to any horse, he recognized the benefits of long association and missed the horse's ready response and stamina. Not to mention saving his feet.

They walked through the pickets after a perfunctory call-and-response of passwords. It didn't take long for them to trek to the command center where the cavalry rested after a long skirmishing reconnaissance. Tate nodded toward an older man lighting a cigar, leaning against a tree.

"That there's Wheeler," he said. "One of the best cavalry commanders this army's got. Hell, may even include the whole South. I dunno, I ain't no horse rider."

Jeremy was impressed only as a country hick could be at the number of uniformed and un-uniformed men milling about. The cavalry was clearly seen, in gray uniforms of comparably well-kept appearance, compared to the hodge-podge of butternut outfits and other colors that the militia tended to sport. In the distance, over the hill, boomed the artillery. Although well protected this far behind the lines, the thunder of the deep, far-carrying low frequencies gave Jeremy a chill that vibrated throughout his bones. Or was it thrill? He could not immediately identify it as either and decided it was likely to be both. In part of it, he saw the obvious dichotomy between the vibrant green of new growth in the forest and the voice of an admirable facsimile of God, something man was doing his best to imitate.

Tate led him to a low tent strung in and among the trees. He saluted the sentry on charge with the same slovenly salute Jeremy had seen him give the lieutenant.

"'Tenant Philips sent a prisoner for questionin'." Jeremy didn't like this reference to him one bit.

"'Hm," grunted the sentry, who went inside the

tent. Murmurs within began and ceased and the sentry returned. He motioned them inside and Tate jerked his head in the direction of the door. Jeremy walked under the flap.

Sitting at a cot next to the table was a small, dapper man. He was well dressed, his uniform clean and even pressed, but something in the man's eyes spoke of vast battle experience and wisdom derived from it. His beard was full, but trimmed into an impressive goatee and as Jeremy watched he sat up and with his finger, brushed the equally impressive mustache away from his mouth as if it interfered with his speaking. And now he spoke, in a smooth patrician accent of the South's merchant nobility.

"Well, masteh Tate, what have you brought us t'day?"

"Prisoner, sir, captured near our command this mornin'."

"And?"

Jeremy interrupted, somewhat to the annoyance of Tate. Anxious to establish loyalties at the beginning, he committed himself before it sounded pretended. "I been along the ridges southeast of here and seen something y'all should know."

The cavalry major turned to him. "And what would that be, my young friend?"

"We got Yankees amoving south on your left side. Not just a few, but a lot of them."

The major's eyes narrowed. "How many?" he asked.

"Don't know no numbers, I just seen a lot."

The major started to say something, but changed his mind.

"What's your name, boy?"

"Jeremy." And then, because he'd heard others say so, he added, "Sir."

"Where you from?"

"Helen, sir, about an easy week's ride from here. I think." His wandering had not exactly given Jeremy a surveyor's concept of the geography.

The major made something between a grimace and a lopsided smile. There was something sad in it. But beyond noticing the lopsided aspect, Jeremy's heart was far from—or far beyond—recognizing his own emotions, much less empathizing with anyone else's and the man's eloquent face did little to convey to him the wisdom attained at a great price. He did not like the silence and spoke again.

"I'll fight Yankees, sir. They're invading my land."

The major didn't know whether that statement expressed ignorance, cleverness, or duplicity. Spies and scouts came and went and it was difficult to know which side they really worked for. He dismissed Andrews, and wrote for a moment on a sheet of paper. He turned to the sentries.

"Take this young… man to that area we've designated as a holding place for prisoners and await further orders. He's not to leave, but will be treated decently, including food."

He looked at Jeremy.

"As you might guess, I have no way of checking out your *bona fides* for a while. I'll check your story. Mister Tate."

"Sir."

"I'll need y'all t'play as courier for a bit. After dinner, please take this to Mister Stevenson with my compliments. No need to wait for a response, it will come in its own time."

The men moved to do the major's orders. Tate caught Jeremy's eye and gave him a quick wink before turning to exit the tent.

One of the sentries said to Jeremy, "Follow me."

And he did.

*

Billy awoke with one of the worst hangovers he'd ever had and soaking wet. Must have been a hot night for him to sweat so much. Henry's face floated above him with a horrendous grin on his face, and he held a bucket of water, he thought. He'd hit that awful face if it would only hold still and not move about like to make him seasick. Too late. He turned his head just in time and lost… nothing. He heaved for a while and when they subsided, he dropped his head and went back to sleep.

Henry grunted and dumped the rest of the water over his friend's head. Friend! They must be friends: no one else would take the time. Billy groaned and rolled around a bit as the water made the dirt floor under his head slimy and too disgusting even for him. Henry grabbed his hair and all but hauled him up to his feet. Billy staggered once, balled up his fist and tried to slug Henry, but the experienced Henry easily avoided the drunken blow and somehow managed to hang on to Billy's hair as he turned and tried to go back down to the floor.

"Whoa, boy," Henry said. He grappled for a chair behind him and thumped it in Billy's general direction. He dragged the man back until he lost his balance and plopped into the chair.

"How about some coffee, Billy?" Henry agreeably asked. The man mumbled some sort of appropriate profanity. He looked awful. His already tangled and dirty hair was matted even worse from the added clay of the dirt floor, alcohol that had missed his face, and the water Henry had flung upon him. The red Georgia clay would never come out of any clothes that mankind ever put to mill and Henry hoped Billy liked the ochre shade he now wore. It was permanent. Henry set a cup of chicory brew in front of the man. Billy groped for the tin cup and took a sip. Without moving his head, he spewed it over the floor. He mumbled.

"What was that?" Henry asked. The man said

something about "sugar". Henry found some corn syrup Sam was storing for alcoholic uses in what passed for a cupboard and poured a small amount into the cup. It took ten more minutes of Henry pacing through the cabin before Billy was somewhat coherent, if not entirely there.

"Bad stuff," he mumbled.

"Oh, I don't know," Henry replied. "You seemed to dig into it without too much, uh, distaste. And our host seems no worse for wear. He's out tending the latest stock of his still."

"'Susetoit," Billy slurred.

"Au contraire, mon ami," Henry started to say.

"Shit, you mumble worse'n I do," Billy interrupted in his uncouth way. His head felt about the size of an award-winning pumpkin, but full of water. If he moved in any direction, he thought it might fall off. After a while, the chicory began to take effect and he was able to make out—albeit blurry and distorted—Henry's face.

"So, what's up?" he asked.

"Well, looks like we have a place to keep our horses for the meantime. He needs some supplies and we've got a couple of things he doesn't mind having. He'll board our horses and keep our extra supplies for the next few months if we need it."

"How d'we know he ain't gonna run off with it all?"

"Couple of things. I sweetened the pot and told him that if everything was accounted for when we got back, there'd be extra, you know, the half now, half later deal. I've cached the currency in a place only I know so neither he nor anyone who gets us is going to get the cash."

Henry grinned.

"I also made it clear to him that it would be in the best interest of his health that the items not disappear during our sojourn."

"How's that?"

"See, he's still a bit afraid of me and since last night, doesn't trust me worth a darn. He still can't figure a man who doesn't have the inclination to drink himself under the table. A man like that scares him. And, I can be a quiet man when I want to be and that intimidates some people."

Billy nodded. Although he would never admit it, Henry had thoroughly unnerved him the first night they'd met. Hence the loud bluff act he'd put on. A quiet man was either yellow or a man not to be trifled with, and Henry was clearly not the former.

"What about traveling cash?"

"I've kept a few dollars on my body, which won't get found except by the most determined and shameless outlaw."

"Your money and your body. Y'all think you got it covered, *I'll* be fine. When're we leavin'?"

"Soon as you're fit to ride, I'd like to get a start on this thing. I want to find that boy, before he gets himself into trouble. If you want to come."

"Sure, I'll come. Ain't got nothing better to do 'cept drink, and I'm too old to do any more nights like that!"

They packed the two horses they'd selected for quick riding and light gear. The wagon they stored in the shed that contained Sam's corncrib. Then, they left. At Henry's suggestion, they cut through the woods to the north this time.

*

He reached Jasper, still following the trail of the gold. The only trade center in town was the mercantile where Henry had bought his gear, and he found it quickly. He knew better than to hold up a store even in this town where he would be seen and pursued. He was too weak, for one thing. For another, it was different raiding in the backcountry where a cabin would lie hidden and unvisited for weeks or even months. He walked through the open doorway and straight to the counter. The proprietor looked him up and down and would have shrugged him off, but for the lesson Henry had taught him the day before: looks often belie the presence of gold. Ginger Beard had none, but he didn't know that.

"Can I help you?" the owner said, somewhat fawning.

"No." Ginger Beard moved through the store looking at various items on display. There wasn't much, nor was he surprised. Any decent stock hid in the basement or out back. He could come back and see what he could find. The storeowner began to get nervous. He didn't like the look of this man and his short answer was out of character, he thought, for someone who had apparently spent some time away from human companionship.

"Things are going cheap," the owner said, helpfully.

The other ignored him and continued wandering around the small room.

"War and all making things real expensive," the owner continued. "But here, I'm willing to swing you a deal."

The other remained silent. The owner was starting to get frightened. That was Ginger Beard's intention. He waited a couple more minutes to let the man really get scared, then looked at him. He did not bother to hide his Yankee accent.

"Looking for a couple men. Can't miss 'em. One's a Yankee's Yankee and the other's a born Southern. Yankee's neatly trimmed, but been in the bush for a while. Southerner's a good old boy, brown beard as long as your waist, overalls. They had a small herd of horses they were bringing along."

"Ain't seen no one."

The man said it just a smidge too quickly, and Ginger Beard knew it.

"No one, eh?" His tone indicated unquestionably his doubt of the man's integrity.

The man started to sweat. "Ain't seen no horses like that come through here since the Army conscripted a bunch of them. And that's been a couple of years."

Ginger Beard approached the counter.

"'Struth, I swear it!"

The thief and murderer brought his face within inches of the other and stared him down. The owner started to back up, but Ginger Beard grabbed the owner's store-bought shirt—his pride and joy—and forced him to look in his eyes. The owner looked at him for only seconds before his eyes dropped to the counter. Ginger Beard didn't move.

"The men. Seen 'em?"

"Saw only the one close up," the owner mumbled, "but there *was* two strangers in town at the same time. One's Yankee, like you said, didn't see t'other."

"Where'd they go?"

"Don't know," then the man shrieked as a knife appeared in Ginger Beard's other hand. "*Really*, don't know! Th-th-th-man b-b-bought some supplies and left. Rode out of town that away two days ago," and the man convulsively pointed with his right hand toward the north.

Ginger Beard released the clerk, who slumped to the floor behind the counter, his legs useless and his britches wet. The soldier didn't like the way things were going. The fools were headed right for Sherman's army and were likely to get picked up for one reason or the other. He turned and walked out of the store. He would poke around the town—especially to the north—and see what kind of sign he could pick up.

That night, he could come back and see what this store really had.

## Chapter 14

Riding any horse has a wonderful combination of sights, sounds and smells only a true horseman can fully appreciate: the squeak of the leather as the horse moves underneath and the rider shifts, the jingle of the various metal attachments on both saddle and bridal, the smell of horse's sweat and even manure. They all combine into a wonderful world that makes the true horseman regret leaving the saddle even at the end of a tiring workday.

General Joseph Wheeler (C.S.A.) had ordered this small group to reconnoiter the ridge west of Dalton that ran to the south. The unit moved as quickly as possible without betraying their presence to similar units of the enemy. They rode over some of the country in efforts that varied from an exasperating trot to a mile eating yet efficient canter. The clouds lowered and it looked as if the already humid air was past saturation. Rain could start at any time.

The captain in charge called a sudden halt. Most of the horse soldiers following him wondered at the stop, since they had heard nothing that might precipitate such a move. The silence caused the uniquely experienced officer his action. There was no sound. None. And this fact in a battlefield, which had sounded like the mother of all thunderstorms the previous days, prompted his next order.

They cantered cautiously through the thick forest and came suddenly upon a wide, muddy track.

Obviously, many feet had passed here and occasional implements and plain garbage, made useless by the moisture, age, wear and tear, lay spread across the way.

The captain conversed for a moment with his advisor and the sergeant second in command (they had lost their lieutenant in a skirmish two days before) barked orders. Immediately, the two chosen riders broke from the orderly line and galloped south, quickly, while two others rode north. "Dismount!" was shouted and the line obeyed. Limbs were stretched and orders were given to comb the area for any kind of clue while being alert at the same time.

The northern riders returned soon. They saw nothing at the battle site: the area was as cleared out—of both men and flora—as if a thousand homesteaders had been at work clearing trees in the isolation of wilderness. As they approached, however, they surprised a small contingent—Howard's 4th Corps, they later identified by the guidon—but no one else. The 4th apparently skirmished against the Confederate holdings on Rocky Face to show a mockery of strength, but there was no doubt the main army was no longer there.

They did not dare wait for the southern riders, but sent a courier in that direction with instructions to meet them at headquarters. He met them in less than a mile and the three of them made it to the captain before the "mount" order had taken effect. They gave their reports. They had gone five miles at an easy lope, wanting to save their horses for when the need arose, when they stopped and heard a noise in the distance. The sound was disjointed and very muddled, but they had no doubt they were hearing the efforts of the Union army in its hasty flank maneuver to the south.

The rain began and the sergeant ordered oilskins put on. Since they were only a reconnaissance team, they could not afford to let their intelligence be marred by the larger detachment of blue cavalry certainly headed their way. They headed back through the trees, galloping when they could, but at never less than a trot.

Two hours later, the exhausted horses pulled into the cavalry command post. The captain strode in and a worried Wheeler conveyed the exploration's results to Stevenson and thus, to the army's commanding general, "Joe" Johnston. Furious at being outwitted by his old friend Sherman, Johnston gave the order to pull out and head south to head off a flanking attack on Atlanta by the Feds at Resaca.

*

Jeremy was called to the major's tent. Nothing worried him, for his grandfather had instilled in him an immovable respect for the truth: and he knew what he had seen. He could handle anything if he knew what he was doing was right. If not exactly just, he wryly reminded himself.

"Well, boy," said the major, playing with his mustache in the same way as before, "seems you're right. 'Course, I got no need for another spy, can't pay y'all anyway and my cavalry's the best eyes and ears this here army's got. Leastways for a running battle."

He hesitated and then smiled, a somewhat lopsided smile, the first indication of a hidden sense of humor he had yet shown.

"'Course, kind of hard for you to cover that distance, anyway, if you haven't got a horse."

"I'd like to fight, sir," Jeremy said. His mind had already been made up and other considerations, such as self-preservation, had gone by the wayside.

"I'm sure you would," said the major. "Listen, boy, I'll send you back to Lieutenant Philips with Mister Tate, and he'll find something for you to do."

"'Bliged, sir," Jeremy said, appreciatively. He thought he'd have a chance with Tate's group: they knew him and really owed him something for shooting his horse.

Tate showed up within the hour—Jeremy stayed under the somewhat benevolent eye of the major's aide for the time—and they walked back together. The orders had been delivered by that time and by the activity of the men, Jeremy knew they were pulling out.

Philips turned out to be a fair man, if too anxious for his subordinates' approval to be totally effective as an officer. His unit at this particular point was the outlying picket to the east and when Jeremy suggested he be placed as a sniper, Philips sniggered.

"Safe spot in the trees, eh?" The mild insult was not lost on Jeremy, but he remembered something his grandfather had taught him long ago: "You shouldn't brag if you can't prove it, and there ain't no need to brag if you can." Jeremy grinned at the lieutenant.

"Give me my gun back, and I'll take on your best man," he challenged.

The lieutenant grinned back. Any diversion for the men was welcome enough in such an environment. They were ready to go, but the main army was still hours from moving. His gun was hunted up, much to the chagrin of its new "owner": he had hoped Jeremy *was* a spy and he could keep the 50-caliber Kentucky long rifle upon Jeremy's demise. Philips introduced Jeremy to Corporal Mackey, the man who had kept a bead on Jeremy the first time he had wandered into Dug Gap. Mackey nodded, the straight-faced expression among the grins in the company. Jeremy looked him in the eyes and saw experience, skill and slight—very slight—condescension.

"You pick it," Mackey challenged.

"Free or with a stand?" Jeremy countered.

"Either for me, but if your being tested for a sniper's spot, we'd better do a sniper's stand."

Jeremy looked into the woods. About 150 yard through the bracken and branches he saw the last gasps of a mountain laurel's bloom hanging from a branch. He pointed to it.

"Y'all see that laurel? With the branch hanging down over the clearing? There's a blossom hanging over it that needs some encouraging to fall."

Mackey's eyes widened slightly—very slightly—and squinted into the green foliage.

"Looks more like a berry than a blossom," he muttered, but the challenged did not answer but lay on his belly and propped the carbine on his hand, supported by his elbow on the ground in the classic prone-position firing stance.

It didn't take him long. He lined the sights and pulled the trigger, after establishing his intentions in less than a second. The gun roared and the blossom moved as if of its own accord, struck by the semi-invisible bullet, but it remained firmly on the tree. The men watching cheered and clapped: it was hard to see how the new boy could do much better.

Jeremy clapped with the others. He was confident in his ability, which allowed him to be generous when appreciating others'. Mackey was not just a good shot, but a great shot and as well the respect he showed his gun demonstrated the truly symbiotic nature of the marksman and his instrument. But the boy smiled. It would be close but it would be fun. The man was good enough and he wouldn't mind losing to him, if that was to be the case. Although he didn't know it, the graciousness and humility his grandfather had taught him was beginning to come back through the muddle of moral degradation.

"Y'all got a bit of rope or strong twine?" he asked the men.

One of them piped up. "Got some in my tent," he said, and ran to get it.

Jeremy loaded the gun with a modest charge, then looked around in the forest and selected four small poles, about five feet long. He took the proffered rope and bound one end of the poles together. Then, he quickly splayed the other ends of the poles so that they formed a simple pod upon which to rest the gun. The slowly understanding men gave murmurs of approval as the device came together. The lieutenant's eyebrows raised slightly and he looked across to Tate, who was smiling broadly. *Sure, and show these Arkansaw boys how we do it in Georgia.*

Jeremy set the gun on the tripod and, before human twitchiness could spoil his aim, set the bore smoothly on the target and pulled the trigger. This time, the blossom came down, detached from the tree. But there was about a half inch of twig adjoined.

There was another bout of clapping and cheering, but Jeremy knew Mackey's shot was the better and he gave a mock bow to the corporal.

"And a fine shot that was, my boy," Mackey grinned, exaggerating his brogue. He was obviously proud to be Irish and he bowed back to the boy.

"Y'all hit the blossom: I missed and that's all there is to it," Jeremy answered.

"Yes, but you brought her down," he countered graciously.

The lieutenant stepped up. "Corporal Mackey's the best shot I know," he stated. "He's our designated sniper, but two can't hurt. Let me call my recommendation on up to my captain, and pending his approval, we'll have two snipers to support the outfit."

And so, it was. Philips had the connection or the confidence of his superiors if not entirely of his men, and they acceded to his recommendation. Jeremy was satisfied. He wouldn't be slogging it through the mud—although everyone knew that they were mainly defensive at this point and charges would be few and selective—and he would be doing something he was gifted at.

The company pulled out with the rest of the Confederate army and headed to what would be the next point of conflict with the Union at Resaca.

*

Ginger Beard approached the shack and almost ran into the half-hidden still among them. Something clattered and he heard the sudden whinny of a horse in a small corral on the other side of the house. He froze. The night settled in again and he moved again. He pulled his revolver from his belt and, similar to previous attacks, quietly dropped his pack where he stood.

Someone moved in the house: whether in response to his foolishness or merely "living" noise, he could not tell. The only real entrance he could use was the front door, which had a very noisy porch in front of it. He stepped up onto the squeaky board. It gave minutely and he continued to put his weight upon it until it gave no more. It remained quiet. He stood up and matched feet. The pottering about inside continued and a disagreeably coarse voice mumbled some bits of song as its owner worked. Ginger Beard moved again in the same stealthy motion, setting a foot on a new board, waiting until its creaking had ceased, then weighting it painstakingly. He was only a couple feet from the door. He peeked through a crack in the door. There was an old man standing silhouetted against a small fire: no other light showed, for some reason. He considered that, then discarded it: the old boy was probably going to bed or something.

He touched the makeshift latch. Metal clicked against metal. He froze again and peeked through the crack. The old man did not move, still mumbling the same old music through his teeth. *Caution be damned!* he thought and kicked the door in.

The old man whirled around, a big twin-barreled shotgun in his hands. The guns fired at the same time—Ginger Beard's because he wasn't ready, the old man's because he was. The old man doubled over as the revolver's slug buried itself in his diaphragm dead center. It cut through that muscle and nicked the large artery running from the heart to the legs before blowing out the back. The man fell back against the mud-daub chimney before sliding to the floor on his rear end.

Ginger Beard threw himself back as soon as the old man turned and his shoulder was all but torn apart as the edge of the shotgun's spread tore a chunk out of the muscle. He landed hard on the floor, breathing heavily. There was silence over the entire cove except for the whinnying noise of startled horses in the distance. He staggered to his feet in a sudden panic, not knowing the condition of the old man.

He needn't have worried. The man gasped as if he had the air knocked out of him: it is hard to breath when your only device for doing so has had a piece taken out of it. He sucked in a bit, then held it and gasped for the next breath. Moisture spread where the arterial blood leaked out of the entrance and exit holes.

"Where'd they go?" Ginger Beard demanded.

The man looked up at him with confusion in his eyes. He was going, they both knew, but he really didn't understand what was being asked of him. He began to fall forward.

Ginger Bear grabbed his lanky hair and hauled him upright. "Dammit, where'd they go? I saw the horses. I know they're here. *Where—did—they—go?*" His voice rose as he desperately realized the man was dying.

"Gone." The man weakened by the moment.

"*No, they're not!*" screamed the Union officer. "They're *not!* Don't give me that bullshit, you son of a bitch, they're *not*. Don't tell me that!"

The artery, pumping through a tiny hole the size of a pinhead, finally couldn't contain the pressure and ripped open. The old man bled out in seconds but the eyes continued to stare into Ginger Beard's face through an eternity.

He looked at the body for an incredulous ten seconds. Then he went crazy, kicking the body and screaming curses at it. Then, loss of blood and shock went into effect. His cursing and kicking both became feeble until finally, the curses died to whimpers and the kicking died to stumbling steps before he fell headlong on the floor.

*

The same squeak of leather and smell of horse accompanied Henry and Billy as they traversed the lower Appalachians in search of Jeremy. The young man was much too good at wilderness skills to make this easy and the uneasy feeling Henry kept getting made him think they'd lost him at times. Billy was incredible in woodcraft in his own right and if it weren't for him, they would have lost the boy altogether. They crossed over the great ridges in north Georgia, just west of the area they called the Cohutta and the rough country obscured the trail even more and killed them with wasted time. It was well into the latter half of May when they had their first big argument.

Billy was convinced Jeremy had gone south to Dalton and the spoor he found bore him out, but Henry's bias against the Confederate army wouldn't allow him to consider following too far in that direction. The Southerners knew the country far better than the North and, Billy's skills notwithstanding, Henry did not think they would escape observation and inevitably, capture. Billy had reservations against the North for his own biased reasons. Henry finally acceded to Billy's suggestion that they stop in Dalton for what he called a "look-see".

Neither of them considered the possibility that

Jeremy would actually *join* the Southern army.

The guns had ceased booming long since at Rocky Face and both armies slugged it out miles to the south, the artillery creating a sound of distant thunder. It rumbled very low and constant with no higher frequencies to herald each explosion. The two men had no idea where or how far away the fighting was, or who was winning. At this point, neither did they care.

"Feels like something's about to happen," Billy muttered.

"It *is* happening," said the experienced ex-officer.

They made their way down into the valley that seated small Dalton town. The day was warm if overcast, and the carpet of dark green stretched below them to end in recovering wheat fields, marred by the passing of war. The terrain rose again on the other side of the valley into the ridges below Chattanooga and they could see the huge west ridge upon which the Rebel army gave their stance at Rocky Face. From this perspective, they had no clue as to who was in possession of Dalton. Therefore, Henry suggested they again walk in after hobbling their horses in a small cove and hopefully, they would be taken for civilian contractors for whichever army happened to be holding Dalton at the time.

As a valuable tactical position, Dalton enjoyed the commerce of the Rebel army and now the trickles of the Union army spent its money here. The town was on the route from Atlanta to Chattanooga and thus had always been on a main north-south conduit for goods and travelers. It was larger than Jasper for that exact reason and Henry hoped they could get food, at least enough to scout the situation. They would see if and when they could come back to collect their horses and travel without the worry of being detained by either side.

Natural caution again required them to walk in separately. Henry found some food staples, although not near enough to sustain them for more than a few days. The price was naturally exorbitant. He paid with the smallest denomination he had—no sense flashing gold around an army—but did not notice the man pretending to peruse the battlefield paraphernalia in the corner. He looked as if he had seen better days (he made Billy look presentable) and his clothes matched suit.

Henry walked out of the commissary-store-wayside stand with a bag half full of food and ignorant of the other commodity he had picked up, who followed stealthily a good pace back. As they headed out of town, Billy joined them, not noticing their new "partner".

"No powder worth a damn," he said in disgust. "Confederate Army cleaned the place out afore they powdered and the Feds made damn sure the locals ain't gonna have none."

"Union's this far south?" This concerned him. They were two healthy men in civilian clothing, no injuries to speak of, and he knew they looked suspicious to any intelligent officer in either army. But the Blue Army had uniforms for *all* its men; the Gray did not, relying on local militias for their men and being a bit short on the textile scene. With the Blue here, Billy and Henry stuck out a bit more.

"Yep, they left about two weeks ago. Battle's down at some place called New Hope Church, from what the locals say."

"Well, what now?"

"This might interest you. Talked to some drinker—I know, but it's the best source of information you'll ever get. Drinkers like to talk. Anyhow, seems some of the army outposts like to sneak off and mix it up with some of the locals, if'n you know what I mean. This boy gets to talking to some local army private. Rumor had it some sharpshooter from the area joined up with the 15th Arkansas. Wouldn't have noticed it, man says, 'cept'n the shooter's local." Billy guffawed. "Local was pissed, boy. 'What'n hell's the kid joining *Arkansaw*?' he sez, "Ain't Georgia folk goodnuff for him?' he says."

"So?"

"Didn't you see that 50-cal Kentucky rifle he's got, the kid, I mean? Took care of that, yes, he did, and 't takes a shooter to care for a rifle like that. Kid's joined the South army." Billy was emphatic.

In some ways, Henry thought, this was not unexpected. He was also a bit worried. Why would a kid like that join an army in an actively running battle, unless he had a death wish of some sort? It seems the kid left half crazy—if not entirely so—but not necessarily suicidal.

"Whatcha thinkin'?"

"We got to find that boy."

"What for? I said it once, and I'll say it again: we ain't got nothing to do with the kid. I'm sorry for his family and all, but he got the bastards what did it and it's done for."

"That's what I'm worried about."

"Huh?"

"Let's just say, I've *been* where he is *now*. I've been there. I don't want to see anyone go through the hell I had to go through to get *my* sanity back." Then, in a more hushed tone: "Besides, are *you* planning on keeping the gold? I'm sure it's his."

The man in the shop watched and listened. He could not be near enough to hear all of it for fear of discovery, but he did hear something about "Arkansaw". That and the shiftlessness of the men, not aware of the comparison with himself, convinced him that he had Southern sympathizers. Maybe spies. Maybe just Southern soldiers who got lost. On purpose? Who knew? A bit of information in the right ear might generate some sort of reward of some kind: if not money, maybe black market, or connections or something of that sort. He nonchalantly turned around and headed back into town. The two men did not notice him leave, just as they had not noticed his presence.

*

"A loyalist, I is," said the man, appearing offended, his hand to his chest. The captain decided not to tell him how idiotically melodramatic it looked. And he didn't need anyone to tell him this man habitually lied through his teeth. "Don't need no goldang Reb down here, messing things up. Sooner this here war's over, sooner things are back to normal!"

Young, some might call naive, but the captain was certainly not stupid: West Point had seen to that. One reason the U.S. Army has always considered itself elite is the fact that it allows for a certain amount of innovation. No: it *encourages* it, within reason and within limits. This captain exercised that liberty.

"Stay here," he said to the man. "You value your life, don't move."

"Yessir, nossir," the man's rapid-fire exchange echoed each order.

The captain walked out of his tent and signaled his sergeant.

"Sir!"

"Jones, take two men to the south side of town, quickly. There are a couple of men suspected of being Rebel spies. Bring them here. Don't shoot them, under any circumstances!"

"Yessir."

And so, walking more casually than they should have been, Billy and Henry were captured by the U.S. Army. Billy couldn't keep his mouth shut as usual, and his accent with Henry's contrast was a dead giveaway. Their captors put them with other Confederate prisoners. There were few left, those captured in battle already having been marched north. There, they stayed, impatient and immobile, for two weeks. Impatient because Henry wondered how Jeremy was doing; Billy thought they were going to be hung.

## Chapter 15

"Yeah, tie it right. Yeah, that's it. Not around the trigger, you hound-dog, you wanna shoot me in the ass? Yeah, there you are… alright."

He pulled the rope attached to the old musket and hauled hand over hand. About fifty feet up in the cloister of branches at the top of the huge chestnut. *Won't take much banging. Easy, now.*

The pre-dawn began to light up the ground below, a grassy slope rolling away from the entrenchments at the top of the hill. He could see both sides now, the South, gray as the dawn below him in the bushes and lined up in the trenches and the Union to the north, encamped in the trees. Both places came alive. Lieutenant Philips said to expect something this morning, but Jeremy didn't think so, not unless the Yankees were dumber than he thought. But that was pretty dumb.

After the fight at Rocky Face when he'd joined this ill-fated retreat things seemed to go downhill even further, as far as the Confederate Army went. The general in command, Joe Johnston—not *Johnson*, as he'd been corrected more than once—had pulled the Gray back minutes before it seemed they'd be overrun or outmaneuvered. Running fights and days of hacking through thick forest had made them more experienced in defensive warfare than any of them had stomach for. They fought major battles at briefly lived positions of security and advantage: Resaca, New Hope Church, Allatoona Pass. And tired, they were.

Then, they had come to Kennesaw Mountain.

The "mountain" is actually a ridge with individual summits running northwest and radial from the industrial town of Marietta, Georgia. Heavily forested from the flats to the tops and apparently steeper than it needed to be for God's Purposes, it made for the perfect defense of a large army. And hell for the attackers. Johnston put his artillery on top of the peaks and filled new-made trenches below with the infantry. Jeremy's troop settled on a little knoll at the southwest end of the chain and had been glad to find himself there instead of Kolp's farm or the top of Kennesaw where the Blues were guaranteed to attack.

Then, about late afternoon, they'd seen a large division of troops move into the neighborhood below them.

Jeremy shifted on his branch. It was not too uncomfortable: large and fairly flat, well shielded with leaves from the sight of any Yankee whose aim was good enough to shoot at him, and high enough to be out of the sight of any ground-hugging attacker. A few hours of this and he'd be glad to get down, though. To kill time before anything became interesting, he took his hunting knife and, climbing above his stance, cut more branches to build himself a nice little cocoon. Not too much: camouflage was better than coverage and he spent the next few minutes trying to make his perch look convincing as well as comfortable. He then scoped the hill, thanks to a pair of opera glasses borrowed from one of the officers. At least he had some brains, Jeremy thought, ready to give equipment where it would do the most good.

The rains that had poured in over the last couple of days made the hill below him sloppy. Hopefully, the weather would stay clear at least for a while, for though the Union was more likely to attack in nice weather, the Southern soldiers had just about had it with the rain. Jeremy felt more comfortable in the trees. A little imaginative work in the branches and he could stay comparably dry, not like those poor dogs below who would wake up with wrinkled hands and feet from lying all night in standing water.

The attack began later that day. It started with the attempt to soften up the defense by the artillery. The rifled Union cannon shot more accurately than those of the South but sometimes, the rifling was not of much use. It was an era where cannons were guided by sight alone in a situation where haze and heavy foliage hid the true location of the entrenched enemy and much was sheer guesswork.

As the *whump* of each cannon's efforts combined with others to start the roar of battle, he squinted into the hot mist that surrounded the hill. Forms of the infantry showed through the heavy haze, but Jeremy waited: he could not see the officers and they were his targets. A file of Yankees moved in echelon up the low grade of the hill.

*Boy, that's dedication for you*, he thought.

Behind him, in echelon also, lay the system of berms and trenches the dug-in Arkansas and other divisions had designed, intended to pour a devastating cross-fire into the encroaching enemy.

"Here they come, boys!" he yelled, about the time Mackey did the same one hundred yards to the north. He could hear the scrambling of the entrenched soldiers below him. Once again, he thanked his stars that he was not down there. Yes, he was a target above the heads of his compatriots, but the tree hid him and he hoped none of the Southerners were foolish enough to rise up for a sniper.

He picked out a… yes, it looked like a captain, yelling at his boys. Well, time for that to stop. Already checked and loaded, he perched the gun on a crook in the tree. He was practically lying down, the more comfortable in his perch and very much at home. As years of coaching from Dad and experience bore out, he let his breathing dictate the elevation of the 50-calibre gun. A shift to the right and he waited for the captain to walk into the sights. A minor adjustment, and just as the bugle signaled "charge!" the target and the sights met. Jeremy immediately pulled the trigger and red flooded the captain's body as it hurled backward.

He giggled nervously. He was not yet healed and the old man of blood came sneaking through the façade of self-pity he had immersed himself in over the last weeks. Damn! Gotta watch using too much charge! Can't waste it, although it was fun to see that Yankee bastard go flying backward! The old man, sated, slid into the background of his mind, but only for the moment.

The killing machine that Jeremy was part of mowed down the charging Union infantry. He reloaded as fast as his perch and common sense would let him, methodical always, his blood cool and calm in the face of the screaming charge. Not one enemy looked his way, although one less-than-perfect shot on a major, he thought, caused the man to question in his direction before he went down. Always, he targeted the officers, for he would not waste ammunition on the common soldier. They were fodder for the cannon and the men below, and his purpose was to kill the heads of the snakes so that the bodies writhed, witless and aimless, to be chopped up and discarded.

The blue wave swarmed up the hill, hampered by woods, but determined. Line after line fell, limbs decimated by cannon, or holes blown through torsos by the brutal mini ball. The noise was intense. Men yelling, on both sides, screams of hate, anger, fear and, of course, agony, and the roar of rifle and cannon contributed to the amazing din never heard before in the ancient forest of that land.

Jeremy kept shooting. He was well supplied with ammunition, for his particular Rebel command recognized the importance of a ready sniper in turning back a determined charge. He had proven himself in the weeks past and he and Mackey had begun an entertaining, if somewhat morbid, marksmen's competition. Lieutenants were worth a nickel, Captains, a dime, Majors counted two bits, Colonels, four. And a General? Generals were so rare in these days of cannon fodder that Mackey allowed five dollars for the first person to pop a general. Jeremy was up by a dime, but that was so close as to count nothing when the targets were so plentiful.

Suddenly, the branch splintered right above Jeremy's head. Some idiot found his perch. He was angry at the fact that he would have to change trees if the battle ever ceased for more than a few minutes. If they knew where he was, they would gun for him directly on the next charge. He scanned the field. There. Some kid some way off desperately shoved his cartridge in the barrel and looked up at him as if to remember the location. Jeremy loaded quickly, pouring the grains of powder in and ramming the mess all the way down the barrel: this Kentucky long rifle was muzzle-loading, but Jeremy was faster than most of the cartridge boys when it came to loading his piece and he didn't have to worry so much about hot metal jamming the workings. He placed the gun on the branch. The boy brought his gun up to sight, oblivious to the surrounding cacophony, and tried to sight between the soldiers running around him. Jeremy shot the young Union private. The boy went down and other bluebellies tripped over him as they backed down the hill.

The sight of the Union soldiers going *down* the hill was so odd that Jeremy found himself confused.

"They're running," yelled a young voice from behind him and a cheer of men's voices crescendoed to a jubilant version of the infamous Rebel yell, full of exuberance and mockery all at the same time. Jeremy watched the Union infantry running down the hill, yet the hillside was not clear. For on the ground lay hundreds of bodies, uniforms useless for all the glory, pomp, political maneuvering and good intentions they now or ever had.

The day progressed, as did the battle. There were swarms of Yankees and the Confederates beat them back, leaving more of the blue-clad bodies on the new grass. The Rebel yell repeated time and again as they drove the Blue from the Gray position. As often practiced in nineteenth century warfare, the battle ceased when the day ceased and as the sun glowed red through the thickening haze of the deep South, both armies wordlessly called a truce and retreated to feed themselves and lick their wounds.

Jeremy lowered his gun to the ground and followed it. He was stiff from the long day in the branches.

Tate handed the gun back to him. Philips stood beside him, full of the battle and excited as the blood pumped to his face. He shook Jeremy's hand.

"*Damn* fine shooting," he said. "I hell sure am glad I ain't on the Yankees' side, I'd be dead right now."

"Yessir, but Corporal did just as good."

Mackey walked up at that point; his face barely visible in the dusk. "Kennedy," he announced, "the count for this battle is three lieutenants, one captain and one colonel, which is, lemme see… six bits, you owe me."

"Sorry, sir," Jeremy grinned. "Think my two, two and two majors kind of beats your'n!"

"I'll be damned." Mackey grinned back. "Them Yanks must have just come up your backside with bull's eyes on their chests. You got all the luck!" He made a careless gesture. "Go grab your grub."

"Sir," Jeremy touched his hat and moved along the berm at the top of the hill. It was too dark to worry about a sniper: besides, there weren't any near enough to shoot. Tate followed.

Little cooking fires popped up here and there and occasionally, he could hear the sizzle of bacon or game in the little frying pans a few unlucky guys toted along. The smell of hardwood smoke from damp logs mixed with the meat cooking set his mouth watering. He was happy they were in north Georgia. The local folk, especially those from the threatened towns of Marietta and Atlanta, supplied them with a certain amount of foodstuffs. Not a lot, granted, and certainly nothing fancy, but it kept them fighting and fed.

*

Ginger Beard saddled the horse he had once ridden. Some tack lay about—some of it pretty good for the old man, so aside from the horses, he knew the gold had been here. The other horses he ignored as unnecessary baggage. They would slow him down and although he supposed he could sell them, it would take too long and he might even get hung as a horse thief. The old man had hobbled them and enough spring grass grew to keep them alive, if not spry. For all his vices, he appreciated horseflesh and oddly enough could not bear to see an animal suffer: in spite of what he thought about humans.

Lifting the saddle hurt. His shoulder was about half of what it used to be in both volume and strength, but he hoped it would come back eventually. It was not his gun arm: that was the important thing. *Gawddamn that old man!*

He had awakened about noon the day after shooting the old man. He was dizzy and faint, still, and couldn't remember where he was or how he had gotten there. His shoulder hurt like blazes and it took some maneuvering on his part to turn his head far enough to see the mess. He groaned: partly in pain and partly in the frustration of knowing he was going to be badly delayed while this thing healed. He got to his knees. After a bit, he could stand and then noticed the sound of flies buzzing in the warm morning and a sour smell lingering about the place. He turned and even his hardened stomach had a hard time with the sight of what was left of the old man. All that was blood in the man puddled on the floor and the warmth of the Southern night and early morning has never been the greatest for preserving carcasses.

He finally stood and staggered outside. A well with a bucket waited for the thirsty within sight. He filled the bucket, drank and then doused his head thoroughly. It helped.

He was intelligent. He knew he could never make it walking and he could not saddle the horses, much less catch them, with one whole arm and short a few pints of blood. He looked again at the shoulder and cursed again luck, God, stars, whatever, and the old man's unanticipated vigilance. The bone was not broken, fortunately, but the shotgun had torn a chunk of muscle out of the upper arm. He could not lift it to save his life and he hoped that nothing was permanent. If it was just muscle, he assumed it would grow back eventually.

He poured the rest of the water over his shoulder and screamed as the inflamed flesh received this treatment. He leaned over to the well's decaying cover and tore off an ill-fixed piece of wood. He filled the bucket and poured more, and kept doing it, biting on the wood until the pain subsided into a distant throb. A piece of cloth torn from some clothes he found made an adequate bandage and he tied up his shoulder as tight as he dared: he didn't want mortification to set in from lack of blood flow.

The rest of the day was taken up by his search for food, laying up a supply of water. Then he napped on the porch for a couple of hours, regaining his strength. The old man had to be removed and dragged far enough from the cabin not to disturb him or the horses and the place needed cleaning. He knew he would be healing at the house a couple of weeks or so and if he left the body, the nasty mess would be unhealthy.

It had been lost time, but he couldn't help it. By himself, heading west into the pit of the War, he could not make up for the loss of one arm before it had healed. Even now, although it was somewhat healed (it was a good thing some quack of a doctor hadn't hacked it off), his arm was handicapped enough that he would need all his wits to both survive and to track down the gold. And he wouldn't be doing this except for the gold: he was obsessive.

He put the little gear he had found, his firearms and ammunition, and the remaining food from the homestead into the extra saddlebags. He selected one horse only, so as to move all the faster. He worked quickly, familiar with the gear, an outfit that had belonged to the troops before that damn kid killed them all.

He mounted and rode out of the cove. The palomino moved quickly at his urging, a large, unnoticed "U.S." brand on its flank, and the trees seemed to part to let them through.

*

It was late June by the time the prisoners actually began to move north. The conditions were pretty bad and they started the walk north that morning. Again, Henry regretted his decision to head South from Pennsylvania in the first place. Billy was in rare form. He cursed everybody and anything eloquently until even their jailers couldn't take it anymore. They cursed him back in good solid Anglo-Saxon jargon and kicked him in the rear to encourage forward motion and a shut mouth.

The Union army had "commandeered" their horses—Billy said it was "just another name for *stolen*"—but they still had their boots. No horse, but it sure beat walking a hundred miles on bare feet like some of the prisoners.

A young lieutenant had the questionable honor of escorting them to whatever prison they were destined.

Young enough to be yet an idealist, he was anxious enough to do a good job at whatever job his superiors required of him. Therefore, whether for humanitarian or pragmatic reasons—Henry wasn't sure, but Billy insisted it was just to make sure they arrived "alive and kickin'" to be hung somewhere—the lieutenant allowed water during the heat and moderate rest stops during the day.

At one of these rests, Henry perked up slightly. While others dozed for the minuscule rest they would get (Billy could sleep anywhere, anytime and his snores let others know it), he continued scanning the road for anyone he knew. For as the prisoners were marched north, occasional Union infantry marched south to supplement Sherman's march to Atlanta and he hoped that an officer might show with whom he was familiar.

The only things moving at this time of the day were the insects and those who were forced to. The sun beat down from its solstice advantage and supplemented the heat in an attempt to beat down the living. The leaves had turned a dark green and under the trees the air grew still and seemingly more humid, if that was possible. Cicadas sawed and there was no other noise, but this changed as a clatter of horses and men in the distance approached.

Henry could never understand how it could be both humid and dusty dry at the same time, but the state of Georgia somehow managed anyway. As horses and men planted feet along the road, they pulverized the dried mud and injected it into the sky, building clouds of dirt in the windless air. He looked into the hot haze as a troop walked down the road. As was traditional, the commanding officers rode ahead with the guidon. Henry stood, slowly. He thought he recognized the cloth pennant, but wasn't immediately sure in the mist. It had, after all, been seventeen years and people changed outfits.

The silhouetted riders materialized, their uniforms becoming clearer as the brown mist became less and less, and the flag grew substantially in the noon sky. The lead rider had a unique look as he sat upon the horse. Henry grinned and hoped he was right.

"Major *Cox*," he shouted, in his best commanding voice. The other prisoners stared at him as if he had lost his mind. Billy didn't stir. The officer turned his head, the now-clear features on his face betraying a sudden confusion and wariness.

"Major *Cox*," Henry repeated. The figure turned his horse to the side, his curiosity getting the better of him. At a word from him, the column passed by with the non-commissioned officers in charge. His aide and several other officers stopped and moved toward the prisoners with him. The officer's gray eyes settled on Henry. The confusion marginally outweighed the wariness as the man tried to place this ornery Rebel prisoner who had the nerve to call out to him by name as well as rank.

"Major Cox," Henry said, doing his best to stay impassive and not panic. He knew the civilian clothes, the context of being chained as a Rebel, travel and dirt obscured his identity. "Allow me to introduce myself."

"I wish you would," the officer said, his brows

wrinkling.

"Ex-Lieutenant Henry Williams at your service, formally of West Point and an officer in the Union Army." Thankfully, the eyes widened. The man got off his horse and approached. To Henry's surprise and immense relief, the man grabbed his hand and pumped it.

"Damn, Henry, it's good to see you! What the hell you doing chained up with a bunch of Rebels? I didn't even recognize you! It's been years!"

"Doesn't surprise me, sir. Part of the reason I tried to get your attention."

"Hell with the 'sir!' You're still a friend. Where's the officer in charge of this bunch?"

"Lieutenant Pickett is over there, Dan," Henry gestured to the young officer who was suddenly primping himself. "Colonel Dan, I mean. I took a wild guess."

Cox smiled. "No offense! You're just lucky I answered to it, eh?"

Pickett hurried to join the duo and Cox's other officers joined as well.

"Lieutenant, why is this man with a bunch of Rebels?"

"Captured, sir, at Dalton. There were reasons, sir."

"Like?"

"They weren't part of the battle."

"They, eh?"

"Yessir, two men traveling together. They were brought to the compound two days after Johnny Reb left. We suspected them of being Rebel spies examining our flank, sir."

Cox burst into laughing, which mortified the already-intimidated Pickett. "Hell, they're as likely to be spies as *you* are, boy! At least this one is. Release them."

"Uh, sir, there'll be hell to pay if I let them go."

"And there'll be hell to pay if you don't. Taking them up to prison, eh?"

"Nossir. We're to hang 'em up in Chattanooga, public-like."

Cox looked at Henry, with his travel-stained clothes and his jacket stained Georgia-clay red; his short, ragged beard and long hair.

"Hmmm, yes," he said, a twinkle in his eye, "I can see why you'd want to hang him, Georgia spy and all." He turned back to Pickett. "Release him, on my authority. Henry, you'll vouch for your partner?"

"Yessir, although he's a rough character, I can definitely attest to the fact that he's no Rebel. He'd say he's not much of anything." He gestured to the oblivious Billy, still snoring in a patch of grass.

"Fine. Pickett?"

"Yessir." He yelled at one of the soldiers guarding the men, who ran over and fumbled with his knife as he none-too-gently cut the ropes that held Henry. He bent over Billy and started cutting.

Billy, suddenly shaken out of his siesta, curled his bound hands into fists and violently punched up into the man's face. There was absolutely no warning. The soldier hurled backwards and hit his head on the ground, hard. He didn't move at first, then sat up comically, shaking his head. Billy, shaking the sleepiness off, wondered why Henry was laughing at him with the tall major he'd never seen before. Pickett looked horrified and complained loudly to the colonel: he wanted to at least hang Billy for socking his man.

Henry reached over and hauled a still-confused Billy to his feet. Grumbling, the soldier got up and cut his bonds while Henry talked to Billy, who would then not shut up.

Henry explained things to Colonel Daniel Cox.

"I can't do anything about your horses," Cox replied. "I guarantee you they are headed south to the battles where they're needed, or, more likely, off on the black market," he added with disgust. "Either case, they're gone and I clearly can't give you any. I think you're crazy to head South, especially if this boy you're looking for's on the Reb side of the line. They're less likely to catch you, but more likely to hang you if they do. If I were you, I'd go back to that old man with the cache you told me about—that was a very smart move, by the way—and head West. I can write you a pass that will get you through the Union forces, at least. That'll get you to Alabama or, better yet, head north and turn West when you get to Illinois. Forget about this whole thing and get out of here while you can."

"I can't. I just can't."

"Why not?"

Henry suddenly changed the subject. "Got any grub?"

"Some. We have a supply wagon with us to ensure at least our arrival at the battlefield."

"Great, I haven't eaten right for days."

"Thought not. Join me for dinner? We bivouac less than a mile south of here."

So, it was still a walk, but there is a big difference between walking as a prisoner in a direction you don't wish to go to your death in a place you've never been, and as a free man walking with a purpose.

*

Ginger Beard walked his horse into Dalton after the hard push from Jasper. The town was busy and although few Union soldiers stood around, Dalton had the aura of an occupied town. Ginger Beard expected that he could pass through as a courier or something. He wished he had not discarded his blue uniform. Ironically, he had changed into civvies for the sake of blending in and now that he had arrived in town, he found that the very act made him that much more conspicuous. He cursed as he looked around him. He stood out pretty well, dressed in civilian clothes and leading a horse.

Immediately, he walked to the side of the street and down an alleyway. He tied the horse to the back of one of the buildings and rifled through the saddlebags for the limited number of coins he'd gleaned from the farmsteads over the last fifty miles or so.

He had not had a drink since he had left the old man's farm, and he was incredibly thirsty now. He knew there was drink in the area: you couldn't have soldiers and not have alcohol. There were eating and drinking establishments in the town, some of them long-standing and some of them makeshift, with a canvas fly providing the only protection from the dust and the rain. It was into one of these he went, casually, with all his senses and wits on alert.

"Gimme a bottle," he demanded, in total command of the situation.

"Cost you a dollar," said the man. It was obviously rotgut alcohol or "moonshine" as some of the locals referred to the homebrews, but Ginger Beard was not really particular at this time. A *dollar! Hell*, he thought, wryly, *the bottle costs more than the drink.* He paid the man and took the bottle. Yes, indeed, it was the raw stuff: probably hadn't even been mellowed for more than a couple of days off the still. Irrelevantly, he wondered where they got the grain this early in the year. The fire flowed down his throat and he had the illusion of being warm and dry and comfortable for the first time in months.

He was unsure how to start a conversation, for he did not want to seem to pry. Fortunately, the proprietor of the drink stand did it for him. He was a typical backcountry man, homespun trousers hung in place by a belt of hemp. Unusual for this warm time of year, the man actually wore a shirt. It was of undetermined color: it might actually have been some shade of white at one time. The brown beard crept up the cheeks like vines on an Ivy League school building and blended on the sides with the bushy thatch of hair.

"So, where you from? I know you're a Yankee, seen right off," the man said, affably.

"Illinois."

"Must be a courier or scout, or something. Ain't no other Yankees 'round here ain't dressed in some uniform or the other."

"Um, yes, that's it. I've been off the front for a break."

"Yep. Good thing. How's it going down there?" The man took another pull at a jug set to his right and looked at him curiously.

"Um, well, it seems to be going well, at least for the Union. I didn't see a lot of the battle, my job being strictly a scout for one of the cavalry units. I ain't dead yet, that's for sure!"

The man laughed appreciably at the irony.

"You don't seem to be too bitter," Ginger Beard prompted.

"Naw, ain't. Some of the others, though, hate it, and the bluebellies 'round here gotta step lively around some of the darker areas in town, 'less they find a Rebel's knife in their guts. Now, as fer me," the man continued, shifting in his seat, "soldiers is soldiers, and don't make no dif' where they's blue or gray. They likes their firewater, and are willing to pay for it. Makes my livin', it do."

The conversation lagged as the two men somewhat companionably drank from their respective reservoirs. Then, Ginger Beard spoke up.

"I've got some friends passing through, scouts, like me, I'm trying to hook up with."

"What they look like? Ain't no one passing on the street but what I don't see 'em. Nothing better to do during the day if ain't no one buyin'. If they ain't dressed in blue, I'll probably remember them."

Ginger Beard tried to recall the limited views he'd had of Henry and Billy.

"Odd pair. One's a Yankee and the other's Southern born, maybe local. The Yankee's medium height, dressed in canvas pants. The Southerner's taller and heavier, with a big beard and lots of hair, dressed in overalls. They may have been riding. Oh, and the Southerner's a talker in a big way."

The man started laughing at that.

"Oh yeah? And they was *scouts*? For the *Union*? Haw, haw. Seen 'em alright. Couldn't miss that big mouthed boy: he's got a mouth that'll make a sailor blush, you should've heard him screaming at the jailers all the way up the street when they arrested them."

"Arrested?" Ginger Beard was concerned. Where, then, was the gold?

"Yep, and it's funny they's both Union *scouts*! Someone's in deep shit, boy. I seen 'em arrested for being *Reb* spies, in marched up north of here, to Chatt'nooga, or something. Probably hung by now."

*Damn!* Time to go. He needed to head north and find them. Easier now. But *where* was that gold? He desperately hoped it was not confiscated.

"Quick," he said, "what did they do with their horses?"

The man looked up with a puzzled expression on his face. "Horses? They sent 'em south with some other's for the cav'ry."

"And their gear? Some of it was mine, I loaned to them."

"Dunno. Probably just gave 'em out to whatever wanted it. 'Fraid you lost your own stuff, ain't never gonna find it now. T'weren't nothing special in there, just saddles, bags and all. You might make a claim for it with the commanding officer, and might get money for it."

Ginger Beard considered. If the gold had been on them, there would have been some sort of ruckus in this town and this yokel would have mentioned it. He would have *screamed* about it. So. They must have cached it somewhere. Tempted to go back to Jasper and dig around the old man's farm, he knew he could spend weeks on that job without any sign of success.

Assuming, of course, that it was at the farm in the first place. It could be there or anywhere in between. No, he had to follow the prisoners north and try: finding them was the first order of business, then he would figure out what to do next.

*

"Say, Jerry, you standing watch tonight?"

"Yep. Early on. Coming up now."

"Can you see if any of them Yankee bastards got some real coffee?"

"Mebbe. Whaddya got?"

"Some weed here. Good pressed and cured. If that ain't no good, got some pecans from the farm my kid brother dropped by."

"Pecans ain't no good. Bastards'll grab 'em from anyplace they'll walk by."

"Not this time of year, they ain't. And they ain't raiding for fun, I hear, just staples and stuff. Ain't no bastard Yankee got time for the fodderalls."

"'Kay. Lemme see. Gimme some of that real stuff and you got yourself a deal."

"Sure, and you'll lie about it, won't you?"

"Done it yet?"

"No."

"Jest gimme some of that good coffee if'n I gets it. I'll be fair about it."

It was about eight o'clock in the evening and the late afternoon settled into a restful night. The air cooled slightly to a comfortable warmth, as the Southern evenings often were, and it was still as a pond. Jeremy grunted as he got up from the tiny cooking fire he and Tate had rousted up, the bacon consumed and its fat well soaked into the biscuity stuff that passed for bread. Small, but his stomach had shrunk over the last months and this filled him. He was tired, dog-tired, but so was everyone else. Yankees, too, he knew, were exhausted and nobody attacked at night: conditions were too easy for friendly fire. Still, one never knew, and spies and skirmishers might come over and create havoc just to be ornery. So, he sighed, grabbed his rifle and stepped over the already snoring bodies of his compatriots.

The insects whirred in this advent of summer and the air was so motionless that he felt he could walk around any parcel of air without disturbing it in the least. Or, to say it another way, he thought, he could create his own wind merely by the eddy of his body as he passed through the evening. It was that time of the year which makes dusk seem to last forever and the sun had only just dipped over the horizon, leaving an odd hazy faint orange glow through the hills.

He stepped over rocks, climbed berms and hopped trenches as he made his way to the front. The trees opened up and the grass fell away from him, its moisture already contributing to the already humid air. His reverie was bounteous, but temporal.

Something thudded at his feet and the explosion of its sender sounded soon after. He jumped and dove into a copse of bushes to the right. A yell from the Blue side, one full of derision and laughter, floated distinctly through the humidity.

"*Hey, Johnny Reb*," the voice shouted, "a bit closer 'an your guys can shoot, eh? I think I see you limping a bit, huh!" Laughter erupted from the Yankee line and worse, giggles arose from the Confederate sentry post less than fifty yards away.

"Yeah, and your mother, too," 'Johnny' muttered as he scrambled toward the post.

"You alright?" the Gray sentry's voice asked in the growing dark. "Probably not a good place to be admiring the view, huh?" You could hear the smile before you could see it.

"Yeah, 'kay, I's wrong, but here now, ain't I? Go on, I got the post for the next couple of hours."

They made the change and the relieved sentries made their way back to the fires far more surreptitiously than Jeremy had done. He sat down and, choosing his position carefully, scanned the grassy slope below him. Nothing. The encroaching night was dead, figuratively as well as literally speaking, but he had too high a standard to sleep on duty.

"*Hey, Johnny Reb!*"

The same obnoxious voice of the sniper who had taken the potshot at him. Jeremy gritted his teeth but after a moment, answered.

"*Yeah!* Whaddya want, Yankee?" he yelled back.

"No hard feelings?"

"'Spose not. Nice shot, if you was aiming for my feet, but I *doubt* it!"

"Ha-ha-ha." The laugh was measured for sarcasm.

"Whaddya got, Yank?" Jeremy decided to stop beating around the bush. It seemed obvious that the Yankee post was as bored as he.

"Whaddya mean, Reb?"

"I got me some t'baccy, Yank, good pressed and old cured. Whaddya got?"

"Stop there, let me ask." Jeremy knew this was a ruse and bargaining would begin. All sentries wandered to their posts in the hopes of making some sort of trade.

And so, it was. Under a very unofficial flag of truce, under the now-dark sky, Jeremy and his counterpart in the Union Army ran out to the middle of the field, hoping no one would see them and take an overenthusiastic shot during this unconventional rendezvous.

It was weird. Jeremy did as his friends asked him to, but for some reason, this time he found it difficult to do business with avowed enemies, men who tried to kill him. Just as he tried to kill them as best he could. There was something odd about walking up to a man, looking him in the face and trading goods with him, knowing he was the enemy. He had found that he actually liked some of them. They were real men, less true to their cause than to their homes and their families. They tried to survive as he was, by killing this enemy who so confidently stood with them.

He liked the night. The night hid all faces and under the blessing of anonymity, he could take the proffered coffee without seeing the face of the man in front of him. Instead, the form handing him the coffee was merely part of a "unit," or a "division", something to be eliminated, as opposed to "some*one*".

The match flared up in front of him and to his annoyance, lit the face of the man momentarily. The pipe glowed and the man sighed.

"Last one," he said. "You boys came at a good time."

Jeremy did not like this one bit. He mumbled something and started to leave.

"Hey, hey, hey," the man said. "Don't take off just yet. We gotta long watch ahead of us and no one ain't doing nothing. Let's jaw." He took another drag.

"Lotsa paper, but no tobacco." He was nothing if not talkative. "Some of the boys take the back pages of their Bibles to roll 'em, paper's good and thin and all, but I don't. Bad luck. Stick with pipe."

Jeremy grunted some sort of expected reply.

"Got family?" the man asked.

Jeremy turned cold in the dark, warm night.

"No," he answered, sullenly.

"C'mon," the man prompted. "Gotta sweetheart?"

"No."

Jeremy's attitude flowed over and the man stood awkwardly on the grass. He tried one last time.

"Getting warm," he said. "Hate fighting in this shit. Least you boys got the light stuff to wear. They make us fight in these damn wool overcoats they call shirts! *You* ought to try running a charge up this hill when it's this hot. Especially when your used to the weather up north. Don't see how you Rebs can live down here in the summer. I'm a Detroit man myself. We got real winters up there."

Jeremy remained silent as the man rambled on. He now had two reasons for not wanting to talk, and the time became more awkward to him. He desperately wanted to leave as the man became more personable to him, and as the images of the dead soldiers and his grandfather and his murdered family replaced the comfortable anonymity of the Southern night. It disturbed the blessed oblivion he had worked up for himself over the last weeks.

"Gotta go," he suddenly said, and he ran back to his post. The man was sufficiently startled that he sent no wisecrack after the running Confederate soldier.

Jeremy arrived at the post, weeping. It wasn't until an hour later that he realized he'd left the loot at the rendezvous and obligation toward his friends made him run out to see if it was still there. No one shot at him and the Yankee had honorably left the coffee in the same spot. Jeremy grabbed it and fled.

## Chapter 16

Standard field rations sufficed, even for the officers, but it was the proverbial feast to Henry and Billy. Their company was unquestionably much better than before as well. Henry asked the colonel what he had been doing since the Mexican War, where they had served together. *Seventeen years*, he thought to himself.

"Well," Cox replied. "After I left Mexico, I was assigned to the frontier for a while. I was up at Fort Vancouver, in the Oregon Territory for a couple of years, working with Phil Sheridan…"

"What did you think of him?" Henry asked.

"Full of himself and a bit too anxious for glory," Cox replied. "He also has a contempt for the Indian that I believe—accurate or not—is detrimental to the Indian Problem. But he's one of the ballsiest tacticians I've ever seen, both in planning and in execution. He'll take some risks that no one dares to call him on, just because he's successful more often than not. He tends also to use men without regard to loss of life or manpower. So, if you survive, you share the glory. Trouble is, you deserve it just by the fact that you *did* survive. Does that make sense?"

"I think so. I saw a bit of that in Mexico. How did you like it out there? Oregon, I mean." Henry became more enthusiastic as he found out more information about the western frontier, this time from a man who had actually *been* there.

"Well, in the words of that old nursery rhyme, when it's good, it's very, very good and when it's bad, it's horrid." Cox sipped at his coffee.

"How so?"

"Let me give you an example. We were on our way north, on a reconnaissance. Now, the Cascade volcanoes are all crowned with glaciers and when the sun comes up in the morning, they turn a beautiful pink…"

"Man oughtta be a poet," Billy sneered. "That's *so* beautiful."

"Shut up for a change," Henry shot back. "Continue, Dan, don't pay attention to him, that's just the way he is."

"We worked our way up to the salmon runs—that's the rapids on the Columbia River where the Umatilla Indians and others fish for salmon. The paddlewheels go up that far. Anyway, we crossed the river and headed up north, along the White Salmon and then up onto the plateau east of Mount Adams, the one some of the Indians call Klickitat. Man, that's grand country! Rolling hills, just waiting for wheat and what-have-you, with that great, snow-covered volcano rising right out of the forests. It makes this place seem claustrophobic with all that open space out there in the back of your mind."

"Sounds like you'd love to go back," Henry observed.

"I don't know. Maybe out on the coast. Portland and Vancouver are looking good, now that the Indians have settled down and enough people are moving out there to make it home. I don't know. To explain my indecision, let me tell you the rest of that story."

"We were headed up to Fort Simcoe, up on the slopes of Adams itself. That's right in the middle of Yakima country and they're pretty touchy about the land around there. The fort's up there to keep an eye on them and to protect travelers and such. Sheridan was in charge of that contingent and I was the only other officer along. Things were going pretty well until one day, we were set upon by a bunch of Yakimas, all full of piss and vinegar and ready to raise some hair. To give old Phil some credit, it didn't take long before we were able to retreat in some order to a small knoll above the creek. We were stuck there for a long time, no water and a bunch of that time in the sun. Funny thing, you don't think about how dry it can get at night, but it sure can, even in the rainy Oregon territory. It seems like it hurt worse then, I don't know why."

"So anyway, the sons-a-guns finally gave up after we'd held them that whole time. I'm not sure I like the Yakimas. Treacherous as hell, although the chiefs swore up and down it was a bunch of rowdy young bucks that had nothing to do with tribal policy. Hard to tell and we'll never really know."

"What's it like fighting them?"

"Guerrilla warfare, complete and total. It's the same thing that can make it tough down here. The Southerners are more at home in the woods, doing that strike-and-disappear tactic that makes it so hard to bring things to a decisive battle sometimes. That's why the Union is having such a tough time in Missouri: they're all homeboys out there and know how to fight that way. If we're going to win in the western frontier, we'll have to learn to fight the same way. The Indian respects bravery and actually likes those who return that respect, whether in war or peace. At least, that's what I've seen."

"Think you can do it?"

Cox immediately noticed the pronoun "you" instead of "we", and felt a twinge of melancholy as he realized Henry was no longer part of that brotherhood of officers they had both been members of in Mexico. He had forgotten for that brief moment and his friend's conversation and the reminiscing made him forget the years that had passed. He took a breath.

"I think so. It may take a while but we can. A lot of it is dealing fairly with them: regardless of some idiots in the army, they're still human and we all still live together. Some of the things I've seen..." Colonel Daniel Cox trailed off. He changed the subject.

"I haven't seen you since the day you resigned," he said. "What the hell you been up to?"

"It's a long story, but suffice it to say, I made it back to Pittsburgh a few months ago."

"Took you that long to get home from Mexico?" Dan laughed.

"Well, I traveled a bit. Anyway, I found out about some dirty dealing my brother was involved with and decided to, shall we say, make a *discreet* exit?"

"Why here? Why in the South, I mean? With all that's happening, why would you want to come down here?"

"It seemed like a good idea at the time. It's a good place for a man to lose himself if he doesn't want to be found. I wanted to go west, to the frontier, but I didn't want him or his henchmen following me, so I headed in an unlikely direction."

"What do you think now?"

"Well, it's been an adventure and one thing's for sure: my brother hasn't a clue where I am."

Billy spoke up, his mouth full of food. "Yeah, and he met me. Saved his life, I did."

Cox raised an eyebrow.

"I suppose you could call it that," Henry said, with barely detectable sarcasm. "We were set upon by a few ruffians and Billy here decided to shoot them all dead before I could stop him."

Billy pouted. "Yeah, would of shot y'all's butt if'n I ain't been there."

"Who knows? Anyway, Billy's a good guy, I guess. He's forgotten more about the woods than I'll ever know. I'm learning a lot." Henry continued to describe their adventures, including the extraneous obligation he felt toward the young woodsman, Jeremy.

Cox considered for a while. "I think you're crazy. Let me think about it and I'll see what I can do for you tomorrow. We have to move out early in the morning."

*

The lieutenant didn't lift his head as he continued scratching at the paper in front of him. "Name," he mumbled.

Silence filled the room, except for the chirping of night animals, and when the silence made evident the fact that no name was forthcoming, the sergeant looked up. The poor excuse for humanity (his humble opinion) looked at him blankly. *Pretty beat up*, the sergeant thought, *probably some local trying to steal some beans or something.*

He spoke up a bit. "What's your name?" he asked, emphatically.

"Dan Johnson."

"Where are you from, Dan Johnson?"

"Here'bo'ts." Ginger Beard did his best to look like the downtrodden backcountry farmer, slurring his words like those he'd heard. He kept his head down, not looking the sergeant in the eyes. The sergeant looked at him sidelong, his long red handlebar moustache—of which he was extremely proud—bristling as he tightened his mouth. He perceived something odd about this man.

"What do you mean *'hereabouts'*?"

"Uh. Jasper."

"Jasper, huh. Where's that?"

"Uh, east a-ways."

The lieutenant turned to the private who attended the man. "What's he here for?"

"Uh, sir, he was caught riding a horse with a 'U.S.' brand on its butt. He claimed to be a scout, but couldn't tell us who he was with, sir."

Johnson—Ginger Beard—licked his lips. He knew he was damned, for he couldn't even lie in this case. He had no idea of the name of the commanders in the area and any other answer would prompt the question: "Why aren't you there?" To claim his old outfit would provoke an investigation whose direction he didn't dare contemplate. Still, an imaginative lie might buy time. He looked at the situation. The Union had commandeered many of the buildings in this town for temporary use and this one lay on the main road. The lieutenant and the private were the only ones here, but he knew sentries patrolled outside somewhere. Not knowing if he was legit or not, the horse had remained saddled and his gear was still in the bags, such as it was. The rifle was also there, although his knife and revolver were sitting on the desk in front of him.

If they detained him, where would it be? If in this building, could he break his way out? He needed food and ammunition, but then… a major risk, he knew, but he did not have much of a choice.

"Your accent doesn't seem to be Southern," the lieutenant interrupted his thoughts. One mental throw of the dice and he decided to risk it all then and there.

"No, it doesn't. As I told the private here, I'm a scout and a courier with one of Sherman's cavalry. Since the general's engaged at Kennesaw Mountain, my services weren't needed as much, so I… was told to attach myself to one of the cavalry squad's heading south from Chattanooga."

"Mmm," the lieutenant grunted. He was too experienced as a non-commissioned officer, in this war and as a human being, not to see something odd about the man and his situation. He *could* be a scout: many of the scouts prided themselves in their disreputable appearances, trusting in the camouflage to delay if not outright hide their occupation from the enemy. But this man…

"Orders?"

"In the heat of battle, sir," said Johnson, "no one thought about writing orders for some lowly detached scout"—even the private thought he lay it on pretty thick— "so the major in charge, a Major Hicks, by the way, if you want to check, anyhow, he said I didn't need any, that the boys up north would be glad to get anybody to help out."

"Yes," said the lieutenant, wryly, "I see. So. No papers, nothing to establish your credibility, and you want me to just let you go with a government horse?"

"Yessir," he replied, trying to keep his answers to a minimum and therefore out of trouble. Then, an idea: "There's more, but it's confidential."

The lieutenant was not entirely the fool Johnson

took him to be. He cocked an eyebrow at him and debated wisdom versus convenience. If there was confidential information, it might show the man's truthfulness: it would sure beat wasting a courier to someone who may or may not exist just for the sake of one stolen horse. There were more important things at hand, not the least was cleaning up this place before following Sherman into Atlanta and beyond, as the case might be.

On the other hand, the "confidential information" may be bogus and a ploy to escape. He decided.

"Private, take this man into the cellar. Is there any access to the cellar in this house besides that outside door? No? 'Kay, take him down there. I haven't decided what to do with him yet. When you're done, go give Captain Lewis my compliments and bring him here. He may be a spy or something and he needs to talk to an officer. Tell the captain that this 'scout', or whatever, may have some information we need to hear."

The private saluted and gestured to Johnson. Johnson cursed inwardly, although he kept his face impassive: the moment was lost and he could never hope to take both of these men quietly without his knife or revolver, especially with one of them visibly armed and the other probably so. Maybe later. The private directed him to the door and they walked outside. They turned the corner to the cellar door. The private was whistling. *Whistling! By God*, thought Johnson with an inward smile. He looked around. There were no sentries in sight and this idiot with the puckered lips was ready to take him at his word, ill prepared for any violence.

The private gestured toward the prone door. "Open it," he said.

Johnson cooperatively leaned forward and undid the latch. He heaved at the door. It was stuck, or at least, he gave that impression. The private, slightly annoyed, leaned forward to give him a hand, but kept the gun available in the other. The combined effort of the two broke the door free and the slab of wood pulled up on the awkward hinges exposing the yawning unlit hole beneath. It threw the private off balance, slightly, but this was enough for Johnson to grab his shoulder and hurl him quickly through the open door. The gun flew forward and something between a grunt and a cry escaped the soldier's lips. There was a dull thud as he hit the packed cellar floor and Johnson leaped onto him, the cellar door slamming shut behind them.

Johnson was ready for the eye-gouging, desperate clawing for life that would ensue from such a leap in the dark, but there was no movement beneath him. He stayed on top, not daring to move, but as minutes passed and nothing happened, he moved to his knees and felt around in the dark. The gun lay beneath them, he could feel, and although the man breathed—shallow and gasping, but breathing—he was out like a light. Johnson felt something wet as his hand fluttered over the man's head: he must have knocked it on some rock or wood. In any case, he was out of action.

Dan Johnson pulled the rifle from underneath the man. He turned to the cellar door and lifted it minutely to see if a sentry or other passerby lurked in the alleyway. It was clear. He locked his arm straight, insuring a one-foot opening and threw the gun through onto the ground. He looked again. Still, no one. With a quick thrust, the door crashed onto its side and Johnson leapt over the sill, onto the hard packed earth above. He grabbed the rifle and disappeared into the dark.

The lieutenant was organizing some paperwork and never knew what happened. The butt of the gun connected with the back of his head as Johnson struck downward with a vicious blow. The skull broke and the man died instantly. Johnson searched the man's pockets—a few dollars, but not much—and retrieved his gun and his knife, both which still lay on the desk. He figured he had some time now, for the private was incapable of notifying the captain and the lieutenant was the only other who was concerned with his whereabouts. It would be a while before either was discovered, but he needed to leave, and soon. He thought he would get some grub or ammo from the supply tent, but only if things worked out. He would see.

He turned on his heel and left the way he came: through the back door. The darkness guaranteed his stealthy exit.

*

"Here they come again!"

Jeremy bellowed the words at the top of his lungs. Haze still permeated the atmosphere, but much less than the previous day. The lines of Union detachments marched in the distance, emerging from the trees at the end of the field. The Kentucky rifle was loaded and Jeremy also had a couple of "reserves" taken from the bodies of Union dead littered about the hillside. He considered them "reserves" because he shot best with his Kentucky, but if fighting got close, speed was more important than the niceties of casual aim. Even if it came to that, he hoped his new, concealed perch would spoil the aim of any who detected him.

As before, he picked out those who seemed to command men. Mackey insisted that sergeants were fair game, but only gave up a couple of cents for one. Jeremy grunted. It was the getting, not the having, he thought, and although the betting staved off boredom, it was only a way to measure the friendly competition between the two of them.

The sun rose higher in the sky as the fighting went on and the heat and humidity rose accordingly. Jeremy was used to it, bred, born and raised in the South as he was but in accordance with the complaints of his trading partner the previous night, he saw the Union soldiers were having trouble. While the heat of battle went on, the heat of the weather stayed low on their priority lists, but once a charge had been repulsed, many unbuttoned their uniforms for some semblance of relief. And after each charge, there were those incapable of tending to themselves in such a way and others who were beyond caring. For the "dead angle" of the Confederate line, as they began to call it, poured a constant storm into the void in front of them and both wounded and dead lay beyond the help of those comrades who were not willing to join them in their agony.

Jeremy wrapped a handkerchief about his face because the stench of the dead in the hot Georgia rose even to his position over the killing field and he had not the recourse hiding from it, like those entrenched behind him. The battle's furor subdued his confusion about killing men with faces and they reverted to the targets they had been in the previous weeks. He continued to shoot, best he could.

Soon, another smell rose in the afternoon air. Jeremy sniffed. Woodsmoke and brush. The exploding artillery and passing of hot balls fired the brush. Although the dead didn't care, the groans of the wounded changed to shrill shrieks as the fire approached and the screams pierced the melee. Jeremy cringed as the agonized voices reached to him above the crowd. He'd heard such shrieks in the man he'd tortured and that memory served to condemn the young man hundredfold for every one he heard now.

He heard a sudden holler to cease fire, rippling through the commands and down this section of the line.

Suddenly, to his amazement, he saw a white handkerchief thrust above one of the berms to his oblique rear. The fool holding it up was the 15th Arkansas commander, Colonel William Martin, who was screaming at the top of his lungs. Amazingly, none of the Union infantry fired upon him, and Martin engraved his words indelibly in Jeremy's brain.

"*Come and remove your wounded!* They are burning to death!" he yelled. "We won't fire a gun until you get them away. Be quick!"

Silence commanded the field now. Not a shot was fired on either side. If it weren't for the screams of the wounded Federals in the brush, Jeremy doubted the bluebellies would move. But from a brushy section on the other side of the field, a private stalked out intentionally, *sans* rifle. He broke into a run as the need for rescue pressed beyond consideration for bodily safety. Others followed him. Jeremy sat up. He even recognized the one face whom he hoped never to see in his rifle sights—the man who'd traded coffee with him—and the fool ran out into the brushy no-man's land to grab a pair of legs and haul the burning victim back to safety.

He could have killed a dozen men in the long minutes it took the Union soldiers to run out, stamp out the fires, and retrieve Union comrades to the safety of the Federal line.

He was distracted by a motion below. Time seemed to have stopped for him as a wave of gray and butternut coats stepped over the berms to assist the Yankees. In a dreamy world, a fluid motion of blue and gray combined, some stamping out or using canteens to douse fires, others dragging the living any way they could out of harms' ways. Jeremy even saw a blue uniform at a wounded's head: the feet were carried by a gray. He noticed that although this area was still, the only other sound besides the murmur of men communicating to finish a desperate job was the distant booming of artillery and the cracking sounds of multiple rifles being fired. There was a reign of peace here that opposed the still-present roar of battle from other parts of the line.

The dream ended as he looked at Martin conferring below with a couple of Union officers, gesturing in a friendly way and shaking hands as if being introduced for the first time at some sort of high-society social function. One of the Yankees produced a small case, opened it up, and presented it to Colonel Martin. From his view high above in the tree, Jeremy saw it contained a pair of ivory-handled pistols, items obviously cared for very much by the Union officer holding it. The officer saluted and Martin returned the salute. Both were apparently affected by the incongruous meeting. Martin's hand dropped to his side. The Union officer said something, a smile on the side of his mouth and Martin returned it. They saluted, a different one this time, one formally ending the truce. Then, he turned and strode up the hill.

"Look smart!" he yelled to the straggling soldiers who were making it back to the berms. "Let's get a move-on, we still got a battle to fight and I'll be damned if those Yankees are going to take this hill!" The gray and butternut uniforms, mixed with those of questionable origin, moved *en masse* up the hill and it was only moments before each side was in position again.

And the battle resumed as if nothing had happened. Jeremy found himself firing again, but the motion was automatic and he found his mind wandering over the last hour's drama. He again did his best to kill men with whom his comrades had worked to save enemy soldiers from dying. His efficiency and his accuracy would again be praised as he marked every officer marching up the hill for a target. Why was he shooting Yankees? Why was he personally not dead? He deserved death for his actions of dealing out the same in the last couple of months and yet, he was still alive. His firing faltered as the old man came up and he attempted to beat him back into his subconscious thought.

When the Yankees beat another retreat, the last, he hoped, for the day, he looked back and down into the trenches. Colonel Martin lay below him, his aid desperately trying to hold the escaping life within the body of the colonel. Martin's face was paper-white and Jeremy knew he was not long for this world. Tears slid unheeded down his face as his confused mind tried to comprehend the justice inherent in this world that would allow such a gallant—no, not just gallant—such a *self-sacrificing* man to die. Enemy Union soldiers lived because of an arguably foolish act of benevolence by a Confederate soldier and now, this officer was paying for that act in the midst of killing others. And those others were the cause of his own death.

There was no resolution in Jeremy's heart to do anything but weep, and he did, prone in the tree, not heeding the calls from his comrades far below.

*

The horse thundered into the darkness and the man glued himself to the mane, cringing as bullets flew by. They shouted behind him amid the reports of various firearms but the man clung to anything attached to the gelding to create the smallest profile possible. As the opaque Southern night enveloped him, the shots diminished and the curses increased. The man continued and cursed as well as the trees flew by, hitting him, threatening to tear him off the animal, but he didn't dare stop or even slow down for a while.

*Damn!* It would have gone perfectly except for that stupid private stumbling on him when he went outside for a piss! He had been cutting into the canvas of the supply tent when the kid practically kicked him in the rear. All he'd needed was some cartridges and a bit of food and he was on his way, but no, someone had to see him.

He'd tried to kill him quick, but he couldn't get his knife out of the canvas before the kid let loose a shout and ran. He debated following for a quick silencing, but he already heard running feet other than the kid and thought it prudent to leave quickly. The horse wasn't far away and he practically jumped on its back. The skittish animal reared and took off as quickly as his heels dug into it. The thick brush that allowed his secret intrusion now prevented his quick exit and he rode down the lane alongside the tent. A sentry with quick ears ran out and he rode him down, whipping his horse into a faster rate. Others joined the ruckus, some of them armed and ready to shoot. And now, he flew for his life.

Behind him, men saddled, many bare-chested in the warm night air, and hurriedly armed themselves. The horses were directed out of the stalls and eight men cantered north on the trail of the man some knew as Daniel Johnson, renegade, but whom Jeremy had personally nicknamed Ginger Beard.

*

As a matter of fact, Cox was unable to deal with Henry's situation the next day at all. A courier had arrived late in the night, urging Cox to make his best time, before leaving to inform other straggling units.

Henry and Billy merely tagged along as the contingent moved farther south, to a place near the site of the Chickamauga battle. There, they made another bivouac and again, were invited to sup with the commanding officer. Small talk permeated the meal, but nothing more substantial. Like a dog on a leash, Billy kept broaching the subject, eager and hungry, but Cox and Henry kept him at bay. After a while, he gave up as hunger forced more trite issues away.

One of the Colonel's weaknesses was good tobacco and he did everything he could to keep his pipe full: easy enough in the South. He asked Henry for his company and, grabbing his matches and other paraphernalia, strode out of the tent. The evening was warm and humid. In the distance, thunderheads grew, barely visible through the haze except for their stark silhouette and the sunset's pink rays soaked their edges with color. There was a rumble in the distance, but neither Henry nor Dan could, in their northern perspective, decide whether it was the last fragments of the day's threatening ore immediately threatening weather.

"Don't dare go too far, but there's enough land around for a stroll," Cox observed.

"Sentries, eh?"

"Yup. Some of these damned puppies want to see

the war too soon, and'll soon plug you as hear your countersign. Buck fever, I guess," he added with a chuckle.

Henry smiled at the allusion. He remembered his first time under fire and he still didn't know if the charge of adrenaline was due to action's excitement or sheer terror. Probably both, he acknowledged. He remembered pulling the trigger as fast as he could until an older and wiser sergeant calmed him down and pointed out that bullets certainly helped. He'd looked down and found he had all his shot, but his cartridges were almost gone. West Point notwithstanding, it definitely took an "understanding" non-commissioned officer to take him under his wing and show him the ropes.

"As I said, we've no horses to spare you and there's nothing I can do about the ones you 'donated' to the Cause. So, you'll have to make it on foot. Same as your guns, although there'll probably be some castaways on the way if you're determined to head South. You've got some money—how you managed to hide that, I won't even ask—so that'll help a bit, but my advice is for both of you to head back to that cache you said you had east of here and high-tail it out of the South. Don't wait for the boy: he'll make it somehow."

"Sorry, Dan, I'm committed," Henry countered.

They continued walking a ways, Cox's pipe sending blue smoke and a fragrance to mark their passage through the woods. He said nothing, for Henry showed a hesitation that indicated a progression of thoughts. Dan waited for him to speak as they made their way along the game trails that were abundant even in the thick, jungle-like Southern forest. Henry finally broke the silence.

"Have you ever spent a lifetime searching for the answer, never knowing quite what the question was in the first place?"

Dan cocked an eyebrow. "Continue," he said.

"After I left Mexico—and my commission, if you recall—I went a lot of places. I met a lot of strange people and had a lot of strange experiences; experiences that weren't always pleasant, but ones that were nonetheless necessary."

"After seventeen years, I would hope so." He paused. "Necessary? How so?"

Henry hesitated. Even though he and Colonel Cox were—had been, he corrected himself—close friends, Cox was pretty much a materialist. He believed in things he could see and touch. It made him feel in control because in that paradigm, he could usually manipulate things one way or the other. He didn't know if Cox would listen to, much less understand, a philosophical discourse on absolute morality.

Instead, he said, "Let's just say I learned a lot over the last few years."

"Yes, and this has to do with…?"

"Bottom line: it has to do with a promise I made to myself and others a long time ago. By extension, it has to do with a promise I've made to that young man."

If there was one thing the pragmatic Colonel Daniel Cox understood, it was loyalty. Loyalty had seen him this far in his career as an army officer and would seem him to the end. Odd thing, Henry knew, was he never thought of the rewards of loyalty: he just knew it was a thing to be done and adhered to. Loyally.

"I can understand that." He took a puff on his pipe and looked into the misty woods.

"Well, if you're *that* determined, I can get you back on the trail. And I can help a little farther than that."

It was Henry's turn to arch an eyebrow.

"My rank does have privileges, or had you forgotten?" Cox smiled. "I'll write you a pass, say you're a civilian courier or something. That'll do you good until you cross the line, then I obviously can't do anything for you beyond that point. You're on your own at that point."

He paused, elaborately scraping out his pipe. He made a great show of accessing more tobacco, tamping it down and lighting it. He pointed his pipe at the top of the hill.

"Let's make a surprise inspection on the outpost at the top of the hill, what do you say?"

Henry nodded and fell in step behind the colonel on the trail. Cox kept talking. The swish of the brush as they passed by made it hard for Henry to hear the officer breaking trail in front of him.

"You know," said Cox, pensively, "I think I could get you your commission back, if you want it. Sure, it's been a few years, but we could figure out something, I think. You were advising overseas, or consulting civilian contracts or something. Neither is far from the truth, from what I gather, and I am positive it served to further your education in any case." Henry thought he winked at him in the lowering twilight. "The important thing is we don't exactly have a plethora of officers around right now. Damn kids keep getting themselves shot."

Henry looked at his boots. It was somewhat tempting, if inconvenient to his mission and status in life. He sighed and Cox did hear a tone of regret in the answer.

"No, I don't think so," Henry reflected. "If I do anything for the army, it might be as a civilian scout out West or something. And I've a bit to learn in that department before I could convince myself I'm somewhat qualified."

Cox turned as he walked. "So, you've got some, say, *moral* objections to serving in this man's army?" Cox puffed, and there was a twinkle in his eye.

Henry laughed. "No, not at all. When I quit in Mexico, I did have my doubts. There were enough of them then for me to quit, to want to sort things out, so to speak. If they supported 'this man's army' then I might have been back. If not, then 'no.'"

"But now?"

"I just sort of lost interest. I enjoyed it back then,

such as it was, both before and up to that engagement, but it seems mighty small right now, compared to some other things I've got cooking."

They stopped about one hundred yards from the top. Cox hailed the trio of men who were keep a watch out to head off any trigger-happy incidents. The passwords and countersigns pierced the silence of the woods and Cox and Henry continued on up. The men saluted and after returning the obeisance, Cox motioned for them to continue as they were. He led Henry to the balding edge of the hill that faced west.

The sunset was fantastic that night. They stood near the top of one of many passes and looked out upon the hills rolling away from their outlook, the brilliant green of the spring growth fading into gray as the light turned red. The distant tissue of the tops of anvil clouds around the bright sphere triggered a spray of vermilion, which seemed brighter than its red source on the horizon.

"That's where I'm heading," Henry said, nodding in the direction of the setting sun.

"Might see you out there, once this war ends and, God willing, I stay alive," Cox rejoined.

"Lot of people being sent out there?"

"Yup. Some of our Reb prisoners join the Union army under the condition they don't fight their own down here. So, they send them west to keep the Indians under control. Blue uniforms on the outside, but all Reb on the inside. They call them 'galvanized'."

"And you'll be heading out there?"

"Even though men are dying by the hundreds in this damned war, there'll still be a lot of them left when the dying's done. They'll send the extra men out West just to be doing something useful, and they'll need experienced Indian fighters to lead them. I suppose that means me. Might help promotion, too. Action never hurts, no matter where it's at."

"So, you think this thing's almost over?"

"Sherman's advance is the last thrust, I'll be bound, to get the South to see the error of their ways. Assuming, of course, old Grant has his act together in Virginia."

The light faded with the conversation and from the east, dark blue washed over the sky. The stars came out and Cox waved at the sentries as he turned down the trail. Henry lingered. He did not miss the symbolic dichotomy here. The gray land below and the dark blue sky above. And red in the West. Momentary they all were, contending with each other, and when they faded, black night would fall. Henry shuddered and followed Cox down the trail as night did indeed command the hills.

## Chapter 17

The dawn never came. The rains came. Jeremy slipped in the mud and with a curse, went down, sliming his britches up to his thigh. His cursing had become most fluent over the last months.

"Jes' gotta love this Georgia mud, eh?" Tate grinned. He'd almost gone down himself.

"Good thing it's warm mud," added Mackey, behind them. "Hard to start any kind of fire to warm yourself in this mess."

"Yeah, well, it ain't gonna get me down. Been in worse," Jeremy answered. He hauled himself out of the ditch, exposing himself long enough for a Union sniper to take a shot at him. Reflex threw him back down into the mud. Mackey and Tate completely lost control. Jeremy grinned back.

The Union attacked in various points of the mountain chain, but the Confederate Army was well entrenched from Kennesaw Mountain all the way down to Kolb's Farm and beyond. The small knolls that formed the chain were ideal for establishing strongholds and the Union commander, General Sherman, would later be prouder of the fact that he *did* attack than of anything he had accomplished by it.

This consistent warfare had seasoned Jeremy and his friends, and both snipers' skills were rewarded and used extensively in their attempts to deprive the Blues of leadership. Jeremy in particular was becoming pretty famous among the Arkansas men for his marksmanship: something, by the way, he thought pretty secondary to his now unused skills as a woodsman. A head-to-head battle did very little to exercise that aspect of his life.

The three men slipped and stumbled down the deep trench, trying to stay low enough to be out of the sight of the Union snipers. They made their way back to the muddy hole they had called home. Mackey had shown skill at building a fire in the large can he had scrounged up from someone. He punched holes in the bottoms to allow air to flow and the high sides of the can prevented the mud and the rain from putting the fire out. With a small pan on top to cook their bacon and other things, the can got pretty hot and was able to make their soaked clothes marginally less wet.

Tonight, food was scarcer than usual, but it was there. Jeremy did use his woodcraft to pull out some edible greens, wild onions and tubers that the somewhat prissy Mackey called "disgusting", but that he and Tate often dug into with satisfaction if not outright delight. It made a stew of sorts that was good enough for all three of them, especially at the end of a long, soggy day.

"I hear we're getting ready to pull out," Jeremy said by way of opening.

"Can't hold the 'bellies for too long, but what we're running out of is men," Tate acknowledged. "And food."

"You 'nd yer stomach."

"As long as the Yanks are losing men, this

retreating'll work, but it's sure tough on morale," Mackey put in.

Tate took a bite and then replied. "Naw, ain't gonna do no good if'n we get stuck on the flats," he said, his mouth full of stew. "And that's where Sherman's driving us."

"So," said Jeremy, "you're thinking that we ought to just hole up here and wait until the Yankees give up, eh?"

"That, or scatter and come back at 'em."

"That'll last for a while," Mackey added, "but someone's gotta run outta food and ammo. Or men."

The rain hissed as it landed on the hot frying pan Mackey had precariously balanced on one side of the fire can. He poked in a couple of sticks and to everybody's relief, they caught fire almost immediately. There is nothing worse than a damp stick that kills a hot fire. In the rain.

"Anybody done a look-see up north?" Tate asked. "I'll wager that 'cept for a few straggling units coming south, Sherm's on his own, to sink or swim, hell or high water. He won't last the summer."

"Yeah, but supposing he does?" Jeremy asked. "You willing to sit here with fall coming on?"

"Ain't fall I'm worried about," Mackey voiced.

"Why's that?" Tate asked.

"Think about these locals, no offense"—Jeremy

and Tate nodded, appreciating his respect— "but they're waiting for us to pull their fat outta the fire. They're supporting us now, more or less, but they'll get tired of it after a couple of months and where we'll we be? They want results now."

"I hear others in the army, the *army*, mind you, are getting frustrated with this retreating stuff General Johnston-sir, is doing."

The three were fairly representative of what they knew of the army. One view was for one final decisive battle. Another was for digging in, killing the foolish Yankees that dared encroach and waiting until the Union got tired of playing and went home. The third weighed both of these arguments, decided to obey whatever orders came and to stay alive no matter what the cost.

The rains continued and they slept as they had been used to, namely, in the mud if not in the trees. The luckier crowded into tents, but the mud stayed in everything. Jeremy was too tired to climb into his perch or even into the tent the three of them tried to share, standing water notwithstanding, and he fell asleep with the others, vaguely hoping the water would run off before he drowned in it. He piled leaves beneath a bush and fell on the heap. He dozed, listening to the heavy drip of water off the trees above, on and about him.

*

Henry and Billy left, finally, after much wrangling with the powers-that-be. Cox did what he could but beyond a couple days' rations for each of them and a pass, he basically set them off in the right direction and turned to his own problems. Before he left, he shook Henry's hand.

"Still wish you would consider my offer."

"Yeah, well, sorry, sir, but that's something that pretty low in my priorities."

Cox snorted. "Priorities! It seems a lot talk about those and don't exactly follow through with them."

"Well, I think you'd think less of me if I tossed aside those priorities for the sake of a commission." Henry smiled.

"It's the same reason," Cox replied, "that I want you to be involved in the army. We need that sort of integrity. But I understand."

Henry hesitated.

"I guess we've got to go," he finally stated.

"High time," Billy muttered under his breath.

"The West is a big place," said Cox. "But if things work out and you happen to drop by some army post, drop a line to me. I'm a career man and I'll be in the Army until I rot, so anything addressed to me will somehow get there. Address it to Washington, and mark it *Indian Affairs*… on second thought, just send it care of the army: it'll get to me."

"Pretty confident, eh?" Henry smiled.

"Yes," Cox replied. "I guess I am."

"If we get west," Henry said, "I'm heading first to Taos, Colorado Territory. I promised a friend I would stay there until a year from September so he could follow and meet me there."

"Pretty dedicated, this friend, and that's a long time to wait."

"Yes, I know, but I promised him I'd be there, so, by God, I'll be there! September, '65, will give me enough time to get there, including this Rebel war, Indian raids, broke-down stages, starvation, thieves and cutthroats, dead horses, *dying* hors…"

"I got your point."

"Did I say Indian raids?"

"I got your point, and yes, you said 'Indian raids'. I got that point, too. I'll be there, too, or send a message, with two qualifying points. If I'm not, I'm either dead or assigned irrevocably to some godforsaken stretch of the earth even *this* army's never heard of."

"Not much difference between the two," he added, grinning.

"Well, all this jawing and ain't we the ones to be shuffling off." Billy's voice broke in, not unexpected and definitely not welcome.

The two men shook hands again and the colonel rather stiffly turned on his heel and set off to shout some fairly incomprehensible orders at some poor, undeserving sergeant. Henry turned as well, somewhat to Billy's surprise, picked up the satchel Cox's aide had most considerately assembled and walked in the opposite direction without looking back.

"Say," Billy called, "ain'tcha gonna wait for your pard?"

Henry stopped without turning and Billy ran up to him with his own satchel. They set off down the trodden earth trail the Union Army had inadvertently left for stragglers to follow. Hopefully, Henry thought, it would lead to a successful conclusion, and he breathed a quick prayer for Jeremy's life and limb.

*

It took a bit of winding through the woods, but those that followed were not matches for Johnson and he left them fairly quickly. He wanted to get back to the road, for all he knew about the two men he was chasing was they were prisoners and headed north. He'd almost got caught this time, but he believed with a little thinking ahead, he could concoct a story that would hold water. Not a courier: he had no idea of any names up north and that would be the weak point. He could just make up a common name— "Johnson", he grinned—and who would know? He'd have to write some sort of bogus note. What about just a verbal command? No, a note would be better. It would support his story. People might doubt what they hear but for some reason, they believed anything that was written down. That's it. He would stop at whatever town showed up and scribble something out. He swore half of them couldn't read anyway.

The road wound through the woods and already climbed up into the hills near Chattanooga. It would be at least a week at the rate he was going before he saw the town. The day turned sultry and promised to be warm. Occasional showers would keep it wet, too. He was getting tired from the morning's ride, not to mention the grueling drive from Dalton in the dark hours. The horse walked tiredly too, its head down and plodding along in what he called "trudge march". He got off the palomino and began walking. It would not do for him to kill the animal. He would break for lunch at some promising valley creek, and to catch a couple of hours of nap.

*

Henry and Billy walked south at a medium pace. There had been rains on and off during the day, some of them very hard and even the spreading leaves of the chestnuts and hickories did not keep them from getting wet. Billy lamented his oilskin—left on the horses that were confiscated—but Henry had long learned to deal with being wet in the warm Southern climate.

*

Johnson led the horse down into the gully. At the bottom was a small river, muddied a bit by the morning's rains. He was in a rocky section of the hills and hoped that the river would clear in a bit, at least in the rocky pools where the turbulence subsided a bit. He moved toward the middle of the stream to avoid the encroaching thickets on the shores. He certainly did not want to be caught napping—literally, he thought—on the road, considering a pursuit that was not guaranteed to have flagged. He went downstream a ways, toward a small, rocky beach that was hidden from the road proper but still had a good view of the ford and any who would approach. He tied the horse to an overhanging branch so that it had access to the water and could alert him to approaching strangers. To facilitate this, he tied a long bit of cord from the saddle to his wrist, with a decent amount of slack. He stretched himself out on the damp beach that was being slowly warmed and dried by the intermittent sun. It didn't take long. He was asleep in spite of his neglected meal and nerves.

*

By noon, things had dried out a bit under the warm sun and the Southern air became extremely humid, although no fog had formed. It would rain again before night, Billy commented. The sun broke through a bit at times, increasingly as the day progressed and steam rose from the road and from their clothes. The deep forest dripped constantly. Each drop found no relief in evaporation, but would run into another, fall to a receiving leaf and onto other drops and slop from branch to leaf to branch to the damp, mulch-covered ground.

Henry enjoyed the walk, although it was more humid than he was used to. The sun, when it showed, created a green translucence that bathed them in its light and the clouds enhanced, rather than reduced, the effect.

They both had food, water was easy to get, and they were free once again. He had some money left on his body and if they had a chance, they'd buy a couple of horses. He didn't think it likely as long as they were in the wake of Sherman's army, but maybe later. If nothing else, the old man still had the other horses. Still, he didn't want to walk the whole way back to Jasper, and the way they were going, it would be a longer walk from… well, wherever they found the kid. He sincerely hoped it would not be long.

They stopped for lunch and water along a small river in the bottom of a gorge the road crossed. The recent rains swelled the creek and the rocky bed scoured the worst of the mud from the water. Henry sat down and opened the satchel. Cox was far more generous with his food than he had let on. There was dried fruit—a gift from the officers' supplies—and some tinned beef. The tinned beef was entertaining to open without a tool, but Henry pulled out a knife Cox had given him and worked away at the lid. Billy took water containers down the trail to the river, where it was less muddy.

He found a small pool captured in the rocks where the silt had settled and the water ran clear. He crouched down and lowered the first container into the pool. Boredom mixed with hunter's habits made him lift his head and look around.

Henry nibbled at the bit of beef he had coaxed out of the tin. Billy strode quickly and purposefully up the bank. He sat down next to Henry and they shared the small meal between them.

Billy spoke. "Seen something down there I don't like," he said. He didn't say anything for a bit, chewing on the meat as well as his thoughts, and Henry prompted him to go on. Billy got up and started putting the remainder of the food in the little rucksack they'd improvised.

"Best move along," he said, quietly. He was obviously serious and Henry followed suit. They walked a couple of hundred yards and Henry asked him what bothered him.

"Remember that palomino we got along with the other horses?"

Henry nodded.

"Remember the blaze on forehead, the small star, and remember the big old 'U.S.' brand on its butt?"

"Yes, you were worried about getting hung for owning it, I remember."

"That same horse is down that crick, hitched to a branch on a little beach not two hundred yards from here."

There was that feeling of foreboding Henry was familiar with but he couldn't pinpoint the source, right now. Billy saw the confusion.

"If it's the really the same one, there's a good explanation. Someone stole that horse. Or the old man sold it off."

"I know that! The old boy didn't sell it: he

wouldn't dare. Aside from us coming back for an accounting, he would have more trouble getting rid of that government horse than we would."

"I was thinking that. So, the horse was stole. And the rest are probably gone, too."

Henry thought. "The cache is still there," he replied. "No one could find that: you don't know it, the old man doesn't know it and sure, no one else does."

"Something else I don't like," Billy considered. "Remember that night we first found the kid and the bodies he'd killed? I heard something in the woods, something like someone stole up and was gonna do us. I got up from the fire and he took off like a band of Injuns was after 'im. Two legs, human. Seems to me there's one of them soldiers roaming about the young'un didn't get to kill. I told you that afore."

Henry acknowledged the possibility. He would not gainsay someone with Billy's woodcraft. "What says it's the same man?" he asked.

"I think he's been tracking us," Billy observed. "He just ain't good at it and it's taking him longer. Think about it. We had all the horses, and he's on foot. He can't stay caught up with us. Then, we cached the horses at the ol' man's place and take off. He makes it to Jasper, and finds a story about two strangers. Hell, he probably went up to the ol' man's place same's we did: to get boozed up and hear some news. Steals the horse and by that time, he knows we're headed west. All's he's got to do is ask 'round about the two strangers. A Yankee and a local boy hanging out together is bound to stick out a bit. Easier 'n hell to track."

Henry didn't like it, but Billy made sense. The smart thing was to go back, get the cache and head west. But the whole reason he cached was to minimize the loss if they were captured or detained. Which they had been. And, thanks to his foresight, there was no loss. Plus, if this soldier was tracking them, the only reason would be for the gold: he knew it was there and he knew they had taken it.

Separating, now, would make sense. Billy was right. A Yankee and a Southerner traveling together would stick out somehow, especially as they had made their mark one or another in the towns they had passed through. But separately, Billy could pass for a local boy and in Union-controlled lands, Henry could bluff his way as a scout or non-uniformed courier.

"Look, Billy," Henry said. "Here's what we'll do. You're more than a match for anyone in the woods…"

"'Cept that young'n," Billy interrupted.

"Maybe so, but you can beat anyone else. Go back to the old man's place: I know it'll be a trek, but it won't take you more than a couple of weeks. I'll give you some money and you can buy a horse if you find one. It'll be that much quicker if you can."

"And you?"

"I'll continue south and find Jeremy."

"I think you're crazy. Ain't no one worth it." Billy leered. "Got a thing for the boy, have ye?"

Henry grew red, angry at the insinuation. Before he knew it, he was on his feet and reaching for the man. Billy backed off, and quickly.

"Just prodding you! Damn, I'm sorry, was just joking. I know'd better." Inwardly, he knew that there was nothing of the sort with Henry and the boy, but Henry baffled him with this obsessive pursuit of the half-crazy—or totally crazy, he wasn't sure which—young man.

"It's not the thing to joke about," said Henry, quietly. Thinking beyond his anger and morals, he knew Billy had indeed been joking and he didn't blame him for prodding him. He knew his pursuit of Jeremy looked odd to most people. But it was a commitment, a promise, and he would finish it.

"Aside from restoring the gold to that boy, there's a second reason for me to go south," Henry said. "If he's after us, he'll keep following the logical direction. Last anyone heard of us, we were heading south. If you take off to Jasper, you'll be going in a direction he'll never suspect."

"He's heading north right now, I'll bet. No way he could be this close if he was following us. He's on the prison trail, I'll bet."

"How long do you expect that to last? We shouldn't take any chances."

"What about the gold?"

"What about it? I could describe the place to you best I could and you still wouldn't find it."

"Try me."

Henry didn't trust Billy: he didn't *not* trust him. The problem was, the gold was neither his nor Billy's and Henry felt he had been put in trust of it. He didn't feel he had the right to tell Billy where it was. He more than half suspected it belonged to Jeremy, but why the kid didn't want it was beyond him. Maybe he just had a different set of values and the gold was—like it was to some Indians—just some shiny metal that wasn't good to eat, maybe made good bullets, but was more of a pain to carry around than it was worth. That was part of the reason he was bent on finding the boy. If it *was* his gold, it was a duty set upon Henry to restore it to him. If it was his and he didn't want it still, that was another thing.

Billy looked hurt at his hesitation, but he could not understand his reasons. Still, if Billy was bent on the gold, he could have had it a long time ago.

"'Kay," Henry considered. "I suspect that gold is the kid's or his family's. From what you said, those soldiers were in the cove for upwards of a week. If they'd already had the gold, they would have lit out for New York or Atlanta or something the moment they had it. So, they were looking for something. Did you see those traces in the creek and the mining implements? Someone had definitely been working there. I think the soldiers came upon him and tried to pry the gold out of him. They never showed evidence of compassion or morality, so I think they killed him and looked for the gold on their own time."

Billy looked wryly at him. He knew what he was

getting at and he was still a little hurt that Henry would think he'd take off with someone else's money. He'd done a little "borrowin'" in his life before, but stealing money was beyond the pale. Henry now voiced the conclusions he had made the time they first discovered the gold on that soldier's body. And in contrast to Henry, he knew why the kid didn't want it. It was a curse, the thing that had killed his family and—the part Henry got right—it was just a shiny metal with less use now that the people he had cared most about were gone.

Henry made his decision and he hoped desperately that he was right. He was by nature a trusting soul, although being aware of this made him at times swing to the other extreme, afraid of being "taken in". But he was also a determined man and a wanderer with no agenda, nothing to do: if he was wrong about Billy, he would hunt him down and make a reckoning.

It didn't take long to outline the directions for the supply cache. The gold took longer, because the location was deep in the woods and cunningly hidden. Besides Henry, only God Himself knew where it was and the chance of someone stumbling upon it by accident would take an Act initiated by Him. Billy was a good memorizer, although, or because his literacy approached maybe the level of cattle, and he repeated word for word the direction he had been given. Henry opened his little reserve of coinage and handed Billy thirty dollars.

"That should be plenty. I'm hoping you might find a horse somewhere in the woods no one knows about. Even thirty dollars should get you something."

"Aw," Billy replied, "these feet've taken me farther'n any animal could. Won't be hurting for food, neither's I've shown you in the past."

"Well," Henry interrupted before Billy could get wound up, "take it easy. I have a feeling the kid's down somewhere below Resaca, where they've been fighting. If we don't see you in Jasper in three weeks, come down to Resaca… no, let's meet in Resaca in two weeks: that should give you enough time to get there and back even if you have to walk there, you think?"

"Make it three and you got yerself a deal."

"Done."

Billy reached out a hand. "Can't say it's *all* been fun, but at least it's been interesting," he said. "Take care yourself."

Henry responded. "You, too."

Billy disappeared into the forests on the left and Henry wondered if he would ever see him again. The man's rough demeanor, his filthy habits and uncouth ways belied what was underneath, and Henry had been through too many adventures to read only the cover of the book. He dismissed his doubts and threw up a quick prayer for the man. Then, he headed south to Resaca.

## Chapter 18

"Yes, they were to have been hung. No, they had escaped. How? Well, escaped isn't exactly the word, since an officer ordered their release. Dangedest thing you ever saw, since one of them boys was definitely a Southerner and the other from the North. Now, you could understand the Northerner being set free, sympathy and all, but why the Southern boy? Beats me, too. Where? Well, the last thing anyone saw of them they were headed south with the colonel that freed them. The whole danged army went south, it seems, except for those of us what got to take prisoners north to Illinois if we've got to go that far."

Johnson sat back against the log. He looked fairly presentable now, dressed in the uniform of a corporal whom he had killed a couple days ago. No use tramping around the Northern army looking like a Southern spy, he'd thought. The pants were tight, but that was okay in this army and the private spouting words didn't notice. The boy rambled on and Johnson didn't bother stopping him. There was a small amount of grub he helped himself to and the warmth of the fire in this rain helped dry things out just a bit. They were camped just a stone's throw, figuratively speaking, from the Tennessee town of Chattanooga after delivering the prisoners to the railroad.

"So, you say you're a courier," the private gushed. "Yessir, I coulda done that, roaming across the country without any officer. Exciting, too, I'll bet you."

"Yes, I suppose so. You see a lot of things you

won't see on the front lines, I'll tell you."

"Say, on your way north, did you ever come across the big doings around Dalton? They say they're after a man who killed a lieutenant and a private while trying to steal from the supply depot. Almost shot him, they say. It's okay for a man to be shot by the enemy, I suppose, in a battle and all, although the dead are dead alike as the Good Book says, but cold-blooded murder is another thing." The young man shuddered. "They say the sarge's head was bashed in so hard there was a dent three inches deep where his skull should have been and there was blood all over the table. Bad doings in this army, I'll tell you."

Johnson controlled his concern and thanked his lucky stars—God was a non-entity with him, and "goodness" was a foreign concept as well—that he had the patience to "jaw" with the local troops. He'd found out two very important things. His prey was headed south—why? he wondered—and the pursuit was still pretty hot. He faked a story.

"Yes, well, I didn't just hear about it. I was taking a break at the town that night, just ready to saddle up and head north, when all this commotion broke loose. Shots were fired and all and I didn't know what the hell was going on. I heard 'After him!' from someone and this horse comes galloping by with this ragged looking man on top hanging for his life. I ducked, 'cause they were shooting at him, but I was in the way."

The private's eyes grew large, impressed with the tale of an "experienced" man. Johnson hoped this would emphasize his “bona fides”: he didn’t need suspicions from this man. Obviously, killing the captain earlier had created some problems and he had been seen with this private. Eliminating such a problem in this way would produce a worse situation and he could no longer be the “innocent” courier.

The private asked if he’d seen “action” and Johnson, gifted as he was in lying, told enough violent stories salted with enough gory details for the next hour to satisfy even the most bloodthirsty veteran-wannabe. The night passed without incident. The next morning, he saddled the palomino, restocked his food supply, thanks to the commissary officer who somehow was convinced of his courier status, and headed south at a very quick pace. He would overtake Cox’s troops and find out what was going on. He did not like going into the teeth of battle, but his lust for the gold was insurmountable and the obsession would have him risk much. His temper did not improve at this lengthening delay.

*

The final assault on the hill began. The rains continued and the Union army trudged through thick mud as their foes flooded the fields with lead. Jeremy lay in his perch looking down on the grimy wet enemy and that enemy came on, despite the efforts of his comrades. He cocked back the hammer on the Kentucky—it was still good to go, in spite of the rain, mud and other abuse—and he prayed the powder was yet dry enough to ignite. The gun *did* fire and he saw another Union officer go down. It was significant that he had brushed off Mackey's enthusiasm for their "game" last night and had turned away without acknowledging the others claims. He still felt bad at Mackey's hurt look, but he could not explain his sudden lack of participation. Now, it was just a job.

About that time, he saw through the corner of his eye another officer point into the trees. The unit around the officer fought far from the guns of the entrenched men, although not out of range of the somewhat limited Confederate artillery or the snipers. He yelled his orders: Jeremy could see it through the smoke his own side's guns poured out. The unit all aimed one—only one—direction and fired *en* masse. To his horror, somehow above the din of guns he heard a shriek from the trees to the north and a gray body dropped out of the trees. He had no thought after a passing regret for Mackey, for the Union officer swung his sword in Jeremy's direction. Jeremy and Mackey had both remarkably shot the same officer and a remaining man of that brotherhood had marked the positions of both snipers.

Automation took over and Jeremy desperately reloaded his gun. He knew he was well camouflaged in a large, bushy section of the tree and made himself as small as possible within that bush. His hands flew over the rod and powder, and his eyes sneaked glances through gaps in the foliage. The soldiers reloaded as quickly as possible. *Powder through the barrel.* He looked again as the soldiers tore the paper cartridges with their teeth. *Wad. Ball.* The officer impatiently exhorted his men. His mouth formed the words, although the din drowned them out: *faster, faster*. Jeremy grabbed the rod and shoved the ball home. One soldier was done, his barrel up, then another and another. One man went down as some spent Gray mini ball plowed into this uncanny group of men that neither retreated nor advanced.

Jeremy took aim as the officer debated on whether to fire early and sporadically, or wait until the whole unit was ready. As if in slow motion, the officer yelled *aim*. They were taking no chances and would fire *en masse* to ensure Jeremy's demise. He settled the bead on the man's chest. The soldiers brought their arms up to point at Jeremy's cozy hideout. His heart beat fast as for the first time, his skill during battle was directly pitted against those of another man and he concentrated, calling up the ice-blood control he had exercised in eons past. He ignored his probably impending death, for the first time in months unconcerned about on which side of Charon he would end up as instinct, training and long habit took over, and he pulled the trigger just as the Union man closed his upper teeth and lower lip in the grimace that presaged the "f" sound. Then, Jeremy curled up and tried to make himself as small a target as possible.

His bullet slammed into the man. It was a perfect shot. Too perfect. It hit the lower sternum and drove the air out of the man's chest. Instead of the grunt that emanates from a man hit in such a way, this officer's lungs were full to the limit with air stored for that command: "fire!" and that word tore out of the man loud enough to order those soldiers under his care. He flew back, his chest split open and bloody from the effect of

Jeremy's ball, and his soldiers pulled their own respective triggers. The rain of mini balls seemed to accelerate on their way to the tree.

Most missed. One scraped his head and plowed a shallow furrow into the skull, deep enough to shower blood over the boy as he lost consciousness. On his part, Jeremy thought he felt an impact, then felt nothing.

If anybody would have noticed Jeremy's plunge, he would have seen another body roll off the tree's limbs and fall an unhealthy fifty feet to the ground. Mackey was dead and Tate did not notice a thing. They would not notice anything ever again, the first casualties of this assault.

Part of Jeremy's ingenuity in selecting his post in this particular chestnut was the somewhat inaccessible access. Tall bushes and small trees—dogwood, wild cherry, azaleas and such—crowded together under the large branches. Growing through these were equally dense poison ivy bushes that years of isolation had allowed to grow extensively. He had found a narrow path through the brush, but his perch was typical of chestnut trees: to get into the thicker foliage, one had to move quite a ways from the trunk. The good news was that his fall was broken. The bad news was that his fall was broken by the various bushes and bracken. If anyone had taken notice of his fall, he would have been less than inclined to go hunting for a "dead" man in thick poison ivy.

When the orders came to pull out for yet another retreat, this time back to head off a flanking movement by the Union Army at the Chattahoochee River north of Atlanta, proper, no one gave a second thought to the boy lying unconscious among the poison ivy thickets of Kennesaw Mountain.

*

The trail had disappeared and no one south of Resaca ever noticed two men of such varying personalities and appearance has having passed that way. Johnson had heard lots of stories about the Union armies and spies and soldiers and scavengers heading south, but how was he to pick his way through that barrel of manure?

He continued south, following the swath of battles. *Damn!* It seemed as if that hard-won leather bag of gold had disappeared. His weariness and sensibility wanted him to give up, head West, or back North, maybe to Texas or Mexico and just give up. His personal lusts would not allow that. It was not close to a fair fight.

The horse moved slowly, tiredly, along the wide, muddy road the armies had used in their pursuit south. It was just after noon but the lowering clouds darkened the sky. The mists settled onto the plain and a great rise in the geology loomed above it like an island. He shivered, the image recalling the night he had lost that gold and when, from a distance, he saw the young man loom up through the mist in front of the troop leader; when torture and death permeated his experience in a new way. It was not horror—his leader had that miniscule humanity that allowed him to feel that emotion and anticipate the proximity of hell; Johnson did not—it was a sense of deep loss. Even that was not the more wholesome pain of a loved one dying or even of famine or homelessness, but that pain known by only those whose investments are of mammon and whose only life is found in Midas' bane.

They were there. He knew it. The mountain called to him with the certainty of a man who knows his homeland, whether he's been there or not.

*

The rain stopped. The humidity exceeded its normal ninety-nine percent more typical of the Georgia summer and fog formed over the fields. There was thunder in the far distance but it faded almost before its presence was understood. Clouds blew across the sky, dark and impotent, having spent their strength soaking the land. The effect was that of a permanent dusk, dark and brooding, and it tried to gather energy for some impending storm, whether made of nature or men.

Henry poked his way among the litter on the north side of Kennesaw Mountain. Nature abhors inequity and the passionate action of the battle was replaced by a spiritless stillness.

No, not spiritless, Henry reflected. The many dead littered the territory, even those whose bodies were no longer there. He, too, shivered in the balm but the warm air seemed to soothe the sadness within his soul even as the darkness brooded. All that was left was a familiar melancholy. Above, the massive hill showed scars where highly motivated men had hacked roads in the woods for their vehicles of war and deep trenches and high berms, built to protect the lives of others who would not leave this place until forced to. And they had been forced to. Knowing only that the Gray Army would have been at the top in the defensive positions, he worked his way up the northernmost hillside.

The great battle of Kennesaw Mountain, the last great conflict before Sherman would besiege Atlanta, had been over for a day. Sherman had tried to take this ridge and had again been repulsed and his annoying, flanking maneuver in the light of a battle literally going south was countered by yet another equally annoying retreat by Johnston. Peachtree Creek, Roswell and other places would retain the memory of skirmishes, conquerors and occupation, but the next pitched battle would be on the outskirts of Atlanta.

The "scorched earth" was a wasteland of churned mud and abandoned woodworks. It took him awhile to ascend, less because of the steepness of the hill than because of those obstacles. Trenches and berms crossed the hill laterally and Henry needed to descend into and climb over them, and the logs that had been thrown askew by the Union artillery contributed to obstruct any logical path that he took.

From the top, he looked southeast. He could barely see the buildings in small Marietta rising above the thickening fogs. Beyond it were farms, small hamlets and Atlanta in the distance. Small-arms fire percussed the distant thunder and an occasional boom from some overenthusiastic artillery officer's command rolled up the hill. The armies skirmished at places Henry had never heard of in his life: Ruff's Mill, Neal Dow Station, and Rottenwood Creek.

He turned and walked along the short ridge. It descended in another hundred yards or so and as he approached the lip, he saw how the line of hills stretched to the southwest in a series of small, diminishing peaks, which faded into the clouds covering the plain.

It was July 4th: Independence Day. A sadness moved over Henry. There were men below, both fighting, nominally at least, for independence. One fought for the independence of all men: blacks from the slavery, and for equality and the abolition of class. The other side fought for the right to deny all of those things. Both believed that the principles of freedom supported either purpose.

From a practical perspective, more earthy things tended to motivate men in such a situation. Some fought for their lives to the detriment of those who would take them. Some fought for glory, honor, and for political and professional advancement. Others fought merely to win, or from another, more sensible perspective, to not lose.

Probably the saddest thing, Henry thought, was that they were both American armies. He had gone to West Point with some of those who were commanding for the South as well as those in the commission of the North. They had gone together through the grief that all first-year initiates received from their superiors, and learned, been tried and tested, had partied and socialized together. They had graduated together and, at least for a brief time, had served together.

"*Stop!*" The voice interrupted the profundity of his thoughts. He turned.

"What're you doing up here?" It was from a soldier in a blue uniform. His cockiness from the Union's possession of the hill was evident: he didn't even bother to point his rifle in his direction.

He looked and now that he was at the edge of the little ridge on top, he could see a small troop of soldiers combing the area. There were one or two prisoners: probably looters, he thought.

"I said, 'what are you doing?'"

Persistent cuss, he thought. Probably thinks I'm a looter, too.

"I'm looking for someone," he said. "I have a letter." He pointed to the pack. The soldier gestured for him to get it, but he raised the rifle at him, just in case. He pulled the makeshift rucksack off his shoulder and loosened the cords that bound the canvas. Cox had been kind enough to put the letter in a small leather wallet, considering the rain would make it useless if Henry ever needed it. He opened the wallet and presented it to the soldier.

The man squinted at the paper. He was barely literate and could read some of the words (important ones like "Major" he knew) but his lieutenant definitely had to see this. He handed the paper back.

"Follow me," the soldier said, lowering the rifle

and, still sure of his power over the “prisoner”, strode off purposefully without observing whether Henry followed him or not.

The terrain was too steep for water to settle and for mud to form but the tiny gullies carved by the rain made the going treacherous. They slipped and stumbled down the hill to where a young lieutenant directed traffic. The soldier conferred briefly and the lieutenant looked at Henry momentarily. The soldier saluted and set off at a less-than-enthusiastic stride up the steep hill.

“You have a letter,” the lieutenant said.

“Yes,” said he, and handed the folded paper to him. The army required educated officers, and the lieutenant was one. His eyebrows lifted slightly as he perused the writing. It perked Henry’s curiosity, but he kept his silence, the mighty impact of the silent battlefield outweighing any trivialities as being captured or hung. The lieutenant handed the letter back and saluted him.

“Is there anything I can do for you, sir?” he asked.

Without considering the unusual gesture and address, Henry asked for some food to enhance his supplies. Then, he took a chance. “I need to know where the 15th Arkansas was entrenched. And I need to replenish my food supply.”

The lieutenant didn’t hesitate. “I’m not too sure, but some of the peripheral Reb troops were down by what they call Kolp’s Farm, I think. The entire Rebel army was pretty solid on this ridge, from the top of the mountain down into that direction."

He pointed down the hill.

"This ridge flattens out a bit, but you can't miss the berms. Just head southwest from here. The Arkansans must have been somewhere along the ridge. If you hit Kolp's Farm, I think there's still someone there for cleanup that can help you. I believe there was an Arkansas troop there. Good luck, sir."

The lieutenant turned to give orders about the food and Henry looked around. Only about fifteen Union soldiers walked around the hill, examining berms and campsites. The lieutenant saw his look.

"Yessir, we're the cleanup crew. There are a few of us ordered to make sure no one's left behind and to do a little intelligence search in the areas the Rebs were at. We don't see much but every once in a while, there's a letter or something that sheds some light on at least this battle."

Henry nodded. It made sense. It was only a day since the Rebs had vacated the site and these Union troops would check on things before they caught up with the rest of the army. Probably cavalry, the eyes and ears of the modern army, noted for speed and a low profile. If so, the horses were somewhere below in a safer spot: no one wanted a lame horse from the awkward terrain.

The lieutenant left and Henry opened the paper. His own eyes widened and then, he smiled.

*May 22, 1864*

*To the officer,*

*Please extend to the bearer, Captain Henry Williams all courtesy and aid, including what may be most unusual requests. He is traveling incognito on a mission of utmost importance to the Union. The 41st is to join General McPherson under General Sherman and requests for verification may be sent there.*

*Colonel Daniel Cox*

*41st Maryland*

"Utmost importance!" Henry smiled again. Dan's tendency to both flout and use authority when it suited his purpose or humor had always entertained Henry, although somehow it never got him into trouble. As long as the reader believed the note to be authentic, Henry could go anywhere with little hindrance from the *Union*. The South was another issue. If the note was not hidden properly, he would be shot as a spy. At least it helped things on this side. Obviously, with the intelligence potential in this letter, he would show it only in dire need, even to Union personnel.

A young private delivered the food and Henry set off purposefully down the ridge. It flattened out as the lieutenant had said and he strode under the canopy of chestnuts and hickories. It started raining again, a light drizzle that somehow cut through the mist and fogs that perpetuated the low areas and the creek bottoms. He was damp, but not too wet and it was warm enough in any case. The eight miles or so to the south end passed fairly quickly and he found himself on a very low ridge that rolled smoothly off to either side, the contour disappearing in to the plains. Berms stretched to either side of the makeshift road the men and wheels had cut through the forest, and the trees on either side bore scars to the viciousness of the attackers and the intensity of the defense.

No one could tell through that canopy of mist that the sun was setting on this Independence Day, 1864, and the gloaming became dark quicker than was wont on a Southern summer evening. Henry wandered in a melancholy reverie for a while along the road until he fell over a log blown laterally from the berms. He lay there, dazed for a moment, until logic asserted itself and he decided to sleep above one of the watery trenches to stay dry.

*No fire*, he thought. He had no matches and dry duff was not plentiful down here in any case after weeks of rain. *It'd be a waste. Such a waste. All things go to waste down here. That kid. A waste. Promising kid. Where is he now? He stands on the edge of a razor's edge, teetering to either direction. One side lays insanity and death: the other has only potential. If it doesn't kill us, it can only make us better*, he thought, *but the ghosts of Kennesaw Mountain are still better and worse than they were. It took me years to find truth and answers and this poor kid has no one and he's running out of time.*

Thus rambling in his mind, he became drowsy. The mist flowed around him and the night creatures settled him into a dreamless sleep.

## Chapter 19

Jeremy stood in the waning rain shower as the water thinned the blood caking his head. He could see in the morning gloom that the place had been cleaned out. There were still the little pickings up in his tree, maybe, but he could barely stand, much less try to climb the massive trunk. He found his Kentucky and one of his "backups". Fortunately, his ammunition pack with several peripheral things attached to it, including his knife, had been hung on a loop around his neck and he never removed it after assuming his prone position in the tree. Unfortunately, lying in the woods during rainstorms did not necessarily insure dry powder. He opened the leather container. The sack containing the powder was tightly wrapped. He opened it and could see the top was damp: useless for now. He pushed his finger in and the damp powder crumbled. Below, it was dry.

He supposed he could start a fire, but he was not particularly cold. Besides the little bit of dried meat he had in his ammunition pack, there was no food anyway and nothing to cook it in. He knew he was in bad shape, the mini ball grazing deep enough to make him lose a lot of blood, but he didn't see how anything more than just surviving would help.

He kicked over a piece of trash that had found its way into the deep trench he and his comrades had called home for the better part of a month. Water still stood in it and more was collecting as a new batch of rain poured down. He didn't care. He lay down where he was and went back to sleep.

*

There was a pain in Henry's gut that got worse as something hard drove deeper with successive thrusts. He groaned, chilled in the early morning, and he was as wet as the rain still dropping on him. The pain did not go away but was accompanied by cursing and, now that he thought about it, some idiot was kicking him, too.

Henry squinted open his eyes. For some reason, he felt worse than a hangover's victim. Maybe he was coming down with something. He looked up. Over the places where the rain wasn't hitting his body stood a man in a Union corporal uniform that was too tight for him, with a ginger-colored beard and a very sour disposition.

"Wake up, damn you," the man said with a healthy prod of his rifle into Henry's gut.

"I'm awake."

The man withdrew the rifle, slightly, and allowed him to sit up. To say Henry was confused was an understatement. He thought this man was another cavalry soldier to check his credentials. He reached for his sack, but the man had already torn through it. The letter of commendation lay open to the world and to the rain, the cheap ink Dan had used running and blurring into the paper.

"I'm on a mission for the Union," he blurted, suddenly panicked at the loss of his paper.

"Yeah, sure you are. Like I'm a *courier* for the Union," the man sneered.

Henry was more confused than ever.

"Where is it?" the man asked.

"Where's what?"

He didn't see the blow coming and the stock of the rifle just about shattered his jaw. It hit too low on his face for his teeth, but his jaw felt like it had been knocked off kilter. He moved his hand up to his scraggly beard, feeling it gingerly.

Johnson swore. It's hard to get a confession out of a man when he can't talk. Now that he was here, he got desperate. He aimed another blow at the crotch, but Henry saw it coming and rolled away. Johnson swore again, torn between using a very effective stock for beating or reversing the gun and shooting the bastard.

His voice raised, but only slightly. He still had some sort of control. "Where'd you *hide* it?"

Henry still didn't know what was going on. He rose to his feet and Johnson flipped the gun so the business end of it pointed at Henry's chest. Suddenly, thunder cracked and the day got darker. Someone in the background whinnied, nervous at the tension in the atmosphere, both human and meteorological. Henry reacted to the horse, and saw beyond Johnson the familiar animal: a palomino with a U.S. brand on its flank. Then, he knew.

"You're not going to get it," he slurred, his loyalty

to Jeremy's gold being just a minor part of his reason. The rest simply involved an innate Irish stubbornness to not give in to the man.

Johnson's eyes widened at the effrontery. Then, they narrowed as determination forced its way to the front of his emotions.

"We'll see about that."

The narrow rifle gauge was formidable when seen from a few inches away. They approached even closer and the man forced the barrel tip against Henry's cheek.

"Where's your friend?" he demanded.

"Gone," replied Henry, "powdered on me when he had no more use. He's a wizard in the woods and you'll never find him. I wish you would: I'm mad as hell at him for leaving me."

"You're a liar." The tension in his body seemed to flow into the gun itself and although Henry did nothing so melodramatic as to close his eyes, he definitely prepared for his advent into the Hereafter. But the man was very good when managing his rifle as a club. He whipped the gun around and the stock slammed into the side of Henry's head. He went down.

"You'll never get that gold," Henry grunted, dazed.

The man straightened up. "Oh, I'll get it alright, if I have to take you apart joint by joint."

Henry held up his hand. "I'll tell you…"

"That's more like it."

"…but you'll still never find it. It's so well hidden…"

"Just tell me."

He told the truth. There was no point in lying, especially since what he had just said was fact: telling where it was made no difference if you couldn't find it once you got there. He wasn't sure even Billy could find it. If he did, the gold would be long gone anyway.

Johnson bit his lip. He was, oddly, one of those who told so many lies that he could see the truth after all when presented to him. But still, suppose it wasn't the truth after all? He looked toward the horse and back at Henry. He was tempted to kill him: he couldn't drag him all over the country with him and he couldn't take the risk of being followed. Jasper was a long way off and if not there, it could be hidden anywhere between. A lot could happen then. But worst was getting there and not finding it.

The voices awakened Jeremy. Neither man had noticed his hidden body—dead and not recovered from the last big assault, for all they knew—lying in the low depression. He lay, not moving for any reason than he was weary. Though weary, his head was clearer than for many weeks, and he wondered for a moment where he lay. A voice rose solitary among the sound of falling rain.

"I ought to just kill you. How do I know you're telling the truth?"

The voice haunted Jeremy, from some point in the past. It bothered him because he knew it was important, somehow.

"I told you the truth. Now, you can kill me, but you won't be doing me any harm."

"What?" The incredulous tone in the voice was evident.

"I'm also telling the truth when I say you won't be able to find it."

"I suppose I could, let's see… shoot you in the gut. Gut wounds take a real long time to kill you. Long time. Several days. If I do it right, you might even last the week. A week's long enough to get the gold, I suppose." The voice grinned.

The other's voice changed audibly from brave to bravado. "Well, do it if you've got to, I got nothing better to do."

Jeremy peeked over the edge of the hole. He peeked between the legs of the palomino, ten feet in front of him. The men disputed about twenty yards away. The one on the ground looked vaguely familiar, but he couldn't place him. Long time ago and far, far away, it was. The standing one looked familiar, too, he thought, but his back was turned toward the boy, and he couldn't be sure. The weirdness of it all made him do a very safe thing. He checked the bore and the workings of his Kentucky long rifle. There was nothing dry on him to wipe it with, so he hoped it was dry enough to fire. The percussion cap was more reliable than most systems, but water could get inside the tube if one wasn't careful. He pulled some of the dry powder from his horn and quietly, very quietly, loaded the gun.

Henry's eyes widened slightly. Behind Johnson, a stick flashed through the air. His imagination? Again, it happened. It wasn't a stick; it was a rod of some sort. Dirty blond hair grazed the ditch's horizon for a split second. There was someone there.

Johnson still tried to make up his mind. Playing for time, he prodded Henry none-too-gently in the stomach.

"Get up."

Henry complied. As he stood, he saw the barrel of Jeremy's Kentucky prop itself on the muddy edge of the hole. Between the legs of the palomino, it was placed and the rifle covered both men. The eyes behind the gun he knew. The rest of the face was muddy and bloody but the eyes were the evidence. There set the insane kid he'd sworn to track down. The rifle clicked as the boy drew back the hammer.

Life on the edge of humanity tends to give the living one the senses of an animal and often elevates that sixth one into levels uncanny. Johnson heard the click and it confirmed that nagging sixth sense that had tickled him the last few minutes. He started to turn.

"*Stop!*" Jeremy yelled. The palomino started and walked out of the way. It cleared Jeremy's view entirely and his target froze.

"Drop the gun!"

The voice carried a frightening amount of authority, a voice that had the will to carry out anything—anything—it commanded. And the means. Johnson dropped the gun, but he grinned. Henry inwardly shook his head. The man was insane, he thought, he had to be.

Jeremy stood in the ditch and stepped over the berm, never taking his eye from the sights nor the rifle from its target.

"Turn," he said.

Johnson turned and shined his full, grinning face upon the boy. Jeremy's eyes widened and Henry thought he knew why. He started to move to the side and Jeremy's concentration broke momentarily.

"Stop," he murmured, shortly. And Henry stopped.

Johnson wasn't sure about who this kid was. Because it was out of context. The last time he had seen him, Jeremy had been lying down, unconscious by the fire, and he didn't get a good look at his face. But he did look familiar. Like the leader who walked into "that good night" before him, Johnson saw that he bore more than a passing resemblance to the family they had butchered and to the old man they had killed at the mine. And he didn't like the look in his eyes.

"What's the problem, kid?" he said, gently. Yes, he could be gentle when he wanted to, and he definitely recognized the need to be so now.

"I think I know you," Jeremy said. He held the

gun rock-steady.

"I don't think so. I'm a courier for the Union, 15th Illinois, I am. Just on my way delivering messages to one of the generals down here and lost my way." He looked sidelong at him when he said this.

"I know you." It was as if Johnson hadn't spoken at all. Jeremy stood and walked forward, the 50-calibre Kentucky looming larger as it approached the increasingly nervous Johnson's face.

Henry hadn't spoken. The drama between these two was far more important than any trivial dispute about a fortune in gold. Two souls hung on the outcome: whether they would go directly or transversely to hell was merely a matter of time unless a decision was properly made. He saw the look in the kid's eyes. There was silence. The rain increased its thunder, pounding on the battlefield, on the mud and those left who were beyond caring. Except for that and the distant roll of thunder—or artillery—it was utterly quiet. But Henry felt surrounded by a great array of witnesses who waited, with held breath, the decision of the young man. In some ways, the battle the dead watched was more important than the battle that had taken their lives.

He moved to the side and this time, Jeremy ignored him. He picked up Johnson's rifle, but did not bother to raise or check it.

As for Jeremy, he now knew well who this man was. Hadn't he stalked him with his cronies through miles of Georgia highlands? Hadn't he eliminated his comrades one by one, trying to increase the fear in those left? He had wondered at the time about this man who seemed to enjoy the terror and pain of his comrades, rather than the reverse. But then, Jeremy's lust for killing and revenge had taken over and blurred images in his eyes and in his mind. But he did not forget this man. The others had died to the detriment, he was afraid, of his soul. And now that's gone, what was left? There was no longer any accounting, he thought, and he was merely a bundle of emotions and thought bound in a moldering body that hadn't the courtesy or brains to give up and die yet.

Johnson was not afraid of dying in the positive sense, for he did not believe in the hereafter and never thought of an accounting in the spiritual sense. But he didn't like the idea of the cessation of being. There rushed through his head the things he could have done—can still do? —with the gold and the sense of loss at being so close to it to be foiled by this youngster. But there was no chance, now, unless…

He moved suddenly to his left, trying to get out of the uncanny nearness of that gun. Jeremy shifted the gun slightly, still lined up. He did not move but for that. Johnson stopped, dead in his tracks. Henry had started to swing the rifle at Johnson's legs, but stopped as he saw that Jeremy hadn't even blinked, but remained planted in the earth.

Now, Johnson was scared. With his humanness dwindled away to a mere atom of what it had once been, the chemical reaction called Fear manifested itself in his body and what sociologists have since learned to call the "fight or flight" response was strong. Jeremy could smell it. His finger tightened on the trigger. Henry held his breath. One word from him might make the difference. But it might save the life of an evil man at the cost of a boy's soul. And he believed with all his might that the soul was far more valuable than the body.

Jeremy closed his eyes. Johnson shifted. The eyes opened instantly, leaving no doubt that there was no room for play with this boy. The eyes closed again and Johnson didn't dare move. Jeremy could hear his grandfather in the distance, entreating him to mercy. But why? There had been no mercy for his dad and no mercy for his family, and all for the sake of a bit of metal. If he killed this man, it would at least be for a reckoning, some sort of justice and not for selfish greed. It was different from the men he had tortured: he knew that was gratuitous. Now, it would be a mere execution.

But wasn't it greed? he wondered. Wasn't it taking something from someone else for his own personal wants—not needs, but wants? The gun lowered slightly and his finger relaxed. Johnson did, too. Now, Henry brought up the gun. The boy now felt the sense of loss. Far deeper than anything Johnson could understand, it almost overwhelmed him and the Kentucky dropped onto the grass. Without a sound, the boy wept in frustration.

Johnson turned and looked at Henry. "I guess you've got things where you want them."

"Do you believe I'll shoot you at the slightest excuse?"

"I believe you."

"I'm taking the horse. I don't believe it's yours and I don't want you following us for a while."

The boy looked up at that and his eyes met Henry's. He thought he knew him now, but could not fathom his presence this far from the cove where his dad made his last gold strike. For the second time in months, the boy's body was far beyond most men's experiences and his mind a clear jar, ready to be filled. He knew nothing. Two types of war had cleansed his mind of anything and Henry knew he needed to fill it with the right stuff. He backed away from Johnson until he stopped twenty yards away: more than the distance required for safety from a lunge by such a man. Without taking his eyes of Johnson, he spoke to the boy.

"Jeremy? Remember me?"

The boy nodded.

"Pick up the gun and put it in the holster on the saddle."

The boy obeyed.

"Bring the horse here."

He brought the palomino, soaking wet, saddle, blankets, horse, everything.

"Get on."

The boy got on the horse. Henry tossed up Johnson's rifle.

At that moment, Johnson ran, desperately trying to get out of range.

Before Henry could stop him, the boy whipped the gun up to his armpit, sighted, and pulled the trigger. Johnson appeared to trip and landed on his face in the mud. He rolled over. And over.

"Oh, God!" he screamed, holding his knee. "Goddamn kid!"

The army animal skittered a bit, then stood still, trained to hearing gunshot over its head. Henry and the boy looked at the man through the pouring rain.

"Didn't want him following us," the boy simply said.

Henry said nothing, but was troubled in spirit. He picked up the reins and led the horse over to the man, who was still writhing on the ground, moaning. He bent over him. The man grabbed him by his shirt and hauled him down. He grimaced in Henry's face.

"D-damn kid, I'll kill him."

"Don't be a fool, let me see that." Henry grabbed the man's hand and forced him to let go. Then, he quickly examined the leg. The shot had shattered the kneecap, separating and tearing the ligaments and wedging between the thigh bone against the now shattered shin. Painful. Probably crippled him for good. Henry felt a little—a very little—sympathy for the animal below him and also felt guilty that he didn't feel more. It was bleeding pretty well: the shattering bone must have gone through some vessels, maybe even an artery. Henry found some rope on the horse and made a tourniquet with a stick. He twisted it until the bleeding stopped.

"Keep it tight and release it every once in a while. If you don't, mortification will slip in and they'll take off the leg. You'll live, I think, more's the pity."

Johnson panicked all of a sudden. "Wh-what? You're leaving?"

"Some patrol'll probably be along anytime. Just keep pretending you're a courier: no one'll know the difference."

"No, you can't leave me!"

"We can, and we will. Others would've just killed you and let it go at that, but it can't be done right now. Not by us."

Henry walked back to the horse. The boy was catatonic, staring into space, the rifle still cradled in his arms. Johnson started screaming again, this time salting the air with amazing curses and other profanity, begging them not to leave him as if they were his best friends and the next moment, cursing them as if they were his worst enemies. Henry led the horse north, this time, along the ridge, the man's curses fading as they moved.

The boy mumbled something. Henry stopped the horse.

"Where we goin'?"

"Home."

"Ain't got no home."

"I'll see you get home. Maybe a long time, but

we'll get there."

"Home."

They walked along for a bit. The rain lessened a little and a slight breeze came. The boy mumbled again and Henry stopped.

"Ye notice I let 'im live."

"Yes, I noticed."

They had a long way to go. Henry had some money left and he thought he might still bluff his way through somehow, in spite of a blurry pass and a U.S. Government-issue horse. He felt pretty tired but he knew he could make it to Jasper, as he had promised Billy. And then, they would go West. To Taos, New Mexico, as he had promised Bart. Then? Who knew.

## ABOUT THE AUTHOR

Jack Ballard is a literal "jack of all trades". A native Westerner, he has been a resident, researcher and explorer in places as divergent as the Arizona desert, the Colorado Rockies, the Siskiyou Mountains of California, the battlefields of the Wyoming plains and the Pacific Northwest. He has published several pieces and enjoys writing in a variety of genres, from historical fiction to action/adventure, from sci-fi/fantasy to even a textbook on audio physics. His novel, *Rockdance*, received excellent reviews and is part of the Dusty Palmberg series of adventure novels set in the modern West. His screenplay, *The Devil's Paintbrush*, was optioned by Boulevard Pictures. He has been a member of wilderness Search and Rescue teams since 1995, a mountain guide, adventure educator and climber in the northern Colorado Rockies. His musical endeavors produced many projects, including work with the *Bar D Wranglers*, the bluegrass project *Long Time Coming*, and the international jazz/classical release, *The Psalms*.